───────────── ★ ─────────────

"Claudia was alive last night, according to her brother. How could she suddenly end up dead and reduced to—to—" Kozol stared at the small pile of bones nearly submerged in the thickly coated cave floor "—that?"

"Not hard at all." The detective kicked his feet up on the keyboard. "Let's say Claudia Santana really was at the Austinland Theater last night. Someone, person unknown, takes her and kills her, here in Austin or someplace else. He takes her and kills her there at the cave, maybe, and dumps the body."

Kozol turned his face deliberately from the screen. He was finding it hard to look at those bones without imagining the living flesh that once was attached. What if the girl hadn't been dead at all when she was tossed in the cave? Would those bugs have eaten her alive?

───────────── ★ ─────────────

J. R. Ripley

Lost in Austin

WORLDWIDE.

TORONTO • NEW YORK • LONDON
AMSTERDAM • PARIS • SYDNEY • HAMBURG
STOCKHOLM • ATHENS • TOKYO • MILAN
MADRID • WARSAW • BUDAPEST • AUCKLAND

To Jon and Jon, without whom...well, you know the rest.
(P.S.: Jon, I always did like you best.)

LOST IN AUSTIN

A Worldwide Mystery/April 2002

First published by Long Wind Publishing.

ISBN 0-373-26417-8

Printed in U.S.A.

Lost in Austin

ONE

"GET YOUR HANDS off me!"

"Not until I've said what I've got to say!"

Tony Kozol pulled his arm back. "So, say it already. We're running late as it is."

Restless fans were raising a din that carried backstage. Since leaving Nashville three weeks before, it was a sound that Tony was getting used to.

And liking.

Brian Love grabbed Kozol again with his good arm, his left. "I'm telling you, wise guy, stop trying to get so chummy with Clint. Soon's my arm's healed up, you're out of here!"

Tony shook his head. Filling in as rhythm guitarist for Clint Cash and the Cowhands was often more exciting behind the stage than onstage. And backstage at the downtown Austinland Theater was turning out to be no exception.

Kozol looked down at Love. "Screw you. I'm just doing my job."

Brian Love was all of five foot four, and that was being generous. He looked like a bundle of chicken wire covered with skin and not an ounce of fat to spare. The tallest thing about him was the pair of cowboy boots he'd had special made with four inch heels. Love thought nobody knew. But it was one of the world's worst kept secrets.

The guy was never without them. Height was an extreme obsession of Brian Love's. Maybe that's why he'd had his red hair shaped into an inch high crewcut kept at constant attention with gel. Every inch counted.

Kozol had once seen Love get caught in a thunder shower back in Memphis and his hair still stood up! At just under six foot, this made Tony a giant by comparison, friendly or otherwise.

"Just doing *my* job, you mean," snarled Love.

"Let him go, Love."

A couple of roadies who'd been watching the exchange from the sidelines, decided the fun was over and moved on.

Tony recognized Rock Bottom's bassoon-like voice and turned. Rock Bottom, the band's bassist, was as big as a bull and twice as ornery if you made fun of his name. Tony had seen it happen once at a bar in New Orleans. Not a pleasant sight if you were on the receiving end of that vision. Whether Rock Bottom was the guy's real name or not, Rock wasn't saying and Tony wasn't asking.

Who'd have guessed that Rock's father was a preacher and his mother a small town librarian and part-time piano teacher? Not Kozol. And with close cropped black hair and a small silver earring in each lobe, he was also the most punked out looking member of the band.

Tony said, "It's okay, Rock."

Rock nodded. "Time to move on. Show time." He gave Brian Love a 'that's it' look and pushed Tony forward with the right two and three.

Rock Bottom had had his fingers tattooed across the knuckles of both hands with the numbers one through five; starting with the thumbs which were ones and ending with the pinkies which were fives. Rock had explained to Kozol on the tour bus one sleepless night that he'd gotten them tattooed as a teenager. Said he did it to help him learn to play the bass. All those books with all those notes...and the fingering system, numbered one through five for each finger of the left and right hand and he still couldn't seem to get it straight. Then Rock had the bright idea of labeling his fingers and thumbs. First he'd used a pen, then a marker when the ink smudged. But even permanent marker eventually wasn't.

A friend suggested tattoos.

And so it was done.

His dad, the preacher, had had a fit. But Rock had become an astonishing bass player. A generally quiet giant who, once he got cranking, could talk for hours.

"This ain't over, lawyer!" Love glared at Tony and then his own broken arm.

AFTER THE SET, Kozol toweled off his guitar, then ran the flimsy rag over his own neck back in the dressing room he shared with the rest of the backup band; the male members, that is. Happily, he was alone then. The two girls in the band, both singers, had their own dressing room.

One nice thing about working as a musician, reflected Tony enjoying an unexpected moment of solitude, was that there was no suit or uniform to change into or out of. He'd keep on the same blue jeans and black t-shirt he'd worn on stage. Tony had barely worked up a visible sweat. After all, Clint Cash was the one jumping around all over the boards, white Telecaster in hand, like the *premier danseur* of a country boy's ballet company.

Clint's musical star had been on the rise of late. Two top ten hits in a row on the Billboard country charts and an album that had gone gold in three months had done wonders for his career. And his ego.

Not bad for a guy who, so the story went, had shown up in Nashville a scant four years before that and had scratched out a living singing backup for everybody else in town. His second album had already done twice in sales what the first album did in the two years since its release. The record company was ecstatic.

Kozol's lone concession to *country style* was the rhinestone studded black leather belt around his waist. From what Tony had seen of the business, if the country music market ever went bust, so would the seemingly inexorably entwined rhinestone market.

Savoring the few moments of alone time he'd stumbled upon, Tony shut his eyes and reveled in the muffled silence. The excited voices outside could have been in another dimension. He decided he'd better leave before his private world was shattered.

Kozol pulled on his Clint Cash and the Cowhands denim tour jacket. Normally wavy brown hair now clung to his head with stage sweat. Everyone else was just getting started with that staple of the road, the after show shmooze. The way Clint said it, "If you ain't shmoozin', yer losin'."

So far, Kozol seemed to be losing.

Tony's fingers wrapped around the keycard in his pocket. At least tonight he would sleep in a real bed. A hotel bed, but at least it wasn't on wheels, going sixty down the highway while he tried to catch some of that elusive thing called sleep.

Towards the end of winter, the Southwest Music Conference ran for four days every year in Austin, Texas. And that's how long they'd be in town. They'd never spent more than a night anywhere else. So this was heaven. The last stop had been San Antonio. The next stop was Tucson.

Kozol made his way down the long corridor to the back entrance. It was blocked. A wiry, Hispanic kid was arguing with someone at the rear door wearing a concert security jacket.

"I'm looking for my sister, man!"

"Get out of here, kid. Your sister's not here." The guy in the security jacket shoved.

The kid shoved back.

"I'm looking for my sister. Help me, please!"

Tony sighed. The kid was looking right at him.

The two men began tussling. The boy didn't stand a chance. The security guard had at least a sixty pound advantage on him. Kozol dropped his guitar and raced over. "Hey, come on, guys. Knock it off." He pulled the big guard off the youth or at least tried to. "Stop it!"

The guard glared and straightened his jacket. His face displayed his displeasure. "This is between me and this little piece of—"

"Piece of what, lard face?" The boy's brown eyes flashed like active volcanoes. The guard took a swing at him and the boy ducked.

The kid swung back.

The guard caught the boy's fist in a hand the size of a catcher's mitt and grinned as he bent the kid's fingers backward. The boy winced. Kozol grabbed their hands and pulled the guard away before he could do some serious damage.

"Are you both crazy?" He scolded them both, then turned to the guard. "Will you let me handle this," Tony said, reading the guard's name off the front of his embroidered jacket, "Rick?"

Rick pursed his bulbous lips and glowered at the intruding youth.

Kozol took that for a yes. "Now," he said, turning to the boy, "what's your name?"

The boy stared defiantly.

"All right," said Kozol, "forget it. Remember, you asked me to help you." Tony shrugged and half turned. "I'm exhausted. I'm going to the hotel. Try not to kill each other."

"Julian Santana!"

Tony smiled. He erased the smile from his face before turning back around. "That's better," he said sternly. "I'm Tony." Kozol held out his hand and the boy gave it a firm up and down squeeze. "Now, suppose you tell me why you think you might find your sister here. What's her name?"

"Claudia. And she is here. I know this. She came to see a friend."

"There, you see, Rick," said Tony. "His sister came to see a friend."

"Listen, squirt," interjected Rick, "I told you before, your sister isn't here. And I doubt if you or your so-called sister even have any friends. So why don't you vamoose? And don't slam the border on your way out!"

Julian leapt forward.

Tony held the boy back and opened his mouth to reprimand Rick when a throng of girls showed up at the door begging to get in.

"Come on, Julian," Kozol said quietly. He hustled the young man inside as Rick turned to deal with the attempted breach at the door. "Let's see if we can find your sister—whatshername."

"Claudia."

"Right." Kozol pushed his guitar case out of harm's way along the wall and headed right down the hallway leading back to the band's dressing rooms. There was a virtual warren of such hallways crisscrossing the area behind and beneath the stage. In that respect, the Austinland Theater was like dozens of other venues Tony had performed at in the past weeks. Life was becoming a blur, like a watercolor left out in the rain.

Doors opened in all directions. Tony was relieved to see most of the doors were labeled.

"So, who was this friend your sister was going to see? It'll make things simpler and beats knocking on all these doors."

Kozol and Julian Santana stepped to one side as a roadie passed them pushing a speaker cabinet on a handcart.

"Hey, Tony," said Kirk the roadie. "How's it hanging?" Kirk looked the Hispanic youth over as if checking him for fleas. "Who's this?"

"He's with me," explained Tony. "We're looking for his sister, Claudia."

Julian, unbidden, described his sister. With a hand, he indicated that she was approximately five-five. "Black hair and brown eyes. *Muy bonita.* Very pretty."

Tony asked, "Have you seen her?"

Kirk shook his head. He was a scrawny twenty-year old kid out of Huntsville, Alabama, with bleached blonde hair, who had dropped out of college to pursue a career in music. "Nah, sorry. Tried party central?"

"Not yet."

The roadie shrugged as if he could care less and went back to work. For a roadie, the times before and after the show were, if anything, the hardest. All the gear, including PA equipment, amplifiers, instruments, cables, recording mixers and digital recorders, special lighting and more had to be loaded up on the trucks after every show. The trucks usually drove all night, following the band buses to the next gig where they unloaded and set it all up again.

Four days in Austin was vacation time for everybody in the Cowhands.

"Party central?" asked Julian.

"That's just where everybody hangs out after the show. Food, drinks, you know."

The boy nodded.

"So, you never said who it was your sister was going to see."

"I—I don't know. She did not tell me. Only that she had to see a friend. Someone she said could help her."

"Great." Tony rubbed his chin. "Look, Julian, are you sure—"

"Yes," the young man replied adamantly. "I am sure my sister she did come in here. I stood outside. I watched her go!"

"You saw your sister come in the theater?"

"Yes."

"So, was it Rick who let her in or not?"

Julian frowned. "I don't know. It is not very much light in the back. And I only saw them for a moment."

Kozol remembered. There was one low watt bulb over the out-of-the-way service door where the band entered and departed. The bright lights were at the main back doors. This was designed to draw the crowds away so the artists could come and go in relative peace.

"But I do not think it was him. The person my sister spoke with at the door did not seem so big."

Kozol gave this some thought. Not that it helped any. "All right," he said with resignation, "let's take a walk and see if we can find her or someone who knows where she went. You realize, she could have gone out the front or one of the side exits they open up after the show for the audience to leave from."

"No," Julian said. "Claudia knew I was waiting for her. If she had gone out another way, she would have come back to the alley for me."

"Yeah, I suppose so." Kozol knocked on the girls' temporary dressing room door which was only a couple of spaces down from his own. "Hello?"

A moment later the door was cracked open by Tanya Tobler. She had changed from her stage costume, a black sequined dress with leather boots that matched down to and including the sequins, into a loose fitting beige gown and not so matching peach colored mules. A black shawl was over her shoulders. Tanya was rarely without her shawl.

Tanya Tobler was one of two permanent female backup vocalists with Clint Cash and the Cowhands. Pretty, but heavyset, she was often mistaken for Anne Wilson of the rock group Heart. With coal black hair, whose bangs fell sharply down her forehead leaving a line that looked sharp enough to cut maple, and the overwhelming figure she herself cut, Tanya often joked it would take a Rubens to paint her portrait, because only he'd have a large enough canvas to do her justice.

Tony had grown quite fond of Tanya. And she was an incredible vocalist in her own right. If success was only a question of talent, Kozol figured she'd be every bit the star that Clint Cash was. Maybe bigger.

"Hi-ya, Tone." Tanya stopped brushing out her hair long enough to give Tony's companion the once over. "What's up?"

"This is Julian Santana."

"Oh, yeah?" Tanya laughed. "Any relation to Carlos?"

Julian said nothing.

"I may be a country girl but I love that guy's music." Tanya started singing. *"Oye como va."* She raised her arms and rocked her hips doing an impromptu dance with her shawl.

Kozol went on. "He's looking for his sister, Claudia. She was supposed to be visiting someone backstage here. It wasn't you by any chance, was it?"

"Not me, honey." Tanya pushed the door open wide. "You decent, Grace?" she asked turning back.

"Lucky for you," replied Grace, as a white t-shirt fell over her chest to the hips of her Wranglers. She was a slender, chestnut headed, twenty-two year old from St. Paul, Minnesota, with a pageboy haircut and matching brown eyes with just a fleck of gold in the centers.

Tony was quite fond of her, too. In another fashion.

"I'm looking for Julian's sister, Claudia. Dark haired, Hispanic, obviously. Have you seen her?" Kozol hadn't taken his eyes off Grace. He had a bit of a crush on her, but had so far stayed away. The gossip he'd had was that Grace was off limits, being one of Clint's girls. Tony, being a relative newcomer and an outsider, had no way of checking the veracity of this. The source of the gossip was, after all, Brian Love, number one source of information, right or wrong, and number one jerk.

"No, sorry." Grace rubbed some lotion up and down her arms. It smelled of lavender.

Julian tapped Kozol's elbow. "It was a man."

"What?" Tony asked, forcing himself to look away.

"It was a man she was coming to see. Claudia said she was going to see *him*."

"Guess that lets us off the hook, Gracie," Tanya replied.

"Yeah, but you're still my number one suspect," parried Kozol.

Tanya blew him a kiss. "Come back anytime, sailor boy. And don't forget my birthday party tomorrow!"

"How could I?" Tony called in retreat. "You've been reminding me for a week!"

"Hey, twenty-seven times around the big ole sun." Tanya pinched her hips. "You would've thunk I'd have sweated off some of this, wouldn't you?"

"You and me both, girl. You and me both." Kozol had been meaning to start an exercise program. For the past couple of years or so. And thought about it even more seriously whenever he met a girl he was interested in.

It wasn't that he was overweight, but he did feel a bit flabby himself. He liked to blame it on the time he was running that fast food joint his Uncle Jonathan had given him. But that had been a brief, miserable and murderous affair and not truly responsible for his lack of muscle tone.

His stint as an attorney had been nearly as brief, and equally miserable. But at least he'd had those heavy law books to tote about.

Now his hands, fingers and forearms, at least, had been getting quite a workout since he'd been with Clint Cash and the Cowhands. Nothing like a little guitar work to firm you up. The fingertips of his right hand were nicely calloused and had stopped hurting a fortnight ago.

Kozol headed towards the open twin doors up the hall from which the sound of raucous laughter and the fog of expensive cigars and cheap cigarettes drifted outward.

Party central.

Tony waved a hand in front of his face. He hated the smell of cigarette smoke. Not that the cigars were any better. He spotted Clint Cash in the center of the room, having an intimate conversation with a bottle of Jack Daniel's.

Half the crew was there, too. Rock Bottom was talking up some young blonde on the sofa. Johnnie Beaton was doing likewise with what looked like the blonde's twin sister.

Hector Orlando, the band's drummer, was tapping out a beat with a drumstick and a bottle of Lone Star.

And Brian Love had one arm, his good one, draped over Clint's shoulder and a thick grin on his face. Love looked up when he saw Tony and grinned even bigger.

Tony got the message. Clint and Brian were buds. And when Brian Love's arm healed up, Kozol would be out of a job.

About the only person who seemed to be missing from this little shindig, so far as Kozol could tell, was Granger Murdock, Clint's manager.

Two women, one playing the part of a tall, haughty model with white skin and dead looking gray eyes and the other, a voluptuous kitten with fox-colored hair, had been snared by Clint.

Other groupies floated around the fringes of his band mates, hoping to attract the attention of Clint or, moving down the food chain, one of the band members. They settled for the techies and road crew when all else failed. Which was why all the guys loved these after-concert parties. It was like a smorgasbord where the food and the fun never ran out.

Hopeful eyes gave Tony the once over as he and Julian stepped in. Tony brushed past a flock of girls who barely looked legal. He approached his boss.

Clint saluted with the near empty bottle of whiskey. Wearing his trademark black Stetson, his long blond hair, now braided into a ponytail, stuck out the back of his head and trailed along the nape of his fuzzy neck like a pet snake. Blue eyes showed the flush of alcohol, as did the dopey grin on his boyish face.

"What's wrong, lawyer? You lose your way?" Brian Love aimed a sneer at Julian. "And who's this?"

"A friend."

"He ain't got no badge on."

Tony looked past Love. Everybody backstage was supposed to wear a visitor's badge. Not that it was a rule rigidly applied. Often as not, most of the revelers at party central had no passes. Rules only applied to the people you were trying to keep out. Friends, groupies, and anybody that made the boys laugh or horny were all allowed entry to these parties.

"Lighten up, Brian," Clint said. "We're all friends here. What's your name, kid?"

"Julian Raul Santana. I am looking for Claudia. She is my sister," explained the young man.

"Yeah," cracked Love, "and I'm looking for my mother." He waved his casted arm around the room at the plethora of female bodies. "Take your pick. Me, I'm getting out of here. The air's starting to stink."

Love gave Tony and Julian a bilious look before he departed. He patted Cash's shoulder possessively. "See you back at the hotel."

"It's about time you showed up to one of our little soirees, Tony."

Cash turned to Miss Voluptuous. "Get this boy a beer, will you, doll." It was a command, not a question. "His friend, too!"

Clint turned her loose. The girl headed for the table where the food and drinks were laid out. At least what was left of it. Food didn't last long in these after show bashes. And the booze went even quicker.

Clint's devilish blue eyes followed Miss Voluptuous's hips. "Name's Amanda." He scratched his head. "I think." Clint squeezed an arm around the model on his right. "Tell us your name again, honey."

"Rose."

"Right," said Clint. "Rose." He beamed at Tony and Julian. "Rose is a model, aren't you, honey?"

Rose managed a nod and took a slow sip of champagne from a glass with a stem nearly as slender as she herself.

"Yeah, I figured," Tony replied. "Listen, Clint—"

Clint's other contender for his attention that night returned with three open bottles of beer. "Ah, drink up, boys!"

Clint took the bottles from Miss Voluptuous and handed one each to Tony and Julian. He kissed her. A reward. "Why, doll, you can read my mind." He took a long pull of the fresh beer and smiled. "Five bucks?" Clint asked, sizing up his shot at the tall gray trash can in the corner.

Kozol agreed. He was in no position to decline.

"Yeah," said Clint with a gleam in his eye. Clint hefted the three-quarter guzzled bottle of Jack Daniel's, turned his back to the trash can, kissed the bottle on the neck and gave it a slow toss over his right shoulder.

Tony took a sip of his own cold beer as he watched the whiskey bottle sail smartly into the can with a crack of sound that rose even above the din of the party. Kozol opened his thin wallet and grudgingly parted with a five.

"Tough break, Tony. Double or nothing on the next one?"

"I don't think so, Clint. I'm kind of in the middle of something."

Clint laughed. It was a good old boy, shoot from the gut, burst of sound. "You're in the middle of something, all right. It's called a party! Come on, get with it!"

"No, really, I can't. We," he said, glancing at the boy at his side, "are looking for Julian's sister."

Julian, who'd barely touched his beer nodded solemnly.

Clint tipped back the brim of his hat and looked across the room. "Okay, that's cool. So, which one is she?"

Kozol looked at Julian and then back at Clint. "I don't think she's here."

Julian added, "No, *Senor* Tony, she is not here."

"Well, I'm sorry, Julian." Clint favored Miss Voluptuous with a smile. "I suggest you both drink up." Clint turned back to Julian. "If your sister's around, I expect she'll show up here sooner or later. It's where all the action is!"

Clint spun again, in the opposite direction, as Scott Day, a local Austin DJ whom Tony had met fleetingly at the afternoon's rehearsal, slapped the star on the back.

"Great show, Clint! Just great!" the DJ said effusively. "You boys were hotter than Texas chili!" Day had short, kinky black hair, which bobbed like stiff waves on his head as he babbled, and a nose that looked as if it had been chiseled off a Rodin.

The DJ looked to Kozol every bit the preppie playing dressup as a Texas cowboy. Looked like he'd seen *Urban Cowboy* one too many times.

With Clint drawing fire from Scott Day, Kozol turned to Julian and said, "Come on, let's get out of here while we can."

Out in the hall, Tony said, "Listen, Julian. You see what it's like around here. We'll try a few more doors, but it's been a long day." He stifled a yawn. "If we don't find her real soon, I suggest you go back to your place and wait for Claudia there.

Heck, your sister might be home already, for all we know. Okay?"

"*Si.*"

"Alright then. Come on." Kozol rattled a couple of door knobs. The doors were unmarked. One was locked, the other turned out to be a janitor's closet. It held nothing more interesting than cleaning supplies.

Julian followed Tony up the little stairs and out across the stage. The hall lights were up and the concert hall cleaning crew was out in force. "Claudia?" called Julian, his hands cupped around his thin lips.

The only responses were the puzzled and amused looks he and Tony received from the clean up crew.

They crossed to the other side of the stage and down again. "We'll loop back here and try a couple of more doors. Then we go home, right?"

Julian nodded and followed.

"You know, your sister could be anywhere—even waiting back at the rear entrance by now. We could be running in circles for nothing. If that security guy, Rick, has any sense at all, he'll have her waiting for you there," Tony said, trying to offer Julian some reassurance. The boy was looking awfully nervous.

Kozol jostled another door handle as he spoke.

Locked.

Tony heard coughing outside the next door and knocked.

"Yes?" came the flat response from behind.

"Excuse me, I'm Tony Kozol. I'm with the band. Clint Cash and the Cowhands."

The door opened. A short, heavy man with receding mud colored hair and a large brass belt buckle in the shape of a bull looked at them enquiringly.

"Uh, hi." Tony began again. "I'm looking for a girl. Her name's Claudia." Kozol pointed to Julian. "It's this young man's sister actually."

The man stepped aside. "Sorry," he said, "haven't seen her. I've been stuck in here for hours."

Tony looked inside. Here was a small, Spartan office with a cheap veneer desk, a couple of file cabinets and no windows. There wasn't even a nameplate on the door or the desk. Not a place he'd want to be stuck for minutes, let alone hours.

As if reading Tony's mind, the man replied, "Not much, is it?"

Tony didn't know what to answer. So he didn't.

"I'm an accountant. Not a big, flashy country star." He swept an arm through air that smelled as boring as the room itself appeared. "Take a look. This is how the other side lives."

Kozol nodded and thanked the man for his time. Why did everyone think his life was so glamorous? After all, he was only a fill-in guitarist.

Mansions and flashy red Ferraris?

Hardly. More like a cheap condo and a barely roadworthy old Saab. And if it wasn't for a former friend of Tony's dad who worked at the motor vehicle inspection station and couldn't bear to see him without a car, the Saab would have flunked Florida's state inspection years ago.

If only this guy knew...

Sleeping on buses. Sharing living quarters with a bunch of guys who shared nothing in common but their all-consuming love of music. Eating meals on the run and on the road. Little socialization outside the band. More hours spent rehearsing. Performing. Packing up. Moving on...

Tony jiggled the next door handle a little harder. He was getting tired. Real tired.

The room was dark. He fumbled along the edge of the wall with his left hand and flicked the switch.

The body was on the floor.

Telmont was there. He marked along the east of the wall,
 with his hand on... under the switch.
The lever was on the floor.

TWO

WITH A STARTLED GRUNT, Tony pulled the door shut so quickly he'd banged himself in the head and was seeing stars.

Little fuzzy ones.

"What's wrong?" wondered Julian.

"Nothing," replied Tony, trying to digest what he'd just seen and make some sort of decision, right or wrong, while a couple of stars paired off in a *pas de deux* doing a fourth dimensional adagio. He leaned against the closed door. "I think we should get the police, Julian."

"The *policia?* What for? Why?" The young man tried to get around Tony. "Claudia! What's happened? Let me see!"

Kozol tried to hold the door. "Julian, it's not what you think—"

Then, unable to resist the terrified expression on the boy's face, Tony backed down. "Go ahead. Take a look."

Tony slowly turned the door handle. "But don't touch anything."

Julian swallowed, nodded and stuck his head inside. Kozol heard a hiss of air as the young man inhaled sharply.

"Seen enough?" Tony carefully closed the door. In hindsight, he supposed he should have been more careful of fingerprints on the door handle.

"It's him."

"What? Him who?" demanded Kozol in surprise.

"That is the man who let Claudia inside this night," Julian said with apparent certainty.

"How can you be so sure? The body's lying face down." With a horrible open wound atop his skull, Tony couldn't help but recall. And he had a sinking suspicion that the body had once held one of the Cowhand crew, a Jack Henderson, a roadie and jack-of-all-trades, who on more than one occasion had proven indispensable to the band. Those days seemed over, if Jack Henderson was as dead as he looked.

"The boots," replied Julian. "I recognize those tan cowboy boots." He looked Kozol in the eye. "That cat with the big teeth on the sides of the boots. Like the saber-toothed cat. The man who opened the door for my sister, I remember now, he was wearing boots such as those."

Tony gave this some thought. "Nashville Predators, the new hockey team." He'd been hearing plenty about them from his bandmates. Everybody was excited about Nashville's latest sports franchise. And Henderson had a pair of custom boots like those Julian described. And he was awfully proud of them.

Kozol had been so busy noticing the blood that he hadn't noticed the boots.

"He is dead?"

"Probably, but we can't be sure," said Tony. "Here's what we have to do." Kozol told Julian to hurry back to where Rick, the security guard, was stationed and tell him what they had discovered. "And tell him to get an ambulance and the police, fast!"

"Okay," agreed Julian. "I will be very quick."

Tony hoped Henderson was alive. But intuition and a whole lot of still, red blood spreading from Jack's head and hair to the floor said he was dead.

Kozol longed to take another look. He inched open the door. The light was still on. The body lay sprawled across the hard floor, arms akimbo, legs out. Nashville Predator cowboy boots. It was Jack Henderson, all right. No doubt about it. Tony could make out the left side of the man's face.

The long narrow room appeared to be a miscellaneous equipment storeroom. A catch-all of theater gear. There were green metal shelves rising to the ceiling on either side laden with coils of rope, electric cables, mismatched speakers, and microphone stands, monitors, racks of lighting and more.

An accumulation of dust had settled over the topmost shelves. A small microphone stand, barely twelve inches tall, the kind that might set atop a piano, lay on the floor beside Henderson's crumpled form. It had a heavy round base with a clear coat of sticky looking blood.

Feeling a sudden urge to puke, Tony turned back into the hallway and shut the door. He gulped fresh air and fought to regain his composure. The whole time he'd been in the storeroom, Tony hadn't taken a breath. As if he subconsciously didn't want to inhale the air of the dead.

Kozol pulled up the sleeve of his jacket and looked at his watch. Fifteen minutes had gone by. What was taking the police so long? How long did he have to babysit a dead guy?

Tony's ears pricked up. Someone was approaching. Rick, the security guard with the winning personality, a long-neck clenched in his big hand, came up the hall, sharing a laugh with Kirk, the roadie, whose hand was equally well equipped. Apparently, dead bodies *were* something to joke about.

"It's about time you guys got here." Tony looked over their shoulders. "Where are the police?"

Rick laughed an on his way to drunk laugh. "Police?" He looked at Kirk and snorted again. "What are you talking about, man?"

Kirk took a sip of his beer. "Ain't no law against gettin' drunk, is there?"

"What are you guys babbling about?" Kozol was getting an unpleasant feeling in his gut. "Where's Julian?"

Rick scratched his right temple with a thumb the size of a kosher pickle. "Julian?"

"Yeah, you know, that kid who was looking for his sister."

"That punk? He got in here? I haven't seen him. But if I do—" Rick twisted the beer bottle's tall throat like he was wringing the neck of a runty chicken.

"What do you mean? I sent him to find you."

"C'mon, Rick," insisted Kirk, "we're missing the party. All the best girls will be taken."

"Right on," Rick bellowed. "Gotta get me some! Wooo!"

"Wait," said Tony, "you've got to call the police!"

"Are you kidding?" asked Kirk. "Clint wouldn't like that. Wouldn't like that one bit."

"Clint," Rick said poetically, "would have a fit."

"Look," commanded Tony. He shoved open the door and pushed Rick inside by his thick neck.

"Oh, shit." Rick's face blanched. He inhaled the rest of his beer. The security guard's eyeballs rolled back in his head. Rick slumped to his knees and fell in an unconscious heap.

Kirk, who'd been looking over Rick's shoulder said, "Hey, that's blood!" He wobbled. Probably from drink and fear.

"Gee, no kidding? That's what I've been trying to tell you two morons." Tony struggled to pull his left foot out from under Rick's belly. "Now, will you please go call the authorities, Kirk?"

Kirk nodded and ran.

In the meantime, Kozol had the dubious pleasure of struggling with Rick's limp form, dragging him out and leaning him against the side of the corridor and slapping the security guard until he stirred. Okay, so that was the fun part.

"Man," Rick muttered, his tongue dangling. "What did you do to that guy?"

Tony scowled. "I didn't do anything to anybody. All I wanted to do was go to my hotel room and crash. What I did was find Henderson in the closet."

Rick looked at the door. "That's Henderson in there? Jack Henderson?"

Tony nodded. "Yeah."

Rick gave a little laugh. "How do you like that!"

"What's so funny?"

"Nothing. Never thought I'd see Henderson in the closet is all." Rick shrugged his big, round shoulders and clammed up. Footsteps approached.

Kirk returned looking like a cowering little mixed breed puppy in the company of two police officers who resembled Abbott and Costello, and whose faces betrayed their own skepticism.

The short, heavy one doing the Lou Costello imitation looked at Kozol and spoke first. "Who are you?"

"I'm Tony Kozol."

"The body in there?" His bantam-sized eyes flicked to the door.

The tall fellow, who could've passed for a young Bud Abbott, twisted open the door. He spoke before Tony could answer. "Bugger's in here, alright."

"Look, can I go now?" Kirk fidgeted nervously. "I hate this kind of stuff."

"Just stand there quietly, sir." The first officer gently pushed Kirk to the side.

Tony caught a furtive look that passed from Kirk to Rick and back again, and wondered what they knew about Jack Henderson, alive or dead. And what about Julian Santana? Were they lying about not seeing the kid?

"I asked you if you knew this guy," said the first officer.

"Oh, yeah. He was with the band," Tony answered. Kozol watched as the second officer tested Henderson's limp left wrist for a pulse.

"Nothing." He radioed for an ambulance and a team. "Could be an accident, I suppose," said the Abbott impersonator, gazing up at the cluttered shelves. "Some of this junk could've shifted and that thing fell on this doe. Whacked him on the back of the head." He nudged the fallen mic stand with his toe. "Heavy."

The first officer asked, "He got a name?"

"Henderson, Jack."

"Poor Jack," muttered Rick.

"Yeah," echoed Kirk with a tone of melancholy only a drunk could manage.

"Who found the body?" asked the Costello clone.

Tony looked over Kirk's shoulder. Several people had gathered around, including the accountant he had run into earlier.

"I heard the commotion and wondered what was going on," explained the sour little man.

"I found the body," explained Kozol. "That is, Julian and I found the body."

"You Julian?" The taller officer loomed over Kirk.

Kirk shook his head violently from side to side. "No way! I don't even know any Julian!" He pointed at Kozol. "He told me to call the cops and I did! That's all I know, officer, really!"

"So, who's Julian?" The tall cop was looking at Rick now who hadn't gotten up from the floor.

"Hey, not me!" Rick pushed himself up from the cold tile. "He's some punk who tried to hustle me and get inside the theater." Rick pointed a finger at Kozol. "He's the one who let him backstage."

All eyes turned to Tony.

"What? What?!" Kozol felt his stomach knotting up. "All I was trying to do was go home—"

"You live here?" the chubby officer wanted to know.

"No. I mean I wanted to go to the hotel." Tony caught a quick breath. "This is what happened." If only they'd let him explain. "I came out of my dressing room and I saw two guys, who I don't even know at all, arguing. Rick and this Julian kid."

"Dressing room?"

"That's right."

"You ain't Clint Cash." The tall cop spit a fleck of debris from his mouth. "I sure as hell know that. I've got his last two CDs."

"No, I'm not Clint Cash," Tony explained. "I'm in the band though. I'm the rhythm guitarist."

"No kidding?" The cop looked impressed now, if only slightly.

"Temporary rhythm guitarist." The words fell like acid rain.

Kozol turned, though he didn't need to in order to recognize that revolting voice. Brian Love.

"And don't you forget it, *lawyer*."

Tony crossed his arms. "I thought you left, Love?"

"Forgot something, that's all." Love grinned evilly. "Hear you killed somebody—again."

Kozol felt a hand on his upper arm. It was the little cop. The long arm of the short law. "You son of a—"

"Bitch, ain't it?" Love's laugh had all the charm of a castrated Boris Karloff.

Several more bodies, all breathing, floated into the narrow hall which was growing warmer by the moment. Some were in blue uniforms. Others wore suits. There was another team of four men from a local ambulance service.

One man in particular moved forward and said with some surprise, "Kozol? Tony Kozol?" He grinned. "Oh, man, I don't believe it!"

Tony shrugged loose of the Costello wannabe. "Will you let go of me?" Kozol studied the face and moves of the man in the baggy gray sport coat and loose charcoal gray trousers, who'd called him by name and, in spite of Tony's immediate troubles, a grin broke loose across his face as he mentally erased a few years from the other man's features. "Izzie!"

Unsure what to do, Costello allowed his apparent chief suspect to free himself from his own weak grip.

The two men shook hands then hugged. The man named Izzie slapped Kozol on the back. Tony felt the cold press of a gun.

Kozol asked, "What are you doing here?"

Izzie grinned. "Austin PD. I got the call tonight about some dude getting offed." He stepped back. "Don't tell me you've got something to do with it?"

Tony sighed. "I had the pleasure of finding the body."

"Interesting. So," Izzie wiped his hands together like a baker getting ready to knead some dough, "where's our victim?"

"Storage closet," indicated the tall officer with a jab of the menacing looking revolver that had recently left its holster.

"Put that away," ordered Izzie.

The officer reluctantly complied.

Izzie stepped around Kozol and the street cops. Isidore Ibanez was on the small side, five foot seven at best, with a crooked grin bordered by thin lips, and big ears.

As Kozol recalled, Izzie's family had fled Cuba for nearby Miami after the communist revolution. Izzie had been one of Kozol's classmates at the University of Miami all those years ago. And, Izzie had been one of his best friends, though time and circumstance had set them apart.

After several moments of examining the corpse, Izzie waved to the men who'd accompanied him. "Let's shoot it and bag it."

The forensics team streamed into the tiny storeroom. Izzie looked at Abbott and Costello. "You guys keep the hall clear."

"Sure," said Costello's stand-in.

Izzie was looking at Rick and Kirk. "We need these fellows?"

"They found your friend here standing over the body."

Costello had a real way with words, realized Kozol unhappily. A real bad way.

"Standing over the body?" Izzie raised his eyebrows.

"Well," elucidated the officer, "standing outside the door here. This one," he jerked a thumb at Kirk who squirmed as if given a warm and fuzzy once over with a low powered laser, "says this Kozol told him to get the cops. So, he goes outside and starts shouting until we show up and tell him to shut his yap."

The Abbott stand-in chimed in. "Yeah, he runs out on Sixth Street screaming 'murder!' and 'police!' Can you imagine? We figured he was just another lousy drunk."

Tony could just about picture the scene. He'd been told that Sixth Street and the nearby Warehouse District were the hotbeds of nightlife in Austin, though he hadn't had the pleasure of experiencing it for himself yet.

The few minutes Tony had spent strolling up and down Sixth that afternoon between rehearsal and dinner had been relatively quiet. Still, he could easily imagine some young man running out in any crowd of drunken revelers and screaming 'Murder!' could be provocative, to say the least.

"You boys local?" Izzie was addressing Kirk and Rick.

"I am," said Rick.

"I work for Clint." Kirk seemed to be holding his breath.

After a pause, Izzie said, "All right, somebody get their names and addresses and send them home."

"Thanks," Kirk said.

Kozol looked at Kirk and wondered how the roadie managed to stand seeing as he appeared so utterly spineless. The thought of which was what probably made him think of his good friend, Brian Love. Tony realized his nemesis was missing. Always appearing and disappearing at all the wrong times. Like a malevolent specter.

"How about me?" Tony asked hopefully. The adrenaline rush he'd experienced on finding the body of Jack Henderson was dwindling quickly now and he was dead on his feet, if poor Jack would pardon the expression. Sleep was what he needed the most.

Izzie gripped him by the shoulder. "Hungry?"

Tony shrugged. "A little, I guess."

"Great, dinner's on me."

Tony, with some disinclination, allowed his old college friend to escort him down the corridor.

They wandered down the dimly lit alleyway behind the Austinland Theater and popped out on Sixth Street. Though the middle blocks had been closed to car traffic for the night, opening the way for pedestrians, most of the crowd on either side stuck to the sidewalks out of habit.

Employees of the various nightclubs stood on the walkways beseeching potential customers with enticements of no cover and/or cheap shots and dollar beers.

"So," said Kozol, as he struggled to keep step with his old friend, "what happened?" Tony sidestepped a stalled blonde who looked to be well over her limit. "I thought you'd be a bigshot Miami lawyer by now."

Izzie answered without missing a stride. "Yeah, that was the plan. I hung with it for a couple of years. Got married. Had a kid. Wasn't happy. You know, the whole nine yards of misery bit. Seems like half America goes through it."

"Yeah."

"Anyway, one day the old lady says she wants a divorce." Izzie stopped and looked Tony in the eye. "It didn't matter to me none. I moved out then and there. Quit my job." The detective was moving again.

"So how did you end up here and a cop?"

"Dunno. Woke up here, I guess. And liked it." He'd stopped in front of a hole-in-the-wall pizza pit. Literally. "Traded in the Brooks Brothers monkey suit for a uniform. Now, here I am back in a suit." Izzie pulled at a loose gray thread on his blazer. "Though I can't afford the good stuff no more." He laughed. "What'll it be? Pepperoni?"

Kozol looked at the greasy brickfront hole in the wall. An equally greasy faced fellow in his thirties was dishing out big slabs of pizza. "This is what you call dinner?"

"Two pepperoni and a couple of Pepsi's!" Izzie shouted through the open window.

"Can I get a side order of Lysol with that?" queried Kozol.

The man behind the counter scowled, causing his cigarette to go up and down like the leg of a high kicking Radio City Rockette.

Tony and Izzie slouched against the wall with their sodas in one hand and double-sized slices of pizza in the other. Somehow it wasn't a scene Kozol could have foretold back in his University of Miami days.

Tony sniffed. At least the pizza smelled good.

"So, what about you?" Izzie asked as Kozol chewed the end of his dripping slice. "Never thought I'd see you working as a country musician. You used to hate that stuff in college. You on some kind of sabbatical from the legal profession?"

Tony shrugged and swallowed. "No. I guess I found being an attorney even harder to swallow that this hunk of molten cheese and stale bread you call dinner." He paused and sipped his soda. "Who knows? Maybe I'll take up law again...someday."

"Sounds like you've got a story to tell, Tony."

"It's a long story."

"Yeah, I know what you mean. Maybe we could start a support group for ex-attorneys!"

The two men ate silently for several minutes.

Izzie tossed the remainder of his food in the trash can balanced on the edge of the sidewalk. "So," he asked, "who's this Julian person?"

Kozol wasn't surprised by the question. He still hadn't figured out if Isidore Ibanez had bought him dinner as an old friend or a determined detective. Looked like the detective might be winning out. "Some kid I never saw before tonight, Izzie, I swear. I only got to Austin today."

"What's he got to do with the victim?" Izzie cursed as a couple of young men in University of Texas windbreakers jostled him, splashing soda on his shirt. "Hey, watch it!" He spat on his fingers and swiped at his white shirt.

It had an interesting effect. Interesting, not good.

"Nothing," replied Kozol. "He was with me when I found Jack's body in the storeroom. I sent him to get you guys, the police, that is."

Tony looked up and down the street. Julian could be anywhere among all those bodies walking rhythmically up and down Sixth Street. "He never came back."

"And he didn't call us," added Izzie. "Must've gotten scared and run off like a Texas jackrabbit."

"I suppose that must be it. Still, it doesn't make sense. Like I said, he seemed anxious to find his sister."

"This Julian could be an illegal."

Kozol had given his friend a passing description of the young man.

"Or it could be there was no sister. Maybe he killed this Henderson character earlier and then remembered something, a detail maybe, like something he dropped at the scene that could incriminate him. Could be he wanted to get back inside the theater so he could retrieve some scrap of evidence he was afraid he'd left."

"Maybe. But I was with the body the whole time."

"So? That only means he never got the opportunity."

"Again, maybe." Tony was finding the theory hard to believe. But stranger things had been known to happen. And he wasn't always such a great judge of character. A character flaw of his own that was forever getting him in trouble, it seemed.

Det. Isidore Ibanez crumpled his soda can and it soon joined the rest of the refuse. "Better get back to work. Where are you staying?"

"Radisson," Tony answered. "It's supposed to be a few blocks from here."

"Yeah, up on Town Lake. Nice location. You could walk, but come on, I'll give you a ride."

Izzie's car was parked behind the Austinland Theater, which, from the vehicles he noticed in the tiny parking area, looked more like a police substation.

"Oh, no," said Tony, as Isidore swung into the entryway of the Radisson.

"What's wrong?"

"I left my acoustic lying around backstage."

Izzie looked startled. "Not that old Martin that belonged to your dad?"

"I couldn't help it. Julian and that security guard were arguing and I was trying to break them up. I set my guitar down and it slipped my mind until now."

"Security guard? You mean the dead guy?"

"No, Henderson was with the crew. I'm talking about Rick."

"Oh, right, him." Izzie thoughtfully chewed his lip. "Don't worry, Tony. I'll pick your axe the minute I get back to the Austinland. That is, if we're lucky and it hasn't walked off on its own. That's one valuable six-string."

"Thanks," replied Kozol. "Let me know, will you?" He knew he wouldn't sleep wondering whether or not his guitar was safe. Maybe one of the roadies would have stored it away for him.

"I will." Izzie released his foot from the brake and raced up 1st Street.

The lobby of the Radisson was nearly deserted. There was a large aquarium to the right and another straight ahead that Kozol could see. An off-duty police officer stood talking to a clerk behind the desk.

So far, the fish outnumbered the landlubbers.

"Hi." Kozol placed his elbows on the counter.

"Can I help you?"

"Yes, my name is Tony Kozol. I know I've got a room here." He fished his key out of the pocket of his jacket. "My manager gave me my key. The bags are supposed to be already in it?" At least he hoped so.

The clerk's fingers had been moving across a keyboard. "Yes, Mr. Kozol, everything has been taken care of. You're booked in with a Mr. Beaton."

"Johnnie?" Tony inwardly groaned in response to the clerk's nod. Privacy seemed to be a thing of the past. "You mean, I'm sharing a room?"

"That's right. You're in room nine-twenty-six. View of the Colorado." He pointed. "The elevators are to your right."

Tony nodded, feeling at least twice as tired as he had when he'd entered the lobby, and rode up in a glass walled elevator that looked south over the town.

The lights of the city below blended into the stars in the sky above. A bridge far below spanned the Colorado River. A lone car, heading downtown came silently across. Kozol felt a tug of envy towards the driver.

A hand, hidden in a recessed doorway, reached out and grabbed Tony as he meandered up the hall in search of his room.

"Hey!" Kozol struggled and turned to face his attacker. "You!"

THREE

"WHERE DID YOU come from? And where have you been?" Tony's eyes scanned the hallway up one side and down the other.

They were alone. Kozol picked the keycard up from the floor where he'd dropped it between his feet and slipped the plastic into the electronic lock slot without waiting for an answer.

Tony peeked inside. The room appeared empty except for the bags piled near the dresser, Beaton's and his own.

"Get inside," Kozol whispered, holding the door. "So?"

The room was warm and humid. Tony tore off his jacket and tossed in onto the nearest bed.

Julian still had that frightened deer look on his face. "Please, I have been waiting for you!"

"Yeah? I know what that's like. I was standing next to a dead body waiting for you!"

Julian lowered his head. "I am sorry, Mr. Tony. I got scared." He ran his long, thin fingers over the side of his scalp. "I was going to get the police, but—"

"—you're an illegal."

"No! That's not true!" Julian stuck his chest out. "I am not. I have papers to visit. My sister, however, I am not so sure."

Kozol stuck his hand out. "So let's see them."

"See what, Mr. Tony?"

"Your papers."

Julian patted his pants pockets. "I—I do not have them with me. I keep them safe back in my room."

"Right," said Tony flatly. "So, what's the problem, Julian?" He pulled off his boots and tossed them across the room near a brown easy chair. "I'm tired. I've got a show to do tomorrow, a man I know is dead and you know what?"

Julian shook his head no.

"I don't care much where your sister is right now. So, go look for her yourself. Call the police, if you want to." Tony flapped his arms through the air. "Don't call the police. I don't care." Kozol's voice rose as he threw open the door.

Julian moved to the doorway. "Claudia is in trouble. She was very afraid. She trusted me to help her. But she would not tell me what was wrong. When she came to America it was months before she wrote." His fingers clutched the door handle. "Mama and Papa grew very worried. I told them everything would be A-OK. Claudia would be a big success in America. 'Don't worry,' I said."

The young Mexican paused. "Claudia never called and she rarely wrote. And when Claudia did write home, she seemed worried, unhappy. Her letters betrayed her. And they told us nothing about her life in the States. All I knew from the postmarks was that she was here, in Austin, Texas. Again I said, 'Don't worry Mama and Papa. I will go to America and see Claudia. I will help.'"

Julian pounded his chest. "So I came to America and I found her the day before yesterday—on the street. Alone. Claudia looked well, but her mind..."

"Maybe she didn't want to see you. Sometimes people run away to escape their families and their pasts."

"No! Something was wrong, very wrong. And I demanded to know what. But Claudia took my hand and told me, 'Julian, don't you worry, little brother. Everything will be all right.' And we agreed to meet the next day."

Tony listened as he leaned against the doorframe but said nothing.

"She was *mysterioso,* you know? She wouldn't let me go with her. The next day, we had lunch. Today again and she told me again not to worry. Claudia said she had an idea. She was going to see someone that she said could help her and that things would be better. Much better. We'd have money. We'd go home. Together."

Julian Santana stepped out into the deadly silent hallway. "I am not going home," he said with a tone of proud determination, "without Claudia. *Adios,* Mr. Tony Kozol."

It was only after he'd thrown Julian Santana out that Tony began to wonder just how the kid had found him at the hotel in the first place. Had he been following him all along?

The rattle of the bathroom door at his back a moment later tossed the question from his mind and nearly caused him heart failure. Tony swivelled around in time to see Johnnie Beaton, stark naked, open the bathroom door, followed by a cloud of steam.

And Beaton wasn't alone. The sinewy young blonde he'd been talking up at the after show party backstage at the Austinland was in tow. And was naked too. It was a better look on her.

Far better.

They stepped out of the dark bathroom. Both were dripping wet. "Sorry, scare you?" There was a mischievous grin on Johnnie's face. "Me and Lola were taking a little bath in the dark. Very relaxing. You should try it, Tony."

Tony wouldn't have minded one bit if Beaton's offer included the girl. He kept trying to look at Johnnie, but somehow his eyes weren't cooperating and kept focusing themselves in on Lola. Her long blonde hair fell to her breasts which in turn rose rhythmically, teasingly, with her every breath.

"That's okay," Tony finally managed to squeak.

"Well," Beaton gestured, "bathroom's all yours if you need it, roomie." Johnnie grabbed Lola's hands.

Kozol held his breath as the naked nymph passed within an inch of him and then exposed her derriere as she retreated. "Uh," Tony managed with almost a whimper, "you want me to leave, Johnnie?"

Johnnie waved him off. "Nah, don't bother me none. You mind, Lola?"

Lola grinned and wrapped her arms loosely around Johnnie. "Nope. We'll try to keep it down though if it bothers you," she said to Tony.

"Too late for that, baby," snickered Johnnie, as he and Lola locked arms around each other's waist and tumbled into bed.

Kozol closed the bathroom door behind him, splashed his face with enough cold water to shock an elephant, waited in the quickly cooling bathroom as long as he could stand it, then quietly slipped into his own bed under cover of darkness.

Tony shut his eyes and turned his face to the wall so he wouldn't be tempted to look at the moving mass of covers on Johnnie's bed.

Life on the road was no bed of roses, except maybe in Johnnie's case...and in Johnnie's case, it was also a bed of Lolas.

As he tried to will himself to sleep, Tony wished he could be angry, indignant even with his roommate and his wanton behavior. But the truth was that all he could honestly muster up was jealousy.

IT WAS TONY KOZOL'S humble opinion that telephones, especially perhaps hotel telephones, should possess ringers of a benign, peaceful nature—the sound of gentle ocean waves, four footers at best licking a long sloping beach, soft rain falling through the canopy of the rainforest, a baby's muffled laughter; anything but New Age music which Tony had come to loathe listening to since his misadventure in Sedona, where another friend of his had ended up dead, much like Jack Henderson—but something soothing to nudge one awake.

But alas, his hotel room had a telephone with a cacophonous ringer like all the others, loud, brash and insolent.

Which put Kozol in a similar mood as he picked up the receiver. "What?"

Tony glared at the clock. It was just past seven in the morning. A respectable enough time in his old life but, as a musician working nights, it stank.

He glanced at Johnnie's bed. Empty and the bedspread, blanket and sheet were on the floor. Maybe it was bath time again?

The racket in Kozol's ear continued, rattling around like a horsefly caught in his eardrum. "What? Who?" It sounded like six over-caffeinated people yammering all at once. Tony tried shouting back. "WHO'S SCREAMING?"

More shouting, then muffled voices.

"Sorry, Tony," Izzie said, "is that better? Crowd of revelers who didn't know when to quit just got hauled through. You up?"

Tony yawned. "Yeah, I'm up. Say, you find my guitar?" Tony had all but forgotten Izzie's promise to call.

"Sure," replied his detective friend. "I've got it right here. I got busy last night and forgot to call you like I promised. How about coming by and picking it up? I'll send a squad car for you."

"No problem. And thanks, Izzie. I really appreciate your holding onto it for me."

"Happy to. You know I always loved that guitar. In fact, I don't think I can resist opening the case and checking it out, not that the old fingers play so good anymore. You wouldn't mind, would you?"

Kozol laughed. "Not at all. Help yourself."

"Thanks. And I'll send a car around for you. Just say when."

"Don't go to any trouble."

"It's no trouble. The station's not far. I can have a squad car there anytime you like."

"How far is not far?" Tony pushed back the covers.

"Only a few blocks."

"Then, since there's no rush, I think I'll just walk it. Weather looks reasonable," Tony said tugging open the drapery. He palpated his bare stomach. "And I could probably use the exercise."

"Suit yourself. Got a pen? I'll give you some simple directions. You won't have any trouble. Like I said, it isn't far to the station."

Tony grabbed a hotel pen and notepad from the night table and began writing. "Got it. See you in about an hour, Izzie."

The Police & Courts Building was on Frontage and 8th Street. There had been no sign of Johnnie Beaton or Lola, so Tony helped himself to a quick shower before heading out; though by the time Kozol had finished his little walk, he'd worked up a big sweat.

The officer seated in the swivel chair at the main desk, which looked more like a miniature airport control tower than anything else, asked Kozol's name and business. Det. Isidore Ibanez was paged and appeared downstairs a few moments later.

"Come on up, Tony." Izzie hadn't changed clothes and it didn't look like he'd slept much either. Kozol followed Izzie upstairs to the only corner of a largish room that looked to have been struck by a spot cyclone.

Det. Ibanez pulled an oak chair, that resembled a detainee who'd been beaten one too many times in the interrogation room, up to the amalgam of busted sticks and bent metal that seemed to be passing itself off as a desk. "Have a seat."

Tony sat and studied his old friend across the expanse of clutter. "Long night?"

"Yeah, a murder can do that to a body." The detective rubbed his thin neck. "Want some coffee?" Izzie was pointing at two brandless Styrofoam cups of java perched on the corner of his desk.

Tony peered over the rims and noticed that one cup contained noticeably less scum on top than the other. "Thanks." He took it.

One sip confirmed his worst suspicions. The coffee, if that was what Izzie was going to call it, tasted like burnt number two pencils. Its odor was foul and elusive.

Tony noticed the guitar case leaning against the wall behind Izzie. It was his. The case still had the old University of Miami stickers on it. "Did you try it?"

Izzie followed Kozol's finger. "The guitar? No, not yet." Izzie swivelled around in his chair and pulled the guitar case up to his feet. "You sure you don't mind?"

"No, of course not. Let's see if you've still got any music left in you. Besides that wonderful squeak your desk chair makes every time you wiggle your rear end, of course."

"Very funny."

"Yeah, I guess you can't be any worse now than you were when we used to let you sit in with us at frat parties."

Izzie grinned good-naturedly and pointed his finger. "You guys were lucky to have me and don't you forget it. I was hot."

Tony wiggled his hand. "Miami was hot. Your cousin Miguel's car was hot. You were lukewarm."

"What? Are you working up a comedy act in case the music business fails?"

"Okay, sorry. So, let's hear something already."

Izzie cast a look at Tony, chewed on his bottom lip for a moment, then popped open the guitar case. Inside lay Tony's prized Martin D-28. It had been a gift from his father, long deceased.

Izzie propped the guitar up on his knee, fingered a chord, C major, and strummed. "Beautiful, man." The detective picked a few measures of an old blues piece that Kozol couldn't quite place.

Izzie paused then launched into a slow, soulful version of *It's A Hard Life Wherever You Go*. His voice was weak and cracked in all the wrong places, but the sentiment was obvious and genuine.

Tony clapped as did the officers who'd stopped working to listen. "Very nice."

"Nanci Griffith tune. I hear she's from these parts."

"You really are becoming a Texan, aren't you."

Izzie shrugged. "Why not? They've got plenty of room. Ought to be able to squeeze in one lonely, lost Cuban." Izzie gnawed at his lower lip some more.

"Is something wrong?" Kozol met Izzie's gaze.

Izzie leaned the old Martin carefully against the side of his desk. Reaching down, he grabbed the open guitar case and set it precariously atop his desk. Det. Ibanez lifted the lid to the center compartment of the guitar case.

It was where Tony kept some spare strings, a capo, an old guitar strap which he had no idea why he kept in there since he never used it anymore, picks—some new, some worn, a guitar cloth which he used to wipe down the neck and strings after playing—okay, so it was really a baby's diaper, but they worked best and it had never been used for its intended creation, and a small pair of wire cutters to clip the ends off of steel strings.

"What?" Kozol asked.

"Take a look." Izzie held the lid with his finger.

Tony rose to get a better look inside his guitar case. He couldn't imagine what on earth his friend had in mind until he saw it himself. A small, clear plastic bag, no more than three inches on a side, sat in the middle of the compartment. And it was filled with a white substance.

Kozol's face turned white to match and he felt a desperate chill pass through his body. "Is that what I think it is?"

Izzie nodded soberly. "Several grams of coke." He lifted the bag and placed it in his inside jacket pocket.

Kozol stammered, "I swear, Izzie, it isn't mine! I don't even smoke pot!" Tony stepped back from the desk, a reflex to flight. "That was not in my case when I put my guitar away last night."

Det. Ibanez looked Tony squarely in the eyes. "We found an identical packet stuffed in Henderson's shirt pocket. No fingerprints though on either bag."

"It's a setup, I swear it, Izzie. I mean, why would I—"

"Yeah, yeah. Relax, Tony." Izzie gestured for his old friend to sit back down and Tony complied. "I figured it wasn't yours. Besides, you'd have to be a pretty cool fish to allow me to mess with your guitar knowing that junk was in the case. First on the telephone. Then here in my face."

The detective was smiling. "And the Tony Kozol I knew would have been squirming like a night crawler on a keen hook about this time."

"You knew." The realization had come up to Tony like the dawn. "You'd already found the cocaine in my guitar case before I got here."

"Yeah," Izzie admitted, "before I even spoke to you this morning." He leaned back in his chair and propped his feet up on his desk. Miraculously, it held together. "I have a confession of my own."

"What's that?"

"I picked up your guitar after dropping you off at the hotel and locked it in my trunk. As soon as I got your guitar out of my car and upstairs here at the station I couldn't resist checking it out. Sorry for the white lie."

"No problem." Tony had to keep in mind that his old college friend wasn't simply Izzie, he was Detective Isidore Ibanez with a job to do. Even if it led to arresting an old friend?

Izzie leaned closer. With a twist, he snapped the guitar case shut and set it aside. "Confession number two." He held up two fingers. "By the time I got back to the station this morning we'd received a call about you. The captain passed the information along to me. Some guy telling us you'd been mixed up in murder before—"

"Love." Kozol grimaced. "That lousy son of a— You saw him last night, Izzie."

Izzie shook his head no. "I don't think so..."

"Sure. Red hair, busted arm. He was there in the corridor. I thought he'd gone, but then there he was. And then he was gone again. Bastard comes and goes like a bad headache."

"Oh yeah, the little guy with the attitude. Almost forgot about him."

"You're lucky. I wish I could." Tony rubbed his temples. "As much as I like the steady paycheck, I think I'll be glad when this gig is up. So, you want to know what Love was talking about?"

"It'd help."

Kozol scratched his chin and started in, explaining his troubles with the mob, through no fault of his own; his troubles with his uncle and the fast food restaurant business, through no fault of his own; and his troubles in the year before with their mutual friend who'd ended up dead in Sedona; through no fault of his own, of course.

Izzie straightened up. "John Ryan was murdered? Dang. I remember hearing about this Wunderkind guy getting it. Some sort of minor celebrity. Guess I didn't realize it was John. Changed his name, huh?"

Tony nodded.

"Gonna have to say a prayer for him," Izzie added somberly,

making the sign of the cross. Then he chuckled. "Hard to picture John as a New Age star though. The guy was hardly cut from John Tesh or Yanni material."

"No," agreed Tony, "more like Sammy Hagar. And he was getting stranger by the year."

"Still..." Izzie paused and the two men passed the moments in their own unspoken thoughts about the past and the dimension of death that hung both their own lives.

Kozol took a slow sip of his burnt pencils, thinking maybe later he'd send off a postcard to one of his friends back home. He wouldn't need a writing instrument, he'd be able to use the tip of his *pencilized* tongue.

Det. Ibanez secured the Martin D-28 back in its case.

"So," asked Tony, "am I busted?"

"Well," Izzie answered, somewhere between a grin and a sigh, "the captain had a fit when I told him my thinking. Never a pleasant bit to listen to. The man's got lungs. He used to play tuba in his high school marching band, you know."

Tony waited for the other foot to drop.

"But," said Izzie, "I explained the particular circumstances to him. I asked him what kind of idiot you'd have to be to stash that garbage in your own guitar case but wipe it for prints."

"Thanks, I think."

Izzie grinned. "Anyone could have planted the junk in your guitar case. I'm sure you didn't keep it locked, did you? It wasn't locked when I picked it up. Not that a flimsy little lock like those things guitar cases have got could keep even a halfway determined thief out."

"No, I never lock it. But I do carry the key on my ring. Except if I'm traveling with the guitar on a plane, then I lock it up—I don't want the case to pop open and my guitar to fall out of the overhead bin. Backstage and on the road, if someone wants my guitar, I figure they're going to take it case and all."

"Sure," Izzie said, "actually much less conspicuous that way. Better to be seen carrying a guitar case down the street than a loose guitar."

Kozol concurred.

"So as much as I'd like to lock you up and confiscate this beautiful axe of yours for my own personal use, I feel I have no choice but to let your scrawny ass go."

Tony relaxed. "Thanks." It was a good thing he had a friend on the force, Tony realized, or he could have been arrested. And whoever had been trying to set him up on a drug charge hadn't been counting on his getting out from under it, at least not so quickly.

Kozol had to ask himself who wanted him out of the way. And why?

"Just do me a personal favor and keep it clean while you're in town, okay? Or the captain will have my behind."

Tony replied quickly. "That's a deal." Kozol gripped his guitar case. "This free to go, too?"

"Yeah."

"Great. Well, I'd better beat it. Clint could be looking for me by now. See 'ya, Izzie."

Izzie nodded and tossed a waist high wave.

Kozol turned and threaded his way carefully through the packed office. He froze and turned slowly, the guitar case banging against his knee, when Izzie called his name. "Yes?"

"Aren't you forgetting something?" Izzie's face was set in stone. His eyes flared.

"Uh, well." Tony squeezed the handle of the guitar case tighter. The handle slipped in his sweaty grip. "I—I don't think so."

"Like a couple of passes to tonight's show?"

Tony beamed. "They'll be waiting for you at the window. Just give them my name." Tony cocked a finger at Izzie and fired. "Best seats in the house."

"That's the ticket," Izzie replied.

KOZOL'S RETURN TO the Radisson was less pleasant.

"Where have you been?" demanded Granger Murdock as he shot up from a high backed chartreuse chair in the lobby.

"Taking a walk," snapped Tony, tired from lack of shut eye and his second hike of the day, having hoofed it back from the police station, this time carrying his guitar.

A detail Clint Cash's manager hadn't missed. He was glaring meaningfully at the black guitar case. "You always take your guitar with you when you go for a little walk?"

Kozol switched his grip from his right hand to his left. Arcs of sweat spread out from Tony's armpits. His guitar seemed to be growing heavier and his fingers were growing numb. Maybe he'd hit a pocket of heavy gravity. The kind that can make you trip and fall down if you weren't careful where you stepped.

Granger went on before Tony could answer. "I know. Maybe it's like a pet, you gotta let it out in the morning to take a big old poop so it doesn't soil the carpet! Is that it?"

"I left my guitar at the theater last night, that's all. I picked it up this morning." As much as Kozol would have liked to sink his teeth into Granger Murdock's hide, the man was Clint's manager and, as such, a major player. If Tony pissed him off, he'd be out of a gig.

"Yeah?" Granger, with a crop of long red hair that would have done a beet farmer proud under his Stetson, crossed his arms. "I hear that's not all you left behind."

Nearly equal in height, Granger Murdock stared at Kozol through eyes greener than the money he seemed to worship. Like usual, Granger wore a blue denim shirt, Wranglers and his bolo tie with the silver end tips; the cameo one bearing the likeness of Patsy Cline.

"What's that supposed to mean?" Tony finally set the guitar on the ground. The aroma of real coffee coming from a complimentary setup near the door tugged at his senses. He grabbed a cup.

Granger followed. "It means—" Murdock lowered his voice, taking in the half dozen or so guests on their way to breakfast and the numerous hotel employees passing back and forth. "It means dead bodies."

"You mean dead body," Tony replied. "As far as I know, there's just the one and he's got—had—a name, Jack Henderson."

Granger pulled his hat to his chest. "Yeah, amen. Jack was a good man."

Kozol stirred several packets of sugar into his coffee and took a swallow.

Murdock was still talking. "But we can't have incidents like this happening. It creates a big stink! You know what I mean?" He popped his Stetson back on his head. "A friggin' big stink."

Tony nodded. What else could he do?

"Clint don't like it."

"Clint?" Kozol's ears perked up. It was one thing to get Granger angry, but the last thing he needed was to have Clint mad at him. "What did Clint say?"

"Well," complained Murdock, "after Clint stopped yelling, he told me to handle it. And that's what I'm trying to do. I've been up half the night making statements to the press, to TV people—all that jazz."

If Granger was looking for sympathy he wasn't going to get it from Kozol who privately took a heap of pleasure in hearing about the manager's travails.

"Now, I love publicity as much as the next guy," admitted Granger. "I mean, it's half my job. But this kind of publicity is murder, no pun intended. And Clint don't need it."

Granger pointed a nicotine stained finger at Kozol's chest. "I don't have to tell you, every bigwig in the music industry is here in Austin for the Southwest Music Conference." Here Murdock shook his head in disgust. "And Clint Cash and the Cowhands end up smack dab in the middle of a murder, for chrissake!"

Tony set his half finished coffee on the mahogany side table. "It isn't my fault, Granger. I'm sorry Henderson is dead. But the only thing you can accuse me of is finding the body."

"That better be all, Kozol..."

"Are you accusing me of something?"

"All I'm saying is that Jack Henderson was a good guy." Murdock thrust his thumbs inside his black leather belt. "Jack was one heck of a worker, gave it one hundred percent. And he was as devoted to Clint as a puppy dog. Clint's pretty broken up about Jack's death, too. Like he's lost a puppy, you know?"

Tony nodded though he thought the analogy a less than kind one.

"And Clint's got a show to do tonight."

"Look," said Tony wearily, looking for a way to end this endless and, as far as he was concerned, pointless conversation, "like I said, I'm sorry. All I did was find the body. And that's what I told the police. Okay?"

"Not okay. You shouldn't have been poking around in the first place."

"And what's that supposed to mean?"

"Clint says the last he saw you, you were heading here to the hotel. Then you go wandering around the Austinland like some old snoop with some Mexican kid, who wasn't even on the guest list, in tow."

Kozol swallowed. There wasn't a lot of privacy traveling with a band on the road. "He was looking for his sister."

"That's interesting," scoffed Granger. "I hear most men are looking for their mothers."

Tony wondered if Love and Murdock used the same speech writers. "Is that all?"

Murdock drew himself up to full height. "There's a band meeting at two. Here at the hotel." He aimed a finger at Tony's chest again. "Second floor conference room and nobody makes any statements to nobody without my say-so, got it? And I ain't giving any say-so."

Tony assented with a slight nod of his head. Of course, it was more from fatigue and trouble keeping his head up than it was from accord.

Granger took a quick look around the lobby and moved in closer. "One more thing," he said in a tough whisper. "Me, I'm a tolerant guy, but Clint don't go in for no heavy drugs. Anybody's caught with the stuff, their fanny is outta here, *capisce?*"

It wasn't until the always charming Granger Murdock had sauntered cockily out the revolving front door that Tony wondered what Granger had been alluding to. Had Clint's manager been aware of the drugs found in Tony's guitar case and on Henderson's body? If so, had the police told him?

If not, how could he have known?

FOUR

KOZOL WAS BEGINNING to feel set up.

Back in his room, Tony grabbed the white pages from the drawer of the night table and began flipping through the listings. After all, he was thinking, who else but Julian might have planted that coke in his guitar case and then disappeared?

"What was that kid's last name?" he muttered aloud, standing over the table looking out over Town Lake, which was for all intents and purposes the lower Colorado River. Tony hadn't yet figured out why the locals had to call it Town Lake.

Looking downward, Kozol noticed Tanya Tobler and Grace Burns, Clint's female backup singers, lounging poolside. Tanya had on a lounge dress so buttery yellow that Tony thought it was in danger of melting out there in the big Texas sun. Lying atop her black shawl, Tanya looked for all the world like a jumbo slab of butter on a piece of burnt whole wheat toast.

Grace, on the other hand, wore a tiny pink bikini and suddenly Kozol realized that he'd forgotten what he was doing with the phone book. Grace, nine stories below, rose and slipped into the water. She moved well. Tanya picked up a newspaper.

He snapped his fingers. That was it! It was something Tanya had said last night, *"Oye como va."* "Santana!" Tony said triumphantly. The kid said he wasn't from around here but he could have been lying.

Kozol checked the directory again. No Julian Santana. No Claudia Santana.

He could call the operator, or call every Santana in the book at seventy-five cents per local call. But then again, the pool was looking good. Mighty good.

A slave to his hormones, Kozol slipped into a pair of running shorts that could easily double as swimming trunks, grabbed a towel from the bath and headed downstairs.

Tanya looked up from her newspaper through dark sunglasses. "Morning, Tone. Looking good." She held a golden-colored glass between her legs. It smelled like some sort of rum concoction.

A sign on the fence read *"No Glass Containers/No Alcohol."* Tanya Tobler, Kozol knew, made her own rules.

"Thanks," Kozol replied with a grin.

"Have a seat."

Tony sat on the edge of Grace's lounger.

Tanya was staring at Tony's white belly. "For chrissake, you're from Florida, Tone, but I've seen albinos with more color."

Tony pulled his towel up over his abdomen. "I don't get out much during the day."

"Saving it all up for night time, eh?" Tanya giggled like a bowl of happy Jell-O.

"Something like that." It was time to change the subject. "You hear what happened last night, Tanya?" Tony looked discreetly as he could manage over his shoulder. Grace was gracefully doing laps in the pool with a hypnotizing rhythm.

"About Jack?"

Kozol nodded.

"Yeah, poor Jack." Tanya pressed her full lips against her

glass, took a modest sip of her drink and leaned closer. "I heard it was murder and that *you* found the body." Tanya noticeably shivered. "That must have been awful, honey."

Her hand rested on his knee. "I'd have just died if I'd found a dead body." Tanya held up her glass. Ice cubes floated in what could have been pure Jamaican rum. "Drink?"

"No, thanks. I haven't even had breakfast yet."

"So, any idea who might have killed him?"

Tony leaned back and closed his eyes. Sunlight warmed his forehead and glowed against his eyelids. He thought about Tanya's question. He'd been so harried, he hadn't given the idea much thought. Even now, the answer to that question was only of mild interest to him. Kozol had barely known Henderson, who'd seemed to keep mostly to himself. "None," Tony said finally. "How about you, any clues?"

"Not a one, Tone." She took a more generous sip of her drink. "And that's just it. If I was going to kill one of us off, I can think of a lot bigger pains on this tour than Jack Henderson. Yourself excluded, of course." Tanya laughed wickedly.

"Thanks, I think," replied Tony. "And I agree with you one hundred percent." A splash followed by cool water dripping over his back made Kozol turn. Grace was standing over him.

"Morning, Tony."

"Hi." Suddenly Tony's tongue felt like a one hundred percent cotton sweat sock with a mind of its own.

Grace toweled her hair. "I heard about last night. You okay?"

Tony nodded. "You heard about it?" Grace seemed to be looking around for something and Kozol suddenly realized he'd taken her chair. He jumped up. "Sorry, have a seat."

They traded places and Grace went on. "Sure, the police questioned everybody. Funny you weren't there."

"Oh, believe me, I was with the police, too. Turns out one of the detectives working the division is a guy I went to college with." Tony took a breath to clear his head. The scent of suntan oil warming itself on Grace's satiny skin was intoxicating.

"Small world." Grace wiped her legs.

Tony's eyes went from her legs to her breasts and back again. He tried not to stare. But he was a guy. It was a losing battle. Kozol cleared his throat. It gave him something to do. "Did you know Henderson well?"

"Not really. Tanya and I had sung with Clint on a couple of tracks back in Nashville. Sometimes Jack was there. Usually, I guess. Helping out Clint however Clint liked. Jack never said much to me though."

Tanya added, "Me either. Can you imagine, Tone? Two fine, healthy young females and Jack never so much as talked us up." She pulled Tony closer. "Actually, my gut feeling is that Jack was *devoted* to Clint—if you know what I mean."

The puzzled look on Tony's face was transparent.

"Tanya thinks Jack was gay."

"What about you, Tone?"

"Yeah, me too."

Grace said with surprise, "You mean, you're gay, too?"

Kozol wasn't sure if Grace was joking or not. But he was taking no chances. He blurted out quickly, "No! I'm not gay! I heard that Jack was, or at least Love used to make cracks about him. Never when Jack was around though."

"Love makes cracks about everybody," Tanya said. "You should hear what he has to say about you, honey."

"Believe me, I have. He's not shy about telling me how he feels about me."

"So, you're not gay." Grace shook her head and arched her back. "I guess that will make your new girlfriend happy."

"Girlfriend?" said Tony.

"Yeah." Grace rubbed her arms with oil. "Very lovely. She

said her name was Claudia and she was a friend of yours. Isn't that the girl you mentioned you were looking for last night?"

"Claudia?"

"Umm-hmm. She was out here a little while ago asking if we'd seen you."

"That's right," confirmed Tanya. Her drink was almost gone now. She tipped her wide-brimmed straw hat over her head. "Pretty girl. Spicy."

"Are you sure, Tanya? She said her name was Claudia?"

"Hey, come on, Tone. I'm not drunk or blind—yet."

"Still...I wonder what she wanted and how she even knew I was here."

Grace added, "She was standing there clear as a pink flamingo."

The two ladies giggled.

"What's so funny?"

"Oh, nothing." Grace rested her hand on Tony's arm. "Claudia was leaning against the railing there talking to us when she slipped off her sandal and rested the bottom of her left foot up on the inside of her right thigh. She looked kind of like a flamingo, you know?"

Tony looked bewildered.

Grace added quickly, "We don't mean to be making fun of her. It was just kind of cute, is all."

"That still doesn't explain how she found me."

"I think she said something about asking the staff at the Austinland Theater where you were staying. Right, Grace?"

"Yeah, I guess so. I don't remember."

"They must have given her the name of the band's hotel. So much for security." Tanya leaned forward, exposing more cleavage than Kozol thought possible. "I told her you were probably up in your room, Tone. She didn't find you?"

Tony shook his head. "I guess I was already out. Or I could

have been in the shower or something." He shook his head and sat at the edge of Grace's lounger. "Can you describe her exactly?"

Grace cocked her head. "Describe her? That's funny, Tony. You don't know what your own girlfriend looks like?"

"She isn't my girlfriend. She isn't even really a friend. Matter-of-fact, I've never even laid eyes on her. She's just the sister of this kid that showed up at the Austinland last night claiming she was his sister and that she had gone inside to visit somebody and that he was trying to find her because she hadn't come back out. And, being an idiot, I not only let him in to look, I helped him."

Grace smiled gently, closed her eyes and gave a photo-like description of the young woman which Tanya obligingly filled in with further detail in her own unique, and highly subjective, depiction.

Tanya ended her characterization by adding, "If you don't mind my saying, I don't think she's your type, Tone."

"Oh? And just what is my type, Tanya?"

The singer held her ample arms out beckoningly. "You gotta ask?"

Kozol smiled. "You're too good for me, Tanya."

"Of course I am. But that's what I like about you, Tone."

Tony raised an eyebrow. "What's that?"

"You know it."

Kozol laughed and before he said goodbye he asked the girls to let him know if they saw Claudia again. Though why, he didn't know.

None of this mess was any of his business.

ON THE WAY BACK UP his room, Tony passed Brian Love in the hall. Love flashed a malicious grin and Tony scowled. Par for the course of their relationship.

Kozol fumbled in the pocket of his shorts for his room key, then realized he wasn't going to be needing it. The door was cracked open. He figured the maid must be inside, before noticing there was no cleaning cart in sight.

Tony pushed the door wide and stepped inside.

Kozol wasn't a fastidious housekeeper but he wasn't a total slob. He'd never noticed Johnnie Beaton to be one either. And this room had all the looks of a ransacking.

Tony paused just long enough to let reality sink in. The image of Brian Love popped into his brain like a malignant tumor. Kozol tore off down the hall and caught up with the toad at the elevator doors.

"You sneaking little louse!" Tony grabbed Love by the shoulder of his good arm and pushed him up against a mirrored wall. The look of abject terror and complete surprise on Love's face gave Kozol courage and not just a little satisfaction.

"You hound me and hound me. You've got a busted arm. Too bad! I didn't break it. But keep it up and I just might break the only good one you've got left!"

Love squirmed but Tony held him fast by his shirt.

"Let go of me! Are you nuts?"

Brian's eyes darted from side to side like steel balls bouncing around in a pinball machine. What was he expecting, Kozol wondered, the cavalry?

The elevator doors slid open and an elderly couple carrying blue paper shopping bags exited, casting puzzled, fearful looks their way.

Tony smiled. "Hey, how are you, folks?" Kozol gave Love a playful poke in the gut. "Hey, we're just messing around. Sorry if we scared you, folks."

Love glared. So did the white haired gentleman as he led his silver haired wife safely down the tight hallway.

Tony listened for the sound of a door opening and closing,

then turned back to his nemesis. "What were you looking for in my room?"

Love leaned against the wall and tucked the end of his shirt back into his jeans. "I wasn't looking for anything. And I wasn't in your room, lawyer."

Tony stepped closer. "Don't play games, Love. My room's been ransacked and you just happen to be strolling by. How convenient. What I don't get is what you were looking for."

"Like I said, I wasn't in your crummy room."

"He was with me."

Tony turned. Rock Bottom stood rubbing his wide chin in a manner reminiscent of Jack Benny. "Rock. Hi. Brian was with you?"

"That's right, Tony. Brought us up a new set list. Got one for you, too. It's in our room. Love said he knocked on your door earlier but there was no answer."

Love cast a you-are-as-dumb-as-you-look face at Tony and stepped aside.

"Love was with you all this time?" Kozol did some mental calculations. He'd only been out of his room a half hour or so.

The big man shrugged. "Why not? It's his room, too."

"You mean, you two are roommates?"

"That's right, dirtbag." Love's yellow teeth flashed. Kozol considered buying the disabled guitarist a new toothbrush and a tube of that whitening toothpaste.

"He brought up the papers, hung out for a spell, then said he was taking off. Why? What's he done?" Rock stepped closer and Brian Love backed up.

"I ain't done nothing." Brian pushed the button for the elevator.

"I heard a lot of yelling," Rock said. "Why all the commotion?"

"Someone ransacked our room, mine and Johnnie's, that is,"

explained Tony. "I saw Love in the hall and thought he might know something about it."

"I ought to sue your ass for slander, lawyer!" The middle elevator doors opened and Love stepped inside, holding the door open with his good hand.

"Yeah, yeah. Just stay away from my room."

"My room's on the same floor as yours and everybody else's. I got as much right to be here as anybody." Love held up his broken arm. "A couple of weeks more, lawyer," he spat, "and you'll be walking the unemployment line. Try signing autographs there!"

Love lifted his arm. The elevator door closed.

"Sorry, Rock."

The big guy shrugged his tree-like shoulders and disappeared.

Kozol checked his hotel room a bit more thoroughly and quickly ascertained that nothing significant was missing. At least not of his stuff. Even his wallet, which he'd stupidly left lying atop the dresser, was intact, including credit cards and cash.

Johnnie's bags were still sealed, except for his toiletry kit next to the bathroom sink. So, if nothing was missing, what was the point? What had the intruder been looking for? Could someone have trashed the room for the fun of it?

A HASTY CHANGE of clothes and Tony was on the bright streets of Austin. It was hours until the band meeting Granger Murdock had called for. And Tony had had enough detecting to last him a lifetime.

Now it was tourist time. Kozol had never been to Austin and a cursory flip through the guidebooks up in his room showed him there was much worth seeing. Except first he wanted to let Izzie know that the girl Claudia had shown up.

Kozol veered up Neches, past the quaint locale of O. Henry's home. It was a National Historic Site now. A fact which Tony found ironic, as William Sydney Porter, O. Henry's real name, had also been a convicted embezzler from his years working as a bank teller in Austin. Some still say he'd been set up or it was all a matter of sloppy recordkeeping at the bank. Porter maintained his innocence though he hadn't done himself or his case much good by flipping out to Central America via New Orleans.

Returning home to be with his dying tubercular wife in 1897, the law soon caught up with him and Porter had spent several years in a Texas penitentiary for his trouble. Then again, it was a great place to write with few distractions and he did some of his earliest and, maybe best, work in prison.

Once free, O. Henry traded Texas for New York and never looked back. The little house on E. 5th Street had to be over a century old. Tony suspected that O. Henry would be glad that his old home and his reputation had been duly restored.

Up Neches, Kozol cut over on 8th Street and stopped once again at the Police & Courts Building. Izzie wasn't in, so Tony left a handwritten message for him saying that Julian Santana's sister, Claudia, had shown up.

Having done his good deed for the day, if not week, Tony took a leisurely stroll up 6th Street. Flipping through a guidebook, that he had no intention of purchasing, at a souvenir shop that shouted Tacky!, Kozol read that the east-west running streets had once been named after local trees. 6th Street had once been called Pecan Street.

A faint head, a twisting stomach and the thought of pecans reminded Tony that he hadn't eaten a thing that day. Skipping the hole in the wall pizza parlors, Kozol decided on a crowded diner on Congress called Las Manitas Avenue Cafe. He waited half an hour for a seat but figured anyplace that busy had to be good.

It was.

After a late breakfast of fried eggs and biscuits, Tony picked up a couple of souvenirs for the folks back home at the curio shop next door to the diner. He picked up a carved wooden frog. You rubbed its rough back with a stick and it made music, well, okay, noise. He also chose a little jewelry box of carved cinnamon bark. He lifted the lid, took a sniff, sneezed viciously and set it on the counter. "I'll take it," he said with watery eyes. He'd give it to a woman he knew back in Florida. She loved that sort of stuff. The frog was for her son.

Kozol marched up Congress towards the Texas State Capitol, the largest of all the U.S. state capitols. It was an architectural sibling of the U.S. Capitol in Washington, D.C., only several feet taller and through no accident.

The Texas State Capitol rises like a granite hill at the top of Congress Avenue, as if Granite Mountain, from which the big stones had come, was trying to reconstitute itself in a more updated and chic fashion.

A beige car, spitting noxious odors, pulled alongside Kozol and honked. Tony turned at the second blare.

Izzie held the wheel with one hand and waved with the other. "Come on, Tony!"

"Izzie? What are you doing here? How did you find me?"

The line of cars, filled with antsy drivers, building up behind the detective's sedan honked impatiently. Kozol hopped in and Izzie sped off.

"I got your message about finding Claudia and went looking for you at the Radisson. When you weren't there, I figured you couldn't be far. Not on foot. You eat?"

"Yeah, real food for a change."

Izzie ignored a red light and passed under the freeway. "A lesser man would be insulted by that remark."

"I didn't know you were so noble. I'm going to have to

sharpen up my insult skills. Maybe pick up a copy of *Don Rickles For Dummies*."

They passed through a neighborhood of well-kept older homes. "So," said Izzie, "you found Claudia, eh?"

"Sort of." Tony gave his friend the run down on what had happened at the hotel.

"That's interesting." Izzie scratched his head. "You see, we found Claudia, too."

"Oh, yeah? That's great."

"Mmmm, maybe yes, maybe no." Izzie pulled into a restaurant that looked to be converted from a primitive gas station. One Kozol's grandpa might have found modern in his day.

"You see," Izzie continued, as Tony followed him across the gravel topped parking lot, "the Claudia we found is basically a bag of bones lying in guano in a bat cave outside of San Antonio."

He held the smudgy glass door to the rundown little restaurant open for Tony. "Sure you don't want something to eat? My treat."

FIVE

"WE GOT THIS SHOT UP from the San Antonio police department earlier this morning. Standard procedure when a Jane Doe pops up. Information goes out around the state, maybe even national—depending—to try and pick up some leads."

Tony listened.

"Normally, I don't pay too much attention, I've got enough on my plate as it is, but everyone was talking about this one this morning. Then a couple of hours later, I heard the girl's name mentioned."

Kozol stared at the photo that had popped up on Izzie's computer screen.

"It's some kind of medical ID bracelet, you know?"

Now Tony understood what he was looking at.

Izzie rubbed a finger against the glass. "You can make out the name right here." He traced a shiny line with his fingernail. "Claudia Santana. She was diabetic. This chain was found around the victim's wrist."

Tony wasn't surprised that Claudia Santana's bones were the chief subject of discussion amongst the Austin police that day.

Izzie pushed some keys and the next image was a shot of Claudia's bones on the floor of Bracken Cave.

Kozol shuddered. It was hard to imagine that what he saw

was real and not some Hollywood magic, special effects cooked up on a dark stage for a campy fright movie where everybody lets loose a bloodcurdling scream just before the knife plunges into his or her chest.

But he was looking right at the screen and there was no denying it. A young woman's body had been reduced to bone in a matter of hours.

"See that crud all over the ground?" Izzie looked at Kozol.

"Yeah, I see."

"Well, some of that is guano, bat droppings. The rest is those dermestid beetles I was telling you about. The way it was explained to me, they survive on the crap that falls like mana from the heavens as it were."

Kozol nodded. In this case, attaining the Holy Reward wasn't such a lofty goal, heaven being the ceiling of Bracken Cave.

"That and any injured, sick or brainless young bats that fly too close to the ground," continued Izzie. "Those nasty little buggers can strip a bat clean inside of three minutes give or take. And the ammonia they produce is so thick you've got to wear a respirator inside."

"Lovely." Tony's stomach did a flip-flop. He wondered how Izzie was managing to keep his lunch down.

"I mean, you got twenty million or so Mexican free-tailed bats in Bracken Cave—that's the largest bat colony in the world! And only twenty miles from downtown San Antonio!"

"But still," Tony said, "to consume an entire body and that quickly. Claudia was alive last night, according to her brother. How could she suddenly end up dead and reduced to—to—" Kozol stared at the small pile of bones nearly submerged in the thickly coated cave floor, "that?"

"Not hard at all." Izzie wiped his hands on his trousers as if to wipe away the filth of Bracken Cave. "San Antonio's only a couple of hours away from Austin by car." The detective kicked his feet up on the keyboard. The computer protested with muffled beeps and chirps. "Let's say Claudia Santana really was at the Austinland Theater last night. Someone, person unknown, takes her and kills her, here in Austin or someplace else. He takes her and kills her there at the cave, maybe, and dumps the body."

"Convenient."

"Neat as anything. You know, it was something on the order of a miracle that the body was found at all."

"Why do you say that? You told me a crew found her and called the police." Kozol sat and turned his face deliberately from the screen. Even though he'd never known the victim, he was finding it hard to look at those bones without imagining the living flesh that once was attached.

And what if the girl hadn't been dead at all when she was tossed in the cave?! Would those bugs have eaten her alive?

Eaten alive by uncountable millions of tiny beetles... A wave of nausea passed over Tony like a southern California earthquake.

"A crew, right. But this isn't like Congress Ave. and it ain't Disneyland. Not a lot of visitors. The Bracken Cave is privately held by the BCI."

"What's that?"

"Bat Conservation International. They're an outfit that deals with conservation issues and bat protection initiatives. The point is, you can't just walk right in Bracken Cave and wander around like some tourist with a Japanese camera."

"Somebody did."

"Yeah, well it ain't supposed to happen. Anyway, a university team from Utah had done a documentary last month on bats and had gotten permission to return for two more days of shooting in the cave."

"And they found Claudia's body." It was all too creepy. Tony longed to get out of the claustrophobic building—it was beginning to feel much too like a cave—and into the sunshine.

"If that film crew hadn't come in today..." Izzie shook his head. "Those bones could've been buried under a ton of guano and debris inside a week, I suspect. We'd never have found her."

"And none of this explains the fact that Claudia was looking for me poolside at the Radisson only a few hours ago."

"I told you it was interesting, didn't I?"

"That you did. I'm glad I didn't know about those bats when we were down in San Antonio the other night. Just the thought of it makes me feel creepy." Tony shuddered. "All those bats."

"You serious? I mean, you've got about a million of them outside your window."

Tony swivelled. The sun shone out the nearest window. "Very funny."

"Not that window, tourist. Your hotel window."

"Right."

"I'm serious. They live under the Congress Avenue Bridge. Didn't you say you had a view of Town Lake?"

"Yeah."

"That means you've got a prime location. Of course, it's a little early in the year for them. But come summer the place is busting out all over with them. They live in the crevices that run along beneath the bridge. The largest urban bat colony in North America is what I heard."

"You're pulling my leg."

"No, I'm not kidding. This is a big tourist attraction for us. Why, everybody knows about the bats." Izzie held his hands about four inches apart. "You see, when engineers reconstructed the Congress Ave. Bridge back in 1980, I think, they created these crevices, that run the length of the span. Purely for structural reasons, mind you. But it turns out the bats love them. And, before long, Congress Ave. was their summer home."

Tony was shaking his head.

"I didn't believe it myself when I first came here. I couldn't figure out why thousands of people were standing around the bridge at sunset that first summer of mine on the force, and I pulled over to see what all the commotion was. Bats. Though like I said, it's a little early in the year for them right now. They winter down in Mexico and come up here to make babies. Sometimes I think the bats have got a better life than mine."

"I think I'll remind Johnnie to keep the windows closed at night all the same."

"Hey, you! Come back here!"

Tony and Izzie turned in unison. The commotion was coming from the stairwell. The sound of many feet pounding down the stairs swelled like frantic African drumbeats warning of the Great White Hunter's approach.

Kozol waited for Tarzan to swing down on a vine and perform a search and rescue operation.

"Stop!"

"Let go of me. Let me loose!"

Angry voices. "You can't just—"

Several flustered police officers and one young man burst around the corner of the staircase.

"Mr. Tony!"

Kozol folded his arms, looking askance. It was Julian Santana. Oh, joy.

Out of breath, Julian came to a sneaker versus tile screeching halt at Det. Ibanez's desk and blurted out, "Claudia, where is she? The man upstairs says my sister is here. Where is Claudia?"

Rough hands grabbed the young man from behind and pinned his arms behind his back.

"Now just what knucklehead told him that?" demanded Izzie. No one fessed up.

One grim-faced officer spoke up. "Don't worry, he won't get away from us again."

Julian struggled valiantly, if vainly. "I want to see my sister! She's done nothing wrong. Neither have I. Let me go!"

"Let him go, Sid."

"But—"

"Let him go." Izzie's face best represented a sour lemon pressed in a vise.

"Are you sure?" pressed the pugnacious young officer. "Hayes was interviewing this guy upstairs when he takes off running like a guilty friggin' ax murderer or something!"

Izzie chuckled. "Yeah, yeah. Tell Hayes it's under control."

Sid let go of Julian's arms and he and his companions barely hesitated before heading off. Izzie pointed to an empty chair. "Have a seat, Mr. Santana."

Julian glanced across the room, a look of desperation on his face like a wild tiger fearing a cold, steel cage.

Kozol looked from Julian to Izzie's computer screen. The shot of Claudia's clean, white bones seemed as big as a freeway billboard now.

"I am not sitting down until you tell me where my sister is."

"Have it your way." Izzie turned to Kozol. He held a worn down pencil in his right hand. "We found Mr. Santana here at a rooming house near the university."

"I see." Tony's opinion of the young Mexican was not a favorable one, considering he was as good a candidate as any for having planted the coke in his guitar case.

Izzie rattled off the address from a slip of paper. "It's in a residential section of town near UT, up near an area known as The Drag. You should check it out sometime while you're here, Tony. The Drag, that is. Lots of handcrafted arts and crafts. Pick yourself up some more souvenirs."

Kozol said he just might.

Julian just remained dumb.

"So, got time to get a little fishing in while you're in town?" Izzie pulled back the pencil and let go an imaginary cast.

"Maybe. I'll see how things shape up. I live by the whim of Clint Cash at this point."

"Great. Let's hope," replied Izzie as he reeled in his catch. "We've got some terrific lakes here in the Hill Country. I picked up a little sixteen footer with a thirty-five horse Johnson engine last year. I keep it docked out at Lake Buchanan. That's the largest of the Highland Lakes, you know. Plenty of stripers, crappie—caught myself a fine largemouth bass the last time I was out." Izzie held his hands a good twenty inches apart. "Best to get out early though, and I know you're keeping odd hours these days."

"Don't worry. That's fine by me. I could use a little R&R. Being on the road is becoming stifling."

"I bet."

Julian sat.

Det. Ibanez smiled politely. "So, Mr. Santana," he began, "let's start at the beginning."

"What beginning?"

"The last time you saw your sister."

Julian glanced at Tony. "Last night outside the theater."

"What time was this?"

Julian shrugged. "Around nine o'clock. Maybe a little later."

"And this guy," Izzie studied his notes, "Jack Henderson, let her in?"

"Is this the man with the saber tooth cat boots?"

Det. Ibanez nodded.

"Si. That was the man who let Claudia into the Austinland Theater."

"Tell me, why would Henderson have let your sister, Claudia, inside? Did she know him?"

"I do not think so..."

"Who was she going to see?"

The young man shrugged. "She didn't tell me."

"And you never saw her after that?"

"No," replied Julian sullenly. "*Senor* Kozol helped me to look, but we did not find her. Only—only that dead man."

"And instead of calling for the police, like Mr. Kozol here asked you to do, you ran."

Julian stiffened. "I did not run."

Izzie smiled. "You fled the scene of a crime."

The young man bit his lip. "I didn't see what I could do and it had nothing to do with Claudia. How are you going to help me find my sister, Mister Policeman? You ask so many questions, but that's what I want to know!" Julian half-rose from his chair.

"Julian—" Tony motioned for the kid to sit.

"You ever fight with your sister, Julian?"

The young man's eyes turned to sharp points. "No."

"Come on, all brothers and sisters fight sometime..."

"Not like you mean."

With a click of a mouse button, Izzie pulled up the photo of Claudia Santana's ID bracelet. "You recognize this?" The detective pointed at the screen with his pencil.

Leaning forward, Julian answered. "It is Claudia's! Where is my sister?" His hands gripped the edge of the desktop.

Izzie scratched the sides of his head. "Where did you go when you left the Austinland last night, Mr. Santana?"

Julian stepped back from the desk. "I walked around a while. Looking for Claudia. Then I went back to my room."

"Anybody see you?"

Once again, the young man shrugged. "I don't know. Why

are you asking me so many questions? You should be helping me find my sister. Do you know where she is or not?"

Tony rose and placed a hand on Julian's shoulder. "Calm down, Julian." Kozol wished Izzie would finish his current line of questioning and get around to asking the kid about the cocaine. Even though Izzie seemed to believe Tony was innocent, Tony himself would feel better if the police could quickly come up with somebody better to pin the drugs on.

Now Izzie stood. He twisted the computer monitor until the screen was fully in Julian's face. Izzie clicked the mouse button once more.

The eery image of pale white bones glowing against a background of bat guano and dermestid beetles filled the screen and even seemed to spill over the edges. Tony could only imagine the foulness of Bracken Cave's air.

Kozol half-expected the little bugs to spill out onto Izzie's desk and begin gnawing away at his fingertips. Instinctively, he lifted his hands from the surface in self-defense.

"Your sister is dead, Julian." Izzie watched the young man closely.

Julian stared transfixed at the screen. A melded look of horror and disbelief molded his face.

"I think you may be involved."

"Oh, come on, Izzie," Tony implored. Maybe his friend was going too far.

Izzie held up a hand in warning.

Julian Santana, a trace of perspiration over his lip, grabbed the nearest thing at hand, a three-tiered plastic mail tray and hurled it at the screen. Papers and envelopes flew in all directions. The plastic letter tray hit the center of the monitor and bounced to the floor.

With a speed Kozol wouldn't have imagined possible, Izzie Ibanez was around his desk and holding Julian by the shoulder in a grip that, from the expression on the young man's face, had to hurt like the Devil had got him in a headlock.

The pinched expression on Julian's face said Tony was right. With his free hand, Izzie picked up his desk phone and asked for someone to escort Mr. Santana to a holding cell. "It's only until you cool off, Mr. Santana."

Julian said nothing. He cast a confused look at Kozol as he was led away.

Tony squirmed. He didn't want to believe Julian had killed his sister. Still, what could he do? "Was that necessary, Izzie? I doubt if he really killed his sister."

"Hey, I know that." Izzie shook out his hand and began picking papers up from the floor.

Tony pitched in.

"The kid's clean. No priors." He looked at the mess. "He's got a temper, though."

"You all but accused him flat out of murdering his own sister, for crying out loud! Who wouldn't overreact?"

Izzie grinned. "That was the whole point. I wanted to hit him hard and see what response I got, if any."

"Happy?"

Izzie shrugged. "Nah. Not one bit. I don't even know that was his sister in Bracken Cave, let alone that he murdered her. All we've got for sure is an apparently missing girl named Claudia Santana and those bones in Bracken Cave wearing a bracelet with the girl's name on it. That's hardly proof positive."

"Seems proof enough to me."

"Could be Claudia came to see you this morning and the victim was only wearing her ID bracelet for some other reason."

"Sounds far fetched, even for you, Izzie."

"Yeah, I know. If we could just come up with a witness who'd seen the girl backstage last night and tie that up with a motive for her murder we'd be getting somewhere. Not that any of that helps my own case, which is the murder of Jack Henderson."

"So what happens now?"

"For me, nothing. We'll see what forensics down in San Antonio turns up. This is their case, not ours. Like I said, I'm supposed to be investigating the Austinland murder, not missing persons."

"Anything turn up on Henderson yet?"

"Preliminary shows blunt trauma to the back of the head. The microphone stand looks like our weapon." Izzie tossed his mail back up on the desk, in no apparent order, and set the plastic trays on top of the loose pile. "But exactly when and why, who knows? You got any ideas of who might have wanted this Henderson guy dead?"

"None so far."

"A jealous husband, maybe?"

"I don't think so." Not judging by the nasty comments he'd heard. More like a jealous boyfriend.

"Give it some thought. And use your ears and eyes. I doubt Henderson's killing was a random thing. Like most murders, the victim probably knew his killer. And you're on the inside of this one." Izzie dropped a photo of Jack Henderson's limp form across his desk.

"Has anyone informed his family yet?" This was fishing. Tony wasn't even sure what family Jack had. He'd never spoken much about his family, at least not to Kozol.

"We're checking into Henderson's background now. He wasn't married. That I know."

"That fits."

"How's that?"

"Oh, nothing." No point in smearing a man's reputation over unfounded innuendo.

Izzie leaned forward and pressed his hands against the desk as if he suddenly feared it might float away. "You've got good instincts, Tony. I can tell. See what you can pick up from what the people around you say and do, my friend."

Though Kozol disagreed with the good instincts part, he promised Izzie he'd do what he could, then asked, "What's going to happen to that Santana kid?" In spite of everything, Tony couldn't help but feel a little sorry for the young man.

Izzie grinned. "I'll let him go in about an hour or so. Like I told him, after he cools off. Can't have a hothead running around Austin bothering the locals or the tourists. Not good for business."

"Uh, detective..." The officer Kozol only knew as Sid was standing near the desk, scratching his jaw with the back of one hairy hand. His right hand rested on his holster. He appeared to be looking for something.

Izzie asked, "What's up?"

"You remember that Mexican, Santana?"

"Gee," Izzie slapped a palm against his forehead, "let me see if I can remember. It's been so long..." He raised an eyebrow. "So tell me already, what's the punch line?"

Sid made a face. "You seen 'em?"

Izzie's eyebrow fell.

"He's gone."

Tony interjected. "Gone where?"

"I don't know. One minute he was in the interrogation room and the next he was gone."

"And who was supposed to be watching him?" demanded Izzie.

Sid squirmed. "Well..."

"Never mind." Izzie rolled his eyes for Tony's benefit. "See what I put up with?"

"You want to put a warrant out on him?" inquired Sid.

"Nah. What for? He's not actually wanted for anything that we can hold him on." Izzie stared thoughtfully at the bones of Claudia Santana. "And I have a feeling that kid's going to be sticking around. Like a little old fly buzzing around my ear that just won't go away..."

Niet, westspider 2017 it settings. Wysos for application. I'm
weight and last 2017. However, a model disclosures in the course
Coaches wave: land. The waves Chip and this is on prince to
waiting agency, the whole add in the environment. We golf of
driver things applying.

SIX

TONY HAD THE uneasy sense of being followed from the minute he left the police station.

It was a sixth sense.

Or maybe it was only a sick sense. Whatever else it might be, it was palpable. Like when stopped at an intersection, sitting in his Saab, and feeling someone's eyes on him. He'd turn and eyes would meet in an awkward ocular embrace across the painted lines in the road.

Of course, in this case, he figured it was the Santana kid trailing him like a relentless, yet hapless, bloodhound.

Kozol headed up 7th Street. There was that tickling sensation at the back of his skull, like a dentist trying to tackle a cavity from the wrong direction. But when he turned his head, there was no one there. So why did he feel like he was being watched?

It was three o'clock. The band meeting had been scheduled for two. Murdock was going to be seething. Yet, if he hurried, Tony figured he might still make the tail end of it. Sometimes these things ran long, like Granger's speeches.

This one hadn't. The conference room was empty.

"Rats," muttered Tony. Hotel staffers were rearranging the tables and stacking up the chairs. Cigarette fumes hung in the air, though Kozol was pretty sure smoking wasn't allowed indoors. That wouldn't have stopped Granger.

And Granger must have been pissed that Tony hadn't shown up. Clint must have been big-time pissed.

It was Hector Orlando that Tony found sitting alone at the bar, ignoring the televisions dangling overhead like seductresses, tempting weekend warriors with their constant sports coverage. Hector's left hand held a glass of something liquid and, knowing Hector, high octane. His right hand beat out a rhythm atop the bar counter.

Hector was a fairly small man of Latin descent mixed with a generous heaping of Texas, as he liked to say. His father was from Guadalajara. His mother was an Anglo from El Paso.

At forty, Orlando might have been the oldest member of Clint Cash and the Cowhands, at least of the onstage players. A lock of oily, black hair, mixed with a few strands of obstinate gray, fell across his left eyebrow, offsetting his nose, which had been broken and squashed savagely to the right.

The nose had been gifted to the exceptional drummer in a wildly out-of-control bar fight he'd been swept up in when he was about twenty years old. Two morons had begun fighting over a woman, who, in Hector's opinion, hadn't been pretty enough to buy a drink for let alone lose a tooth over.

The barroom brawl had spread quickly and finally engulfed nearly all the remaining patrons and finally the band, who first had struggled vainly to keep playing despite the turmoil. When a barstool crashed through Hector's bass drum he took offense, rose and shoved the ape who'd thrown it. For his sass, Hector got his nose squashed. For his innate orneriness, the ape had received a chair across his knees.

Hector considered himself and the ape even. After all, he now possessed a nose that added character to an otherwise ordinary face. The ape merely had a permanent limp which did nothing for him.

Hector waved to Tony.

The drummer reminded Kozol of a fiddler crab gone awry. Hector's left arm was small, shrunken. Tony suspected polio, though he'd never asked and Hector had never told. The drummer's right arm was huge, muscled and overdeveloped in comparison. If Hector walked sideways, he'd be a fiddler crab.

"Thirsty?"

"Sure." Tony jumped on the empty barstool beside the drummer and ordered a Sam Adams. A baseball game played itself out silently on the TV overhead.

Hector took a healthy swig of his drink. "You sure know how to piss people off, don't you, Kozol?"

"You think so?" Tony could think of any number of people he might have annoyed, on any of several fronts. But he didn't think Hector had been one of them. Then again, he could have been wrong.

The drummer drew an uneven line across the bartop with the moisture which grew from the bottom of his glass like clear, gooey dew. "Yep."

"You have anybody particular in mind, or are you just making a comment about my award winning personality?"

Hector chuckled. "Both maybe." He scooped up a handful of salted peanuts from the nearest bowl and rolled a nut across his tongue before mashing it. "You missed the band meeting."

"I know." Tony took a swig of his Sam Adams. "So, did I miss anything important?"

Hector shrugged. "Murdock's burned for one thing. All this murder business. It's got everybody nervous."

"It isn't my fault."

Hector looked at Kozol. "Who said it was?"

Tony turned his attention to his beer bottle. "Murdock seems to want to blame me for it and all I did was discover Jack's body."

Hector made the sign of the cross. "Old Murdock only wants to keep this under control. He doesn't want anything to get in the way of this tour. There are a lot of big bucks riding on this one."

"Yeah. I know, I know."

"Speaking of which, there was some talking of letting you loose."

Kozol swivelled on his stool. "That bastard, Love. He's been wanting me out of here since the beginning!"

"Actually," replied the drummer, "that'd be Murdock again."

"Not Brian?"

"Nope."

Tony frowned. This could be bad. "What did Clint say?"

"Not much. Said he'd think on it." Hector wet his lips. "With Clint, that could take a spell."

The pile of bills at home in Florida appeared magically before Kozol's eyes. "You think he'll fire me, Hector?"

"Man, I don't know. I gave up knowing anything a long time ago. And nobody tells me nothing. I'm just the drummer."

"Tell me, Hector," Kozol said after a moment, "who do you think murdered Jack?"

The drummer's eyebrows did a playful tandem dance across his shiny forehead as he sucked the last bit of alcohol from his glass. "Clint, of course."

"Clint?" Tony couldn't believe Hector really meant it. Still... "What do you mean?"

"Clint Cash and the Cowhands kills everybody."

"But you don't seriously think—"

"Death seems to cling to Clint like a bad smell. You ever been skunked? Can't get the smell gone no matter what you do."

"What on earth are you talking about?"

The drummer paused, caught in some apparent inner conflict. Tony waited for an explanation. It didn't come.

When Hector did speak again, he'd changed course. "I heard about the drugs they found on you."

"Not on me," replied Kozol, defensively, "in my guitar case. And the stuff wasn't mine. Somebody planted it."

"Yeah, I know that," said Hector with a wave of his small arm.

"You do? What makes you so sure?"

"You don't figure for the type. Besides—"

"Besides what?" Hector was developing an irritating habit of leaving what seemed to be the most important things unsaid.

"Nothing. Be careful, is all."

"Trust me. I plan on keeping my hands and my nose clean."

"That's all you gotta do to survive in this outfit."

"You don't sound so thrilled to be in the band yourself, Hector. Ever think of moving on to something else? You must get other offers."

"Me? I'm like a little old flea, complacent, you know? Riding the back of this old, mangy mongrel. Now, another dog might come along and be looking pretty good, but who knows? They're all dogs, ain't they?"

It seemed more a statement of fact than a question worth pondering and Tony let it hang there in the air between them like an unsteady soap bubble. The little drummer's river ran deep. Deeper than Tony had suspected. Besides, he wouldn't know what to answer anyway. Hector was probably right.

"Hey," Hector grinned, "you know what they call a drummer without a girlfriend?"

"No, what?"

"Homeless!" Hector patted Tony heartily across the back and dropped a ten dollar bill on the bar. "See you at the show, Tony. Don't be late for that!"

Kozol watched the drummer exit. And though his gait wasn't sideways like a crab, Hector weaved—just enough to create the illusion of that fiddler crab gone awry.

"Hey."

Tony twisted around.

A fellow in a pink paisley shirt, which hung like a pair of overlarge curtains from his rounded shoulders, over the soft mound of his belly and down to his knees, nursing a big yellow drink, was rising from a nearby booth. He set his glass on the bartop next to Kozol's near empty Sam Adams.

His pudgy face was pale as paper and he looked like Uncle Fester from *The Addams Family*. The man wore a pair of eyeglasses that Kozol found somewhat familiar. After a moment, he realized they looked awfully similar to the pair his mother used to wear.

Paisley man chuckled.

Tony, for no sane reason, found this annoying and he glared at the man. Waiting.

The stranger pushed his glasses up his nose and said, "Odd character."

"Excuse me?" Kozol wasn't sure whether the guy meant Tony or himself. Between the two of them, Kozol's vote went to Mr. Paisley Curtains.

The man chuckled once more. Not a pleasant thing to listen to. It sounded like a baby machine gun burping off key. "Your friend. He's Hector Orlando, the drummer with Clint Cash and the Cowhands, am I right?"

"Yeah, you're right."

"Wow! I thought I recognized him. I love Clint. And that Hector is a thumping good drummer. The best!" He held out his hand after, Tony noticed, wiping it across his wet lips. "I'm Roger. Roger Daring. Are you with the band, too?"

"Yes. Temporarily, that is. I play rhythm guitar." Tony reluctantly shook the man's soft hand. It was as cold as the ice in the glass Roger kept reaching for.

"What's your name, bud?"

"Tony Kozol."

"Pleased to make your acquaintance."

"Same."

Mr. Paisley Curtains, Roger, jumped onto a barstool, which Tony expected to sink into the ground like a limp toadstool under the unsustainable load. "Have a seat."

Instead, Tony edged back. He needed his space.

"You know," Daring said, in low conspiratorial tones, "I heard what you guys were talking about." Roger glanced at the television screen. "I'm not much of a sports fan. I follow the football scores. That's about it. So, I couldn't help overhearing."

Tony was thinking of telling Roger that he heard his mother calling when Mr. Paisley Curtains grabbed his arm and said, "I read about that murder last night, too. Jack Henderson. Part of Clint's entourage, am I right?"

Tony nodded. "Right again." He extricated himself from Roger's grip and wondered if the guy was ever going to go away.

"You think he meant it?"

"Do I think who meant what?"

Roger leaned closer as Tony leaned back. His breath stunk of pineapple juice and saliva. "Hector Orlando. About Jack Henderson's murder. Do you think he meant it about Clint Cash being responsible?"

Kozol leaned back further. It was like a dance of opposition. If Roger had been any closer they'd have been kissing Hollywood-style and Tony wasn't ready to go that far. He turned his head and took a breath of non-putrefied pineapple air.

When Tony turned back, he said, "No, of course not. Why,

I don't even know what Hector meant. But Clint sure isn't any killer. He's a singer, for crying out loud."

Now it was Tony's turn to move closer. "Besides, I should know." Kozol downed the last of his beer and called for another.

"How's that?"

Tony raised his eyes meaningfully. "I was there."

"No!"

Tony nodded. "I saw the body."

Roger whispered as the bartender strolled past. "Do you know who the murderer is?"

Kozol twisted his lips. "No, but I've found out some things. You see, I've got a friend on the force here. And I've got some ideas of my own."

Roger pressed in. "Really?"

Tony told his anxious listener about the rumors he'd heard floating about like distant thunder clouds—about Jack Henderson, about his bandmates, and even about the body in Bracken Cave.

"Kozol!"

Tony spun around. That irksome voice belonged to one Granger Murdock, who stood about a dozen yards away, dressed in black from his cowboy hat to his boots. His arms were wrapped around his chest like competing pythons. "You missed the meetin'."

"Sorry, Granger. It won't happen again."

"Yep." He tapped his foot. "You and me got to talk."

"Now?"

Murdock nodded. Once.

Kozol shrugged. "Duty calls," he said to his bar mate, slipping away from his stool. On the way, he grabbed his beer.

"Sure," replied Roger. "Nice talking to you. Real nice. Maybe I'll see you around."

Tony turned. "Sure. Maybe."

Granger's eyes narrowed like the muzzles on a double barreled shotgun sighting up a quail. "Who is that?"

"I dunno," replied Kozol. "Just some tourist."

Murdock studied the man in the pink paisley shirt and baggy shorts. His sneakers had holes in them.

Roger, Tony noticed, had returned to admiring his drink. Probably waiting for another lost soul to share a moment or two with. What a way to spend a vacation.

"Some folks just got no sense of style," Granger commented. He ran a finger along the fine edge of his black shirt. "You'd think a grown man would know how to dress."

"Face it, not everyone has your class, Granger."

Murdock nodded once more. "True." He slid into an empty booth and motioned for Kozol to do the same. "You're on thin ice, Kozol."

Tony didn't like the sound of that. "How do you mean?"

Murdock toyed with a gold-plated cigarette lighter. His fingertips rolled it round and round. Granger popped the lid open, popped it shut, popped it open again and pressed an inch high finger of fire into the air before shutting it again. "There's been some grumbling. Some talk of letting you go even."

"I don't get it." Tony laid his hands on the table. "Is there a problem with my playing?"

"Nah, you play okay."

Okay? Coming from Murdock, Tony decided to take that as a compliment. "So what's the problem?"

"We've had some complaints about you. You're trouble."

Tony rose, bumping his hips against the tabletop. "Me? That's ridiculous and you know it!"

"Is it?" Murdock had a sour, resolute look on his face. "You've been with us for all of a month or so and I've got a dead friend and I've got the police sniffing around looking for a murderer and some friggin' drug dealer. Maybe even one in the same."

"That's all got nothing to do with me."

"The way I hear it, you've been around murder before."

"That doesn't make me a murderer, Granger."

"No," Granger agreed, "it don't. But it does make you a fistful of trouble and bad publicity—which we don't need."

"Exactly what are you telling me?" If he was fired, Tony wanted to know it and get on with his life. Maybe take a little fishing trip for a week or two with Izzie, if he could get some time off, too.

Murdock looked up and said stonily, "Consider yourself on probation."

"Meaning what?"

"Meaning nothing else goes wrong and it's smooth sailing for all of us. Rock the boat and it's you who's gonna get bucked off this bronco into the cold, hard wind."

Kozol's head spun amongst the raging mixed metaphors. Nonetheless, he agreed.

"Have you been to the conference yet?"

"No," Kozol replied. "I haven't had the chance."

"Well, see that you get the chance tomorrow."

"Why's that?"

"Clint is speaking on a panel along with several industry bigwigs at eleven tomorrow morning. It'd be good if *everybody* in the band was there. Show some support."

"I'll be there," pledged Tony.

"Ever been to one of these music conferences?"

"No, never."

"Well, just give your name at the check-in. You're all paid up. And when you get inside, you'll get a goodie bag that'll give you a hernia the size of a baseball. Better'n Halloween."

Tony could hardly wait. "Goodie bag?" Tony thought of little plastic bags filled with cheap plastic toys and candies. The stuff children's birthday parties are made of.

Murdock nodded. "A truckload of CD's, magazines, demo cassettes, you name it." Clint's manager rose. "Clint's doing his 'Whispering' Bill Anderson imitation tonight. At the end of the number, we all applaud."

"Sure, Granger." That meant they'd be doing a cover of *Bright Lights And Country Music*. Tony had long ago realized that show biz and disingenuous went very much together. Clint had been doing the Bill Anderson bit every few shows and the crowds ate it up. If Murdock wanted Kozol to clap, he'd clap. Tony smacked his hands together lightly.

Murdock gave Kozol a dead-eyed look. "Work on it." Granger headed for the bar and Tony took this as his cue to leave.

On his way across the lobby, Kozol caught sight of Mr. Paisley Curtains, Roger Daring, climbing into a late model white two-door sedan. There was nothing remarkable about the vehicle, if you discounted the fact that painted on the side of the door were the call letters KKAU, and they belonged to a local TV station whose channel number followed.

This was not going to be Tony's lucky day. He had the sick suspicion that Roger Daring was a news reporter. And, like a moron, Kozol had spilled his guts out to him.

As the probable reporter drove off, Tony started mentally planning his new resumé. He had a feeling he was going to be needing it soon.

Real soon.

Like maybe tonight or tomorrow, when the next edition of the news came on and Granger Murdock spilled the rest of Kozol's brainless guts all over the sidewalk.

Not that Tony would blame him...

SEVEN

THAT EVENING'S REHEARSAL stank like a piss-soaked cigar.

It wasn't anybody in particular. At least Tony wasn't pointing any fingers. Everybody in the band was uptight and nervous. Barely on speaking terms with one another. The tension was as palpable as wet clay in Tony's hands.

Hector was avoiding him. Brian Love snarled. Murdock paced. Even the normally placid Rock seemed edgy and distracted—as tense as a high E string about to snap.

At one point, Rock and Tony broke up a fist fight that started up between Brian Love and Hector Orlando. The two men had been trading barbs all through the rehearsal and finally Love had snapped and thrown a microphone stand at the little drummer, sending the floor tom into his side and knocking Hector off his throne.

And the two men, with only the two good arms between them, launched into a spirited, yet comical and unbloody, no-holds-barred wrestling and punching fest that showed no signs of abating until Tony and Rock stepped in and pulled the two breathless men apart.

When Kozol had tried to ask Hector, who usually seemed so cool and unflappable, what the problem was, the drummer's only comment had been, "I hate that jerk." Then he stomped off the stage.

That had left Tony with no room to maneuver in his questioning as he could merely agree. Love was a jerk. Kozol figured that would make a good title for a country and western song. *Love Is A Jerk.* Maybe he should try to write a country tune? Who knew? He could be the next Conway Twitty or Ray Stevens...

Only Clint had seemed immune to the agitated atmosphere, joking and carrying on like the good old boy he longed to be. Part of the Nashville elite.

Grace and Tanya stayed at the back edge of the stage, singing their parts as they arose. No more, no less. Kozol sat with them at a small table backstage after Clint called an end to practice. Tough to keep going without a drummer.

Three beers kept them company.

Kozol surveyed the empty Austinland Theater stage. High watt bulbs had been powered down and provided only dim light and ghostly shadows. Kirk was untangling, or tangling depending on what one thought of his motor skills, some speaker cable at the far end.

Otherwise, the place looked deserted. Unless the Phantom of the Austinland was lurking about. Clint and the rest of the band probably wouldn't get back until nearly showtime.

"Wasn't there supposed to be some dinner with the bigwigs going on?" Kozol asked nervously. If he missed showing up to another band function, Murdock would have his hide.

"Canceled," Tanya replied. "Granger said something came up."

"I wonder what."

"Do you really care, Tone?"

Kozol chuckled. "No, I guess I don't."

Grace was looking pensive and remote.

"Come on, kids," chided Tanya, "let's not let all this negative energy pull us down and into the void! Besides," she added, "remember? It's my birthday and I don't allow any of this frowning stuff. You got it?"

Tony smiled. "Yeah, I got it. Sorry. It's like dancing on a live wire around here lately."

Grace agreed. "I'll be glad when we move on." She pushed her beer across the tabletop. "A new town, a new outlook."

Tony nodded solemnly—his eyes lost in the light freckles of Grace's exposed chest. She was wearing a flattering yellow tube top and jeans.

"Speaking of outlooks," Tanya said, "any news from your friend on the Austin PD concerning Jack?"

"No. Nothing much. They had a kid—you remember that Julian I had in here last night—"

Tanya nodded. "They think he did it?"

"He's sort of a suspect, but I don't expect anything to come of it."

"Well, I hope they catch the bastard, whoever it is." Tanya folded her arms around her imposing chest. "Jack was a piece of heaven."

Grace said, "If you say so."

"Is that supposed to mean something?" snapped Tanya.

"No," replied Grace quickly, "only that I didn't know him well at all." She patted Tanya's hand. "Not like you did, Tanya."

Tanya's big mass settled like a mountain following an aftershock. "That's right. You take my word for it. We lost a good man."

"I know, Tanya," Grace said apologetically. "I didn't mean anything, really."

Tanya grinned broadly. "And speaking of a good man," she announced, "I'm going shopping."

"Buying yourself a birthday present?" teased Tony.

"Only if I can find a man who fits!" Tanya pulled at her dress. It was an overwhelming purple thing. "After I change into something decent. I don't know what I was thinking when I paid good money for this thing. All the kiddies think I'm *Barney!*" She warbled, "I love you, you love me..."

With that, Tanya Tobler dove into the background like a big purple sun shriveling away as the light years sped by.

"See you lovebirds later!" came the muffled cry from the dark corridor. This was followed by the sound of a goodnight to the security guard, swiftly followed by the sharp clack of a door closing tight.

"Lovebirds!" Tony said in disbelief. "That Tanya is something else." A slight pink tint had spread across his cheeks.

"Yes, she is." Grace ran a hand through her hair. "So," she said, a quiver in her voice and an unfathomable look in her eyes, "you want to?"

"Want to what?"

"Do it."

Tony suddenly noted the odd sensation of all the blood in his body rotating to and from various regions, including some that had never seen blood, before at dizzying speed. Corpuscles propelled themselves round and round like *Speed Racer* in the *Mach 5* trying to catch *Racer X*.

And, somehow, oxygen must've stopped reaching his brain. There was a definite shortage of element 8 and rationality. "Uh, do it?"

Grace grinned mischievously. "Yeah, you know. Have sex."

Kozol shifted in his chair. He felt a tingling along his scalpline which he guessed was a rapidly forming ridge line of sweat. If he didn't calm down, it would soon be pouring down his forehead, branding him for the buffoon he feared he already must resemble in the eyes of Grace.

It's not that he'd never had sex before or even had a problem with going to bed with the girl. It was her bluntness about it that had surprised and unnerved him. Not to mention those stories he'd heard about her and his temporary, but powerful, boss, Clint Cash.

Still, he couldn't let little things like that get in the way of his, if not better, at least male, judgment. "Sure."

"Okay, let's go." Grace picked her slender calfskin purse up from the floor. "Your place or mine?"

Tony grabbed his jacket. He shrugged. "Not much difference, is there?" Then he remembered his roommate, the inimitable Johnnie Beaton. "Then again, I am sharing a room with Johnnie. He might be there..."

"And I'm sharing a room with Tanya, of course. But since she's going shopping—" Grace slid her arm through Tony's. "I suggest you be a gentleman and walk me to my door."

Kozol, resting the urge to do so at a gallop, matched her step. Time to succumb to the moment and enjoy the feel of a woman's arm entwined with his own.

"Tanya forgot her shawl." He pointed to the chair where Tanya had been seated. The black shawl was draped over the back. "Shall we take it?"

"No. We'll be back in a couple of hours, anyway. Might as well leave it."

A couple of hours? Tony could only hope he'd live up to expectations.

GRACE'S HOTEL ROOM was thankfully empty of other occupants. Tony tossed his Clint Cash and the Cowhands tour denim jacket on the dresser. They were custom jackets, in multiple shades of sequins, playing out a scene of mountains and a purple sunset. It was a depiction based on the cover of Clint's new album, *Go West, Young Man*. The tiny sequins shimmered like a rainbow on fire.

But Kozol had stopped looking at sequins. Grace, standing beside the open window, had gently rolled her tube top down to her waist.

She turned towards Tony, one eyebrow raised, then helped him remove his shirt. Her hair smelled of strawberries.

The lovemaking was everything Kozol remembered love-making being with a twenty-two year old. Though the last time he'd had sex with a girl that age, he'd been twenty-three himself. And, although Grace was a good dozen years younger than he, Tony was relieved to find that some things never changed.

When it was over and neither could wrestle any longer, Grace stroked Tony's cheek and wept quietly on her pillow. When Kozol asked her why, she only shook her head.

Waking from a hazy half-sleep, one hunger satisfied, they agreed to have a quick dinner before the show in the hotel's dining room. They strolled up Congress Avenue afterward, hand in hand, over to Sixth and the Austinland. Along the way, Grace had spotted Tanya through the doorway of a dark tavern where she'd roped a young man in polished cowboy boots and tight Wranglers. Tony was keeping a nervous eye out for Clint.

Tony bid Grace an awkward goodbye at the door to his dressing room.

"See you soon." Grace tilted her head and smiled a little as Tony quickly kissed her cheek.

On impulse, Kozol took her wrist. "Do you want to go some-place afterwards?"

Grace held two fingers up to his face and rubbed the stub-ble that spouted from his chin. "Tanya's party is tonight, re-member?"

"Oh, right." Tony's face displayed disappointment, then alarm. "I forgot to get her a present!"

Grace laughed. "I wouldn't want to be in your shoes." She looked at her slender silver wristwatch. "Only about an hour and twenty minutes until show time, too." She stood on her tip-toes and kissed his nose. "We'll think of something after the concert. Now, I've got to start getting ready."

"Sure." Tony watched her leave, then, glancing at his own watch, as if he'd magically come up with an extra hour, he frowned and took off down the hall, bumping into Rock on his way out.

"Careful, Kozol. What's the big rush?" Rock, a black jacket forcibly draped over his shoulders, with a black t-shirt under-neath, sporting his typical black Lee jeans, pulled tightly over his black cowboy boots, looked for all the world like a highly-polished, giant obsidian boulder on legs.

Rock's hero in the world of haute couture was the Big Man, himself, the Man In Black, Johnny Cash. No relation to Clint, though Kozol suspected that's what Clint was hoping to imply. Tony had heard that Cash was not Clint's given last name.

Tony wished Rock would switch to flat-soled shoes or sneakers, anything to level the field a bit, so he wasn't always having to crane his neck back drastically to look in the guy's face and not at his pecs. "Sorry, Rock. I've got to run out for a minute. Tell Murdock I'll be right back, if he asks."

"But he's already asking! You know how he gets this close to show time. The opening act is already out there," protested Rock.

"Just tell him, okay?" Kozol was down the hall and out the back door.

Running into the nearest store, Tony picked out a bottle of perfume, a rose-colored scarf, a funky looking white hat—Tanya was also a big hat collector—and the latest Carlos Santana CD which he'd spotted in the window of a record shop on the way back to the Austinland. After all, Tanya had said she loved the stuff.

Tossing everything into the largest bag, he glanced at the

time and raced to the theater. It was only twenty-three minutes to scheduled show time. Clint and Granger would be getting ready to string him from the tallest tree about now. Tony rubbed his neck and hoped such punishment had been outlawed in Texas, but he wasn't quite sure. At least he hoped the trees weren't too big around these parts.

There had been no time for gift wrap either. Maybe Grace could help him out with that after the concert.

Loping between the parked tour buses, taking long strides accompanied by shorter and shorter breaths, Tony slammed into the door of Clint's bus as it flew open in his face. His parcels slipped from his fingers. "Oh, excuse me, Clint," started Kozol, in a daze.

Then he stopped, for stepping down, with his back to the door of Clint's bus, which had been painted specially red, white and blue like a Chet Atkins guitar, was none other than Julian Santana. "You again!"

Julian swivelled, a mask of fear on his face. "Mr. Tony! You scared me."

"What were you doing in there?" Kozol was wheezing. He tried to peek inside the bus, yet could see nothing but the driver's empty seat. "Clint in there?"

Julian nodded. "I came to look for my sister."

Tony collected his gifts from where they'd been scattered beside and beneath the big bus. He dusted himself and his presents off. "I haven't got time for this. You're going to get yourself in trouble, if you aren't in any already." Kozol looked at his watch. "Which I am. I'm due on stage."

"But, Mr. Tony—"

Kozol ran toward the backstage door and started banging. Glancing back, as he waited for security, he saw the Santana kid running in the opposite direction. The door to Clint's bus was now shut.

Backstage was a blur of activity.

Tony overheard Granger Murdock's booming voice shout out angrily, "Where the devil is he?"

Tony cried, "I'm coming!" His dressing room door lay open and the room was empty. Kozol tossed Tanya's gifts under the makeup table, wiped the perspiration from his forehead with the back of his sleeve and ran as quickly as he could still manage up the crowded hallway to the offstage waiting area.

He'd passed the half dozen members of the opening band coming off. It was some local Austin outfit that the record label had wanted to showcase. Kozol recognized Peter Magnuson, from the A&R department of Clint's label, AWE Records, and that disc jockey—what was his name?—Scott Day, congratulating the lead vocalist, a young kid with a pimply face and a cowboy hat that looked thirteen sizes too big and so heavy it might just drive him into the ground up to his ears like a pile driver.

Clint Cash and the Cowhands were waiting to go on while the road crew and the local techies readied the stage. Granger, standing across the way, looking this direction and that, was yelling at everyone in his sight. Decked out in a lime green, rhinestone studded suit, with dangling white cowhide fringe, Brian Love stood at Granger's side, looking more like some exotic tropical fish than a human.

The two redheads could have been said to resemble a couple of roses, especially Love in that green suit of his. Fish aside, Love looked like a gangly rosebush. But about the only word that came to Kozol's mind that had anything in common with both men and rosebushes was a form of the word prickly.

"I swear I'm going to wring his neck if he don't show up soon." Murdock grabbed Kirk. "Go check the men's room again."

Kirk looked at Love who waved for him to go.

Tony gestured. "Hey, it's all right. I'm here!"

Granger ignored him.

Kozol walked over.

Tanya approached from the other side. She hitched her shawl up over her shoulders and rubbed up against Tony. "Warm me up, Tone. It's too darn cold back here."

Murdock scowled. "You know Clint likes it cold as a witch's box. So don't complain, Tanya."

Tanya rolled her eyes for Tony's benefit.

"Sorry I'm late, Granger. I didn't mean to make you go looking for me."

"Who in tarnation is looking for you?" He glared. "Not me, that's who."

Kirk was back.

"Any sign of him?"

"Nah. Sorry, Granger. I even searched the ladies' room." The kid smirked. "I can look some more, if you want?"

"No." Granger tilted back his hat. "Just make sure everything is set up proper on stage." He cursed. "It's hard to get anything done right around here without Henderson. Whole damn operation is falling apart." Murdock tapped his watch. "Have everything ready in five, Kirk!"

Tony turned and mouthed in Tanya's direction, "What's going on?"

"Nobody can find Hector," she replied. "I wouldn't worry about it, though, Granger. You know Hector. He's always on time and he's never missed a show that I know of. He's a real professional."

"Yeah," Love chimed in, "now, if only he could keep time."

Kozol waved a hand in front of his face, clearing the air. Love's beer breath seemed to be hunting him.

Love grinned. "You know what they call somebody who hangs out with musicians?"

Tanya groaned. "Please..."

Tony frowned, expecting another lawyer crack.

"A drummer!" Love's laughter went unaccompanied.

"Yeah, yeah. Come on, Brian. Help me look outside," ordered Granger.

A vision of Clint's red, white and blue tour bus popped into Kozol's head. "Maybe he's with Clint?"

"Nah, Clint's up in the control booth with Levine," Murdock replied.

Levine, Tony knew, was Arthur Levine, the president of AWE Records. "That's funny, I—" Hadn't he just seen Julian talking to Clint? Come to think of it, he hadn't. Julian had only implied so.

Murdock was looking at him. "You what?"

"Nothing."

"Right," drawled Granger. "Well, thanks for all your help, Kozol. Now, if you don't mind..."

"Yeah, yeah. I'm leaving."

Love lightly reached for Tanya's forearm. "What do you say, Tanya? Keep a couple of good old boys company?"

Tanya laughed and said, "Sure. Best offer I've had all day."

"And don't you go too far, Kozol," ordered Granger, taking giant steps in the direction of the rear doors.

"Don't worry, I'll be around. Hey," Tony called, "do any of you know where Grace is?"

"Why, last time I seen her, her arm was hanging off of Clint's!" Love replied nastily, without so much as turning around.

Tony fumed. Even without seeing the bastard's face, he knew Love had been smirking. Kozol wondered if Love could possibly know that he'd slept with Grace.

Theirs was a small world, but he wouldn't have thought the news could have traveled that fast. Had Love seen them going into Grace's hotel room together somehow?

Kozol asked a stagehand for directions to the upstairs control booth. There was a narrow, nearly vertical stairway at the front of the Austinland leading to a low-ceiling room with a large plate glass window staring down at the stage like a giant ogre's shiny eye.

Seated around the broad PA mixer and some recording gear were three men. The man with the salt and pepper hair and thick jowls Tony knew to be the theater's show director. He was softly giving last minute lighting instructions to a subordinate.

The other fellow was wearing baggy shorts, from which his spindly legs stuck out like match sticks. His red Converse high-tops completed the picture, looking as they did like sulfurous match tips. This was a sharp contrast to the overdeveloped torso and arms which threatened to rip his cotton t-shirt to shreds. This was Otto Owen, another integral member of Clint's crew. He was the FOH. The front-of-house man. A sound man and more.

Owen was also a body builder in his spare time, though apparently he considered his body to exist only from the waist up.

Owen was saying to the stage director and his assistant, "I want to run two clusters, flying right and left, ground-stacked with subs off the auxiliary." As FOH mixer and production manager, Otto Owen's job was making sure that everything to do with lighting and sound ran smoothly.

"Owen?"

Owen twisted his thick neck, prying his eyes away from the sound board with apparent difficulty. "Yeah, what's up, Kozol? Hector finally get his ass here?"

"No," Tony replied. His eyes swept the tiny room. There was a door, closed, in the rear side. "Isn't Clint up here with you?" What he really wanted to know was where Grace had gone, but he dared not ask.

"Nah, he cut out a little while ago."

"Oh, Mr. Levine with him then?" Tony asked, ever the subtle investigator.

"I dunno." Owen flexed his arms, scratched his head with uneven fingernails and picked up a smouldering cigar.

So that explained the smell. It was like a Havana tavern up here, thought Kozol.

Tony was wondering what to do next when the FOH added, "I think they said something about going back to the studmobile until we could get started." A cloud of smoke followed his words across the room.

Again, Kozol wanted to ask who "we" meant, but didn't. The last thing he needed was for the crew to start razzing him about having a crush on Grace; who was looking more and more like one of Clint's girls, after all. And he didn't need to ask what the studmobile was—that was the crew's nickname for Clint's bus.

"Thanks anyway."

"No problem."

Visions of Clint and Grace locked in a fervent sexual embrace in the back of Clint's studmobile shot through Tony's head as he bounced down the stairs.

Clint's bus was near the back of the building in a cluster of trucks and buses. The door was closed. Tony knocked lightly. No answer.

Feeling like a twelve year old and a fool, assuming the two were not interrelated, he pressed an ear against the side of the bus at the spot where he figured Clint's bedroom would be.

Did he hear something?

Was it the sound of violent lovemaking?

A stranger in a security t-shirt walked past, giving Kozol the eye. Tony pulled away from the tour bus and made a show of looking for something in his pockets. The security guard glanced at the pass hanging around Kozol's neck and moved on.

Tony hurried back to the bus's door and knocked again. Louder. "Hey, Clint! You in there? It's me, Tony!" He pressed an ear against the door once more, this time his left. Maybe it had a more powerful receiver.

Tony didn't know if he was hearing something or imagining something and he didn't know which was worse. But he had to know.

Pulling his head away, the narrow door fell open with a tiny squeak, like a doormouse complaining of being roused from a deep sleep. Tony's heart jumped up to moderato. He stepped up on the threshold. "Clint?" he whispered. "You in here?"

The bowels of the bus were dark but for a lone light coming from the extreme rear of the vehicle. That was the sitting area, where Clint would hang out listening to music, watching TV or composing on the road.

Tony quietly tiptoed his way there. "Clint?" He felt compelled to whisper. The sitting area was deserted. The TV was off. The CD player was off. Only the lamp on the table by the sofa seemed to have requested a jolt of electricity.

Kozol turned the lamp off and made his way forward. On impulse, he stopped at the door which led to Clint's sleeping quarters. It was closed. Clint's traveling bedroom was on the driver's side of the bus, towards the middle. The kitchen area and bathroom were opposite.

Were Clint and Grace lying behind that door on Clint's narrow bed, holding one another in a naked embrace, and holding their collective breath waiting for him to leave?

Tony was about to try the old ear trick once more when a clatter came from the galley. Kozol swirled in panic. The noise continued. But it wasn't human. Tony pulled open the galley's accordion-style door and smiled in the direction of the refrigerator. He opened the icebox door. The icemaker was working alone. Putting in some overtime. Doing its business.

Kozol let out a long, slow sigh of relief and faced Clint's bedroom once more. Tentatively, he tried the handle. For a moment, he thought it might have been locked from the inside. Were they cowards?

Then it turned.

The room, short and narrow, was dark and the shades were down.

Kozol waited for his eyes to adjust to the gloom. A trace of lavender scented the air. There was a vague heap on the bed, which was little more than a glorified bunk. Its shape became more solid as his eyes adapted to the shadows. Two lovers caught in the act?

"Clint? You awake?" Tony moved closer. "Grace?"

Kozol's hand groped its way up a lamp base resting on the table at the bedside until his fingers found the switch. Light filled the small room like an explosion. "Hector?"

EIGHT

HECTOR WASN'T LISTENING.

Though he was looking in Kozol's direction. If you could call dead eyes staring your way looking.

Hector lay stretched out unevenly atop Clint's bed; still wearing the black jeans and t-shirt Tony had seen him in earlier. But last time they'd met, they'd both been breathing. That was only true of half of them now.

Hector Orlando's big right arm clutched the bedspread. The smaller left arm hung uselessly at his side, much as it had in life. Kozol noted a redness across the drummer's neck, visible even through the stubble of a day's growth of hair. Tony couldn't help wondering how long hair could keep growing after death. Hadn't he read somewhere that it kept sprouting for a considerable time afterward?

Careful not to touch anything more in the space, Tony backed out towards the bedroom door. An icy hand grabbed his shoulder.

"What the hell is going on here?"

Kozol turned, pulling loose from the icy grip that fixed him. "Clint!"

And standing beside him was Grace. She threw a look at Tony that seemed to be pleading. But for what, Tony didn't know or care.

Clint's cold blue eyes glanced over Kozol's shoulder and across the cubicle that was his bedroom. "What the—"

"It's not what you think." Tony followed Clint's look. Even as he spoke, Tony realized how bad things looked. Clint had just caught him in his private bus, not to mention hovering over a bandmate's dead body. "It's Hector. He's dead. I think it was murder."

Grace let loose a stifled cry and ran back along the narrow hallway, her hollow sounding footsteps raising the tension.

"It's okay, honey," called Clint. "Don't be scared." Clint turned to Kozol. His arm blocked the door. "So, what happened? What are you doing here in my bus? And why is Hector lying in my bed?"

Kozol swallowed some air. "Everybody was looking for Hector. He was missing."

"I know that," cracked Clint. "Tell me something I don't know already."

"I was taking a look around, too. Helping out." Tony kept his back to the corpse. "I thought I heard a sound this way. I tried knocking but there was no answer. Then I tried the door handle. It wasn't locked, so I came on in."

"I always lock up," countered Clint. "Too many nimble fingers around always tempted to lift something of mine—a guitar, a shirt. Hell, even underwear! There's a lot of crazy fans out there."

"Well, it wasn't locked when I tried it," insisted Tony. "Anyway, I came inside and found Hector lying there. We've got to call the police, Clint."

Clint sighed. "Damn." He tapped his fingers on the side of the wall. "It'd be so much easier if we could bury people in our backyards like dogs, you know?" lamented Clint. "I mean, I loved Hector. But why the hell did he have to go and get himself killed in my bus?"

Tony couldn't help himself. "Gee, I'm sure he's real sorry about that, Clint."

"Yeah." Clint waved a deprecating hand. "I know."

Tony rolled his eyes.

Zoom! Swoosh!

Couldn't hurt Clint Cash with a close range barb even when it was aimed with surgical precision at his own thick skull. Couldn't so much as raise a blip on his consciousness.

"You call 'em, Tony," ordered Clint. He stepped across the hall into the kitchen area and opened a top cabinet from which he removed a bottle of Jim Beam. "I need a drink. It's what we'd come here for in the first place. You want one?"

Kozol shook his head no. "I don't think we should be touching anything, Clint. Fingerprints, you know?"

Clint grinned. "Don't worry, I'll skip the glass. He held the bottle up to his lips and sucked. "Lip prints only, see?"

"I'll use the backstage phone. Please, don't touch anything else." Kozol exited the front of the bus. The killer, if there had been one, had to have done so also. It was the only way on or off unless they'd used a window.

Grace was slouched over the steering wheel, sitting like an over-sized ragdoll in the driver's seat. She was sobbing. Tony wanted to reach out and hold her. Offer her some comfort. Something other than the Southern Comfort which was all Clint was probably capable of tendering.

But Tony didn't. Maybe that was Clint's job anyway, no matter how he did it. Kozol was just the hired help.

Tony flashed his badge to security which seemed heavier than usual, not that it had done a whole lot of good so far, and reached for the phone on the wall beside the door.

"Kozol!"

Tony spun around. Granger Murdock and Brian Love were approaching. And fast. He punched 9.

"Where have you been?" Granger's breath was a lovely blend of tobacco and whiskey.

Tony figured they ought to bottle the scent and sell it as cologne to these wannabe cowboys. The same ones who bought all those Harley Davidsons that they rolled out on Sundays and let rot in their garages the other six days a week.

Granger was still talking. "I mean, it's enough I gotta look for that reprobate drummer, but I expect everybody else to stay in their dressing rooms until we can get this goddam show started!"

Kozol balanced the receiver in his hand and said, "I found Hector, Granger."

"You did?" Love said.

Tony nodded. "He's in Clint's bus and—"

Murdock jabbed Brian in the ribs with a pointy elbow. "Go get 'em and kick his sorry butt all the way to the stage."

"Sending Love's not going to do much good," commented Tony.

"Why not?" Granger wanted to know. "Is Hector drunk? And don't be telling me my business. I don't care if he's six sheets to the wind, I want his ass on stage playing the drums right now."

Love snarled like a mad bulldog smelling blood. "Yeah, these boots were made for kicking butt. I don't care if Hector is drunk'er than a skunk. I'll get his sorry ass on stage."

"If you do get him on stage, it's going to look awfully peculiar."

"How's that?"

"Having a dead man propped up on his drum throne? I don't know, it strikes me the folk in the audience might find it a little odd. Of course, I'm sure you'll get some publicity out of it. I can't say it will be good, but—"

"Shut up, Kozol," said Murdock. "What do you mean dead

man?" Granger grabbed at the two words and spit them back in Kozol's face.

"Yeah, dead man. You know, like in not breathing. No heartbeat."

"Are you trying to be funny?"

Tony shook his head and waved the phone in Granger's face. "I was just about to call the police." Kozol punched 1.

"Wait just a minute." Murdock grabbed the phone from Tony's hands and slid it carefully into its cradle. "Let's think about this. I mean, we've got a theater full of people out there expecting a Clint Cash show."

"Music people," interjected Love.

"Hell, yeah. The president of AWE Records himself is out there." Granger settled an arm over Tony's shoulder. "Maybe we ought to put off any telephoning until after the concert..."

"But—"

"I mean, follow me on this," continued Murdock, neatly cutting off Tony's attempted protest like a kid in daddy's Corvette cutting off granny in her Camry. "The man's dead. He ain't gonna mind waiting. The show will be over in an hour, two tops!"

Love was nodding like a dime-store sycophant.

"Let old Brian here sit on Hector for a while. Then we call the police. Why, I'll even call them myself. But if we call the police now, they'll be swarming all over the place like flies on a cow patty. Creating a scene. A huge friggin' scene."

"But, Granger—"

"Think about it, Kozol. Folks will panic. Why, they're already getting anxious out there waiting for the show to get started. Hear them?" Murdock cupped a hand to his ear.

Tony didn't need to follow suit to hear the restless chanting coming from the seats.

"If we don't get this show started soon, there could be trouble. Maybe a riot. Who knows how many innocent people could get hurt?"

"In the first place," answered Tony, extricating himself from his manager's grasp, "Clint is already babysitting Hector. And I don't think he's too happy about it, or about having the body in his bus to begin with. I don't think he'll take too kindly to the idea of Hector lying around in his bed another couple of hours while rigor mortis sets in either. Don't ask me why, it's just this gut feeling I have."

"Clint?" Brian said quickly. "Clint's with the body already?"

"That's right," Tony replied. "And in the second place," he continued, facing Murdock, "how in Heaven's name are you going to have a concert tonight without Hector? Have you got another drummer somewhere who knows the set list? Because unless there is an understudy in this outfit that I don't know about, and waiting in the wings somewhere nearby, there isn't going to be any show!"

Granger slammed his hat against the side of the wall. "Shoot!"

Tony only wished Murdock's head had been in it. "Listen," Kozol said, taking a stab at bending a little himself—after all, Murdock was probably right about the panic and confusion bit if word leaked out about another possible murder—"a friend of mine is in the audience. At least, he should be. He's with the Austin PD."

"That little detective friend of yours?" Love said.

"That's right. I remember that I left him tickets for tonight's show."

"Oh, that's just great..." mumbled Granger.

"But that's just it. Don't you see? It is great. I'll go fetch him, discreetly. And I'll explain the situation." Tony shrugged his shoulders as if shifting a burden. "The rest is up to him. He makes the call."

"I don't know, Granger," Love commented, stirring the pot one last time.

Murdock shut him up with a wave of his hand. "I'd say we've got no choice. Find him," he said. Murdock grabbed Tony by the shirt. "But be quiet about it."

Kozol nodded and skirted along the hall at the side of the theater. He made his way quickly to the stage and placed himself behind a wall of speakers that rose to his shoulders. Now all he had to do was figure out where among all those faces Izzie was seated.

A quick attempt to systematically scour the seats told him that was going to be nearly impossible. He'd have to get closer. Tony pushed past the security men guarding a small stairs to the left of center stage and entered the audience. People began shouting at him—demanding explanations. What was going on? When was the show going to start? Where was Clint?

"I don't know, I don't know." Tony repeated this mantra over and over as he wove up the aisles. Finally, near the center of the fourteenth row, he spotted Izzie. Kozol waved to get his friend's attention but it was no use. Izzie was busy talking up an attractive dark-skinned girl seated beside him.

"Excuse me," said Tony, pushing his way through the crowded seats and taking several unintentional kicks to his shins along the way.

"Hey, Izzie!"

The detective looked up. "Hi, Tony, my man. How are you doing? And what are you doing here?" Izzie turned toward the girl he'd been making amorous faces at and said, "This is the guy I was telling you about who is responsible for our being here." Izzie gave Kozol the thumbs up. "These are great seats, man! Center stage, just about level. Thanks again, Tony."

Izzie squeezed a possessive arm around the girl. "This is Marta. Marta, Tony."

Hi's passed back and forth in a quick volley. Marta was an attractive Latin woman tucked into tight jeans and a tighter yellow sweater that left conspicuous bulges in all the right places. By comparison, Izzie's baggy brown trousers and vintage ZZ Top t-shirt looked like found clothes. And the sandals on his feet weren't helping the look.

"Uh, listen, Izzie," began Kozol, awkwardly aware of the faces watching them, "could I talk to you for a second? Something's come up."

"Sure, shoot."

"Um, in private?"

"Aw, c'mon, Tony," protested Izzie. "You don't have to worry about Marta here. Nothing you can say will embarrass her or anything. Will it, honey?"

Marta smiled and held Izzie's arm. "I think your friend wants to speak to you alone, Isidore, and so you should go." She held a long, smooth finger with a finely chiseled and polished nail up to his chin. "But don't be so very long. Okay?"

"Thank you," said Kozol. "It really is kind of important and I wouldn't interrupt your date if it wasn't. And, it isn't you," he stammered. "It's just not something I can say," Tony dropped his voice, "with all these people around."

Marta nodded. "I understand. Go now. Shoo!"

Izzie smacked his girlfriend on the cheek and rose with a groan. "This better be good," he said, following in Tony's wake. "The show's going to start any time."

"Don't worry," replied Tony. "It's good. Besides, the show's not going to start without me."

"Hey, that's right!" Izzie slapped Kozol on the back. "Lead on, Macbeth!"

Tony pushed forward, once more through the crowd and up the stage.

"Wow, I never thought I'd be on stage with Clint Cash and

the Cowhands!" Izzie said with glee, as he set foot on the boards. "Is that Clint's guitar?" Izzie reached for a hollow bodied electric guitar propped up near the corner of the stage. It was red.

"Leave that alone," Tony called out.

"I only wanted to touch it. I'm not going to hurt it."

"Will you come on?" motioned Kozol. "This is important, Izzie."

"Alright, alright."

The two of them halted backstage. Murdock and Love stopped talking and were staring in their direction. Izzie followed Tony's gaze. "So, what's up, Tony? Are you going to formally introduce me to the band?"

"You might say that."

"Of course, I met some of them during my investigations concerning Jack Henderson. Of course, that was in an official capacity. Let me make sure my hands are clean." He wiped them vigorously up and down against the sides of his trousers as if that would help.

"There is one person in particular I'd like you to meet."

"Who's that?"

"Hector." Kozol rolled the sleeves of his jacket up to his elbows. He was heating up like a slow cooked Christmas goose. "Hector Orlando. And I'd say your hands are clean enough for him. Then again," Kozol added, "you might want to wear gloves."

Izzie sighed. "Tony, my old friend, I think you spent too much time in the New Age. You make no sense at all." He banged a palm twice then thrice against the side of his head. "You're too deep for me. But then again, so's an outhouse."

Murdock and Love appeared before them. "You tell 'em, yet?" asked Murdock.

"More important—did anybody hear you?" quipped Love caustically, as if he could do it any other way.

"Not exactly. Izzie, this is Granger Murdock, Clint's manager. And this is Brian—"

"Yeah, yeah," Love said. "He knows who the heck we are."

Izzie arched an eyebrow and said with amusement, "Yes, we've all met or at the least crossed paths." He appeared to be giving Love the once over. "The other night and," continued Izzie, "if this is about Jack Henderson's murder, I can assure you and Mr. Cash that the Austin Police Department is doing everything in its power to apprehend the person or persons involved in this heinous crime."

Izzie was sounding more like a bureaucrat than a cop, if you asked Tony.

"Though at the moment," the detective went on, "there is nothing more I can tell you, gentlemen." Izzie shuffled his sandaled feet back and forth.

Granger glared at the policeman's ZZ Top t-shirt and rubbed the sharp, front edge of his Stetson between his thumb and forefinger. "It ain't about Jack."

"No, Izzie," Tony said. "It's about Hector Orlando, Clint's drummer, like I was telling you."

"What about him?"

"He's friggin' dead," Brian chuckled.

"Something funny about that?" asked Kozol.

"Nah, and I don't expect it'll affect his timing much. If you ask me, it might even improve it!"

"Shut up, Brian," ordered Murdock. "Show some respect." He turned to the detective. "Do we have to do this here?" He made a show of looking around the room. People were scuttling in all directions. Others stood about looking like useless scenery enhancements. "It's like goddam Grand Central Station, for chrissake. Don't you want to look at," he dropped his voice, "the body?"

"Sounds like a good idea," Izzie answered. He turned to Tony. "You see the girl I'm with?"

Kozol nodded.

"You owe me big time for this one, Tony. Couldn't you have simply phoned the police station?"

"We wanted to keep this quiet. And since I knew you were in the audience..." Tony paused. "Sorry, Izzie."

The detective's lips took a sudden downturn. "Say, there isn't going to be any concert either, is there?"

Love couldn't let an opportunity to speak ill of the dead pass. "Can you hold a pair of drumsticks, detective?"

Izzie kept his eyes on Tony.

Kozol shrugged lamely. "Sorry again, Iz."

"This really stinks bigtime. Let's get this damn thing over with. Where is this body?"

Murdock provided the answer. "Clint's bus."

Izzie's eyes couldn't help but pop a gauge. "Clint's tour bus?"

Tony said, "Yes."

"I'll be damned. Wait until Marta hears about this," Izzie exclaimed, as he followed Murdock, Love and Kozol out the Austinland Theater's rear exit.

Clint himself stood at the door of the red, white and blue studmobile. He leaned nonchalantly against the side of the steel bus. "I couldn't bear standing next to a dead guy anymore," he explained, "so I stepped out."

"Where's Grace?" Tony asked.

Clint's thumb jerked up over his shoulder. "Still in there. Crying her eyeballs out."

Love leapt up onto the first tiny step, using his good arm. Det. Ibanez stopped him with a firm hand. "Wait," said Izzie. "I'd better go first." He turned to Clint. "Anybody else been in or out?"

"Just him." Clint pointed to Kozol.

"You?"

"I, uh, found the body. I guess I should have told you."

There was a pregnant silence all around as the detective rubbed his right ear until it was bright pink. "Wouldn't have hurt."

Izzie bounded up the three steps and paused at the driver's seat. Grace was huddled in the large captain's chair, forehead resting against the leather steering wheel, small hands clutching its sides. "Ma'am?"

Grace slowly glanced upward. "He's dead." She sobbed and coughed, her chest heaving with the difficulty of trying to breathe at the same time.

"Yes, I know. Miss Burns, right?"

The young singer nodded.

Izzie looked down at Kozol. "Would you come up and take the lady inside, Tony? Maybe get her something to drink." He patted Grace lightly on the shoulder. "I'll be in shortly to take statements from both of you."

Grace looked at Tony with pleading chestnut eyes. He held out his hand.

And she took it.

NINE

TONY PULLED OFF his jacket and draped it over Grace's pale, bare shoulders.

"Thanks," she muttered softly, hunched over as if bearing the weight of the world on her back and not merely a yard and a half of denim.

Kozol led Grace into her dressing room. There was no sign of Tanya and she was a little large to be hiding behind the sofa cushions, after all. Grace collapsed onto the smallish, olive green sofa against the far wall and fell silent. It sagged.

"Well," began Tony, "if you're going to be all right, I'll be going."

She looked up. The life had gone out of her face, the twinkle had left her eyes for the stars from whence it had come. "Can't you stay?"

"I don't know. I mean..."

"Detective Ibanez did ask us to wait here."

Kozol looked about the room as if he was lost. Maybe he was. "You want me to?"

"Isn't it obvious?"

Tony sank into a chair at the dressing table. "Nothing is obvious anymore." He ran a nervous hand through his hair, ridding his scalp of a half-dozen strands in the process. Oh great, he thought miserably, now he was losing his hair.

"What do you mean?" Grace wanted to know.

"Nothing," replied Tony. "Then again, everything."

Grace looked up at him from across the room with near-lifeless eyes.

"I mean, I'm not sure about anything at all—" Tony met her gaze. "You, me, the murders...being in this band."

Grace stiffened. "You're not thinking of quitting, are you, Tony?"

Kozol's laugh was a hollow one. "More likely I'll be fired first."

"No way. Clint loves you."

With a steady gaze, Tony asked, "Does he love you?"

Grace turned away from Tony's pinning look.

The pounding, which Kozol mistook for his heart, was the dressing room door, shaking like a leaf in a sudden squall. Tony sighed and rose.

Tony didn't know which of them had been saved by the interruption; him by not having to hear an answer he wouldn't like, or Grace by not having to give an answer she didn't want to utter. Perhaps they'd both been saved.

"That must be Izzie." But when he opened the door, it was Rock Bottom who faced him. "Rock."

"Hey, Tony." He tipped his head respectfully in Grace's direction. "Hi, Grace. You two okay?"

"Sure, thanks. What's going on out there? I feel like a prisoner cooped up in here."

"Nothing much," answered Rock. "The police have taped off Clint's bus. He's madder than a homeless hornet. Threatening everybody in sight with lawyers and all."

"Glad I missed it."

"And Granger had to get up on stage and announce that the show has been canceled."

"What did he tell the fans?" Tony pictured an angry mob tearing Clint's manager apart limb from limb.

"Just that Clint was sick and would have to reschedule."

"I'm sure that went over well."

"Granger spoke his piece and then some guy in the front row threw a beer can at his puss and he took off like a jackrabbit being run to ground by a coyote." The big man was grinning. "That was a sight!"

"Wish I'd seen that." It was better than most of the sights he had witnessed lately. "What about Hector?"

Grace let out a whimper.

"The medical men are taking him out now. No way I could watch." Rock shivered. "Listen, Tony, could I talk to you for a sec?"

"Yeah, go ahead." Tony waved the bass player inside.

Rock hesitated, refusing to cross the threshold. "No." He glanced awkwardly at Grace. "I meant outside. In private."

Pushing his eyebrows together, Tony replied, "Sure, I guess. Are you going to be okay?" He looked to Grace. She nodded and stared into space. Tony had a feeling she'd let the sofa swallow her up if only it could.

Rock moved aside and Tony stepped into the hall. Rock closed the door behind them.

"So, what's up, Rock?"

"I wanted to ask you about the murders."

"You said murders. What makes you so sure Hector was murdered?"

"I heard the cops talking. Seems pretty sure."

"So? What about them?" Kozol asked hotly. "You don't think I'm responsible in some way, too? Do you?"

"No, it's not like that, Tony." Rock tugged at the sleeve of his shirt. "I was only wondering if you had any ideas. That's all."

"Ideas?" He studied the big man. "You mean like who the murderer might be?"

"Yeah, that's it."

Tony leaned back against the wall. "No," he said slowly. "Jack got clobbered, as far as we've all heard, and Hector..." Tony shrugged. "We'll see what the coroner has to say. Anybody could have committed both murders, even you or I. Or it could be there are two murderers. If you ask me, it's not likely. But who knows? Maybe you have some ideas, Rock?"

Rock took a step back. "No, not really. But I listen to what's going on. People always think the big guys are stupid. Like in the movies. I'm not."

"I never thought you were."

"I figured you might like some help."

"Help?"

"Sure, everybody knows you used to be a lawyer." The bassist's gaze met him square on. "And they say you're something of a snoop."

Kozol's laugh hid his pique. "Gee, thanks."

Rock scratched his head. "Bad choice of words, I guess. I didn't mean any offense. I only meant that you might know how to look into things. Figure them out."

"Find a killer?"

"Maybe. Yeah, maybe."

"And you're going to help me?"

Rock grinned like a big kid. "Yeah, maybe."

Tony smiled back. "Okay, Rock, I'll tell you what. If I find anything out, I'll let you know and you do the same for me. Deal?"

"Deal."

"Though I'd be more than happy to let the police handle this one. Besides, we'll be on our way to Tucson soon enough."

"If the police let us go."

"Yeah." Tony paused. "If they let us go..." Kozol couldn't make up his mind if sticking around would be good or bad. Nice to hang out in a room, even if it was a hotel. Nice to do some fishing with Izzie. Likewise, nice to see if there was something like solid ground with Grace?

"Somebody call a cop?" Izzie strode up between the two men. He was clutching a Clint Cash and the Cowhands commemorative tour t-shirt and Clint's latest CD.

"Hi, Izzie, been shopping?"

"Heck, no! Granger Murdock gave me this stuff!" He thrust it in Tony's face. "Can you believe it?"

"Good for you," Kozol said. "But isn't it illegal or something? Something in the statutes about accepting gifts and bribes?"

"Only matters if he's guilty." Izzie looked at his stash. "Besides, I came here tonight as a fan not an officer of the law." He pulled his new t-shirt on over his old one. "And if he is guilty, I suppose I can give it back." Izzie added, though he didn't look too happy at the thought.

Izzie didn't look happy at the thought.

"I give up," Kozol said with a shrug. "You remember Rock, don't you?"

"Sure, how are you doing?"

"Fine." Rock looked like he wanted to run.

"You know anything about what happened tonight?"

"I know Hector's dead."

"No, I mean anything else. Like, did you see anyone in particular hanging around Clint's bus at any time?"

Rock appeared to be giving this some thought. "Nah."

Tony wondered what he himself would answer if Izzie asked him that same question. Why was he protecting Julian Santana anyway?

"If you think of anything, no matter how small, you let me know."

Rock took this for a dismissal and lumbered off with a nod.

"So," said Izzie, picking a pebble out of his sandaled toes, "let's get your statement down. Then I'll get the lady's and we're out of here. Miss Burns inside?"

"Yeah. Go easy on her, Izzie. She doesn't know anything and she's taking it pretty hard. She's just a kid."

"Yeah, you remember that yourself."

"What's that supposed to mean?"

"Nothing," Izzie said. "But I've seen you get all goofy over a girl before."

"I do not get goofy over girls!" replied Kozol huffily.

"Yeah, right." Izzie fished in his pockets and came up empty handed. "You got anything to write on? And a pen?"

"In my dressing room, I suppose."

"Let's go."

"What about Grace?" Tony nodded toward the closed door.

"I'll get an officer to fetch Miss Tobler to keep her company." Izzie waved at a man in uniform holding down the rear entrance.

Kozol said, "Tanya? I haven't seen her lately."

"She's over in Clint's dressing room."

The officer stopped in front of the detective. "Stay here and keep an eye on Miss Burns until I can send Miss Tobler over to sit with her, got it?"

"Sure, Izzie." It was the Bud Abbott impersonator. That meant, to Tony's chagrin, that the pudgy Lou Costello wannabe was likely lurking about. Kozol wondered if he was the only person who saw the similarities and the opportunity for a tribute, perhaps at the next Austin Policemen's Ball.

Tanya was located and sent down to console her cohort. Kozol promised he'd look in on the girls when he was through.

"Okay, Tony," began Izzie, one leg planted on a chair, the other on the ground, once the two men were alone in Kozol's sparse dressing room, "tell me what happened."

Tony paced the room. Up and down. Up and down. Never had it seemed so tiny. He slowly related what he remembered of that evening, explaining how Hector Orlando had been missing and everybody had been enlisted to go searching for him.

It was mostly the truth. Though Tony's own searching had been more on the order of finding out where Grace was, who she was with, and what she was up to. But what was a little disinformation between friends?

Kozol told Izzie how he had stumbled upon Hector in Clint's bus, then been discovered himself by Clint and Grace.

"Boy, when you stumble, you really stumble," remarked Izzie. "You'd make a great bloodhound. Why, you'd be the Jerry Lewis of bloodhounds!"

"Very funny. I'll keep that in mind when I'm pondering my next career change." Which could be sooner than later.

"So, you found Hector—lying in the dark, in Clint's bunk. Notice anything else odd?"

Tony shook his head no.

"Hear anything?"

"No, I thought I did, but it was nothing."

"So, it was sheer luck, good or bad, that you happened upon Hector's body in Clint's bus?"

Kozol didn't know if that was a question or a statement. He hoped for statement. He had to be very careful about leaving out the part about what he had really been doing—searching for Grace—and how he'd only found Hector's body by accident.

Tony couldn't see that it would serve any purpose except to make Izzie think he was a jealous idiot. An image his old friend seemed only too eager to subscribe to.

"I guess that's enough for now. I'm going to take down Miss Burns' statement. I've already got Clint's. Not that he had much to say. He might be the star, but he's not exactly the brains of this outfit, is he?" Izzie looked amused.

"No," Tony answered. "Come to think on it, I'm not sure there is a brain to this outfit. Maybe that's the problem. What exactly did Clint tell you?" That he and Grace were going back to the studmobile to do the horizontal hokey pokey?

"Like I said, not much. Only that he and Miss Burns went back to his bus to have a quick drink while they waiting for the concert to start. He wasn't too pleased to find you already inside."

"I'll bet."

"Not to mention the dead guy in his bed."

"Yeah, Clint has already expressed to me his deep regrets about that."

"Tell me, are he and the girl doing it?"

"If by doing it you mean what I think you mean and if by girl you mean Grace—"

Izzie nodded in the lascivious affirmative.

"—I don't know," finished Kozol sourly. "And I don't care. What about Julian Santana?"

"What about him?" The surprise on Izzie's face was clear. "You think he's got something to do with Hector Orlando's murder, too?"

"I'm not saying that. I only meant that after the scene in your office earlier today—"

Izzie interrupted. "What? The kid got pissed and left. Contrary to what most might think and we'd like them to believe it, people do not have to cooperate with the police or even come downtown with us without being arrested on some charge. Though that's a sad state of affairs, if you ask me. But look who I'm telling. You're a lawyer, you know that."

"You haven't seen him?"

"Santana wasn't being held for any crime so when he left the station that was the end of it. At least, I thought so. You're beginning to make me curious now. But as far as I'm concerned, that kid can keep on looking for his sister until we get a ski lift atop Mount Bonnell, for all I care."

At 785 ft., Mount Bonnell, Tony had read, was the tallest point in Austin. Somehow, Kozol couldn't picture this as competition for Vail. In the first place, they'd need some snow and not the kind found in the case of his Martin.

"Want some advice?"

Tony waited for it. He knew he was going to get it whether he asked or not; people who asked Tony if he wanted advice always did give it, no matter what his reply.

"I'd stay away from that kid, if I were you, Tony. I have a feeling that trouble follows him like a hungry mongrel and he's got his pockets full of stinking fish."

"You paint a pretty picture."

"Don't I though."

"Speaking of pretty—sorry about spoiling your date with Marta. What did you tell her?"

A look of horror transmogrified Izzie's pleasant face from laid back Latino cop to *"oh-man-I'm-in-big-trouble-and-I'm-sorry-baby"* boyfriend.

By the time Tony managed to stop laughing, Izzie was gone.

Catching sight of his shopping bag on the floor, Kozol scooped it up; gifts for the birthday girl whose party was likely canceled. At the very least, there was one less guest on the list. Hector wouldn't be needing any party hat. More like a death mask.

Tony knocked on the girls' dressing room door. Tanya opened it. "Hello, Tanya. Everything okay in here?" Tony peered over her shoulder.

Tanya stepped aside, a finger to her lips. "Yeah, Tone. Be quiet, would you? I just got Grace to sleep."

Kozol studied the young singer curled up on the sofa now, her face pale, her breathing shallow. At least Grace could rest. "I'm not surprised to see her fall asleep. Shock and stress can do that to a person. Sooner or later the body shuts down. Self defense."

"Sure. Of course, the little sedative I gave her helped her on the way."

"A sedative? Was that really necessary?"

"She asked for it."

"Detective Ibanez isn't going to like that, Tanya. I think he still wanted to ask her a few questions."

Tanya looked lovingly at the sleeping girl. "If you ask me, she's better off. This day has been shot to ribbons. Speaking of which," Tanya said, putting her hands on her hips for effect, "I could use a shot myself." She slithered up to Tony and put an arm around his waist. "Buy a girl a drink?"

"What about Grace? How's she going to get back to the hotel? We can't leave her lying here."

"Don't worry. Clint said he'd handle her. He went to get his coat."

Handle her.

Sometimes Tony wondered why the heck he ever opened his mouth at all. Don't ask the question if you don't want to hear the answer. Something any decent lawyer should know. Would know.

But then, he was no lawyer.

TEN

THE WAITRESS who handed Kozol his cola wore a black satin G-string, a stiff black collar around her slender neck with a bright white bow tie whose whiteness matched her teeth when she smiled, and little else besides the high heels that pushed her rear end up in a not unpleasant fashion.

At least she wasn't wearing much more than Tony could see. And he looked everywhere.

Tanya pulled a small bottle of Captain Morgan Original Spiced Rum from her purse. "The girls are allowed to run naked so long as you bring your own booze."

She topped off Kozol's glass with rum and then her own, sipping up some of her soda before doing so. Tanya placed the bottle on the table between them.

"Interesting place you picked here," replied Kozol, forcing himself to twist his neck back in Tanya's direction, though the image of his waitress working her way sinuously between the little tables still held his mind like a silvery mirage in a dark desert.

Kozol raised his glass. "Happy birthday, Tanya."

Glasses clinked.

"Thank you. And thanks for the presents, Tone. You're too wonderful." Tanya ran her free hand along the new scarf which she wore with apparent pleasure around her neck.

Tony glanced at her new hat. He was glad she liked it. Tanya caught his gaze. "I think it makes me look sexy." Tanya mimicked a standard model's pose, hands and arms framing her face. "What do you think, Tone?"

He smiled. "I couldn't agree more." His eyes drifted across the crowded room. It was a mostly upscale crowd at The Tender Rose by the looks of it.

Though Tony couldn't imagine why Tanya had chosen the place to celebrate her birthday, he wasn't complaining. He looked back at his companion. Her face had taken on a tired, troubled substance, as if some unseen hands had come along in the shadows and remolded her face like it was made of clay.

"You okay?"

"Yeah." Tanya jiggled her drink. "Just thinking about Hector, I guess...and Jack."

Tony patted her hand. "We're all going to miss them. I had a drink with Hector only this afternoon back at the hotel."

"Really? What did he say? I mean, how did he seem?"

"About the same." Tony thought. "Maybe a little tired."

"Aren't we all."

"How long did you know Hector, Tanya?"

"Oh, we've been with the Cowhands together all along. And of course, I'd seen Hector around Nashville, at the clubs or working in the studios. We were even in another band together briefly with an act that went nowhere."

"Who was that?"

"Freddie Riley and the Carburetors, I think. You know how it is in the music business, you tend to run into the same circle of musicians over and over." She let out a low sigh. "I'll miss him."

"You know," said Tony with a moment's hesitation, "Hector did say one thing." Though Kozol hated to bring it up. The ice he was standing on was thin enough as things stood.

"What was that?" Tanya tilted her head forward. She held up her glass. Only the ice cubes remained and they were sinking fast. "By the way, if you spot our waitress, see if you can catch her. I need a refill."

"I'll keep a look out," Tony promised.

Tanya smirked. "I bet you will, honey." She plopped her glass down on the wooden table. "Now, tell me, what was it that Hector said?"

"I was asking him if he had any ideas about who might have wanted Jack dead."

"Did he?"

"That's just it. I don't know. When I asked him, he said that Clint killed Jack."

"Clint?" repeated Tanya with obvious surprise. "That's a hoot."

"I think he meant it metaphorically. Hector said that Clint Cash and the Cowhands kills everybody."

"Maybe, but it pays good."

"That it does." This stint with Clint Cash and the Cowhands had so far been the longest stretch that Tony had been employed since being disbarred from practicing law in Florida. Tony spotted a dancer standing on one leg with her back to him. She was leaning against the bar. From a distance, she reminded him of someone he knew but he couldn't figure who or where.

"So, do you have any idea who amongst us might be dealing drugs?" Tony waved to the waitress as she crossed his path and she set another round of cold sodas between them. She was still wearing little more than a smile. But she wore it well.

"Are you talking about the coke found in your guitar case?"

"That's right."

"Heck, that could have been anybody, Tone. Lots of folk hanging around at a concert, you know that. Plenty of them on drugs, if not dealing them. Might be an employee at the Austinland, or somebody backstage on a pass—anybody. It doesn't mean it was someone from the band."

"No, I suppose not. But it doesn't rule them out, does it?" Tanya shook her head.

"And why plant the stuff in my case?"

Tanya smiled weakly. "Because it was there?"

"And I just happen to be unlucky enough to put it there and—"

"And it was handy and somebody needed someplace to stash the drugs for a few minutes and then couldn't get back to it? Maybe because the police showed up?" Tanya spat out one plausible explanation after another.

"So you don't suspect anyone in the band? Or even one of the crew?"

She shrugged noncommittally. "I'm not saying it isn't possible. But who?"

"I don't know," Tony replied unhappily. He helped himself to a refill of Tanya's rum after first pouring one for her. "Jack Henderson maybe? It could be why he was killed. A drug deal gone bad. He wouldn't be the first. And Henderson had another packet of coke on him."

"Drugs?"

Tony nodded.

"And he got killed before he could get it back out of your guitar case."

"It's one scenario."

"Hector, too?"

"I don't know," Tony was forced to admit once again. "I wouldn't think so. But then I've given up even pretending that I know anything about people or human nature for that matter."

Tanya laughed. "You're getting awfully jaded, Tone. Maybe Grace will be able to bring you around."

"More like push me over the edge," replied Tony, somewhat cryptically. He couldn't stifle a yawn.

"Tired, honey?"

He admitted he was.

Tanya patted his hand. "Say no more. It's been a long day. One of the longest. Go. Go back to the hotel, get undressed and get into bed."

"But it's your birthday—"

"Forget about it. You've already brightened it up with these lovely presents." She stroked her new scarf. "Get some rest. The world will look better tomorrow."

"Okay, you've convinced me." Kozol rose. "Aren't you coming?"

"Nah, like you said, it's my birthday. Think I'll finish my drink then wander around the Warehouse District a while."

"I'll keep you company."

"No, thanks. I'll be fine. You look beat. You've got bags under your eyes bigger than my shopping bags when I come back from the supermarket. Besides, having a hot young stud like you on my arm is going to keep the rest of the stallions away."

"You're one wild woman, Tanya." Tony gave the birthday girl a kiss goodnight.

"See you in the morning, Tone. Don't worry too much about the killings. The police are on the job, after all. And the two murders might not even be related. Hector could've been strangled by some crazed groupie."

"In Clint's bus?"

"Why not? Kinkier that way. Maybe she wanted to pretend it was really Clint Cash she was humping and not the drummer."

Tony shook his head. "Too weird."

"Amen to that." Tanya sipped her drink. "And getting weirder every day."

"Sounds like a fractured Beatles song."

"Keep it in mind, Tone. There are a lot of deranged groupies out there. Sick puppies, you know?" Tanya leaned closer. "Maybe one of them is our murderer? Maybe," she said playfully, "our groupie is out to kill off all the Cowhands? I could be next." Tanya pointed a finger at her bounteous bosom. Her finger turned slowly in Tony's direction. "Or you."

Tony scoffed at the idea. "So far, I haven't had the pleasure of considering groupies to be much of a problem."

"Give it time, Tone. Give it time. Once the girls get used to seeing your face around, you'll be holding them back with a cattle prod." Tanya's eyes twinkled playfully. "That is, if you want to."

"My luck, it will be the boys." Kozol rubbed his chest subconsciously as he headed for the door and fresh air; Tanya's pointing finger having left an indelible mark.

The wind was blowing. Tony pulled his shirt collar up tightly around his neck. When he looked up, it was to see Julian Santana, eyes wild as a conflagration, watching him. "What are you doing here?"

"Looking for Claudia."

"Try San Antonio," Tony replied callously; his mind calling up an eery picture of those pale white bones stretched out in a sea of bat guano.

"What's that supposed to mean?"

"It means your sister is dead, kid. Go back to Mexico or wherever you came from. Do not pass go. Do not collect two hundred dollars. Your sister is dead. Two men I know, or rather knew, are dead and I think it's all related somehow. And I don't know if you've got anything to do with all this bad business or not. You'd better hope you don't."

"I don't."

"So why don't you go home?"

"Because my sister is not dead and I am going to find her."

Tony exhaled a million emotions; the biggest of which right then was just how tired and frustrated he felt standing on the cold sidewalks of Austin. "You've seen the photos on Izzie's computer."

"Computers can be wrong. So can pictures. It isn't Claudia. Claudia is alive." Julian's eyes glowed with fire. "I feel her in here." The kid tapped his heart.

Kozol wanted to snap that what the boy was feeling were probably the after effects of all the cheap Mexican food he'd likely been scarfing down since he'd hit town. But even Tony recognized the doubtless insensitivity of doing so. Instead, he asked, "What were you doing in Clint's bus?"

"I told you before, Mr. Tony. I was looking for Claudia."

"And did you find her?"

"No, of course I did not. I am looking still."

"And maybe you killed Hector Orlando in the process? Why? Did he kill your sister?" Julian was shaking his head side to side. "Did you think he did or that he knew something about her disappearance?"

"No!"

"Or did Hector surprise you breaking into Clint's bus and you were afraid of him turning you in and afraid you'd go to jail? You couldn't have that and so you strangled him!" Kozol hammered the young man with questions hard as nails.

Julian clenched his teeth and his fists. "I did not kill him," he said slowly. "I have killed no one."

"Then why run?"

"Because everybody would think I had done it! You think it!"

The kid looked ready to bolt. "All right, slow down," said Kozol. "I'm not thinking anything. I don't know what to think." He rubbed his face. "Lord, I should have told the police about seeing you coming out of Clint's bus in the first place though."

"Why didn't you?"

"Because I guess deep down I don't think you're a murderer." He looked at the young Mexican. "An obsessed unbalanced psychotic, a fool with a hot temper, maybe. Absolutely. But a killer?" Tony released a shrug. "So what did you do, follow me here?"

"No. I was following Mr. Cash."

"Clint?" Tony looked back at the Tender Rose. "Well, he sure didn't go in there. In spite of the distractions, I think I would have noticed."

The young man jabbed his chin in the direction of a narrow flight of stairs between two buildings. The Tender Rose occupied the store front of a three story edifice and a pharmacy filled the ground floor space of the taller building next door.

"Up there?" A tiny neon sign stating simply G's hung over the black door.

"Yes."

"What is it?"

"I do not know. I knocked on the door and a man in a black suit answered. He would not let me enter."

"Are you sure it was Clint you saw go in?"

Julian nodded. "You could go see him?"

"And say what? Excuse me, Clint, boss," Tony added with emphasis, "but Julian Santana—you remember, that kid who was looking for his sister?—well, he followed you to this place and he wants to know what you're doing here, please?" Kozol shook his head as if to clear it of stupid ideas. Not that it ever worked. "Oh yeah, that'd go over great, just great. You promise to break my fall and pick me up when I get tossed back down those stairs?"

"Never mind," Julian said sullenly. He looked measuredly at the stairs, like a runner sizing up a hurdle. "I'll go. I'll make them let me in."

Julian lunged at the first step. Kozol clenched the back of the kid's shirt and spun him around. "You wait here, hothead. I'll check it out."

Tony reluctantly climbed the steep steps and knocked on the heavy door. Moments went by...

With a moan that could have come from the Undead, the door swung open. A man in a dark suit over a crisp white shirt stood in the entrance. He had a potato shaped face and his ears stuck out so violently that it was all Kozol could do to keep from doing the guy a favor and reaching out and pushing them back for him. Like he used to do with his Mr. Potato Head toy as a kid.

The man's eyes were sharp and calm. His lampblack hair was immaculately coifed in a sweep from front to back across his Idaho head. "Yes?"

Tony looked past the man, or at least tried to. But he was too big and the hall was too narrow. Tony saw nothing, though a tangled scent of cigar tobacco and sweet perfume leaked out. "Hey," Kozol held out his hand, which the gentleman ignored, "how are you doing? I'm Tony Kozol—of Clint Cash and the Cowhands?" He dropped his hand. "Uh, I was looking for Clint?"

The man tightened his gaze.

Tony shifted uneasily and tugged at his collar. The big brute's pupils were on the verge of disappearing completely. "He said he'd be here."

"One moment."

The door closed in Kozol's face. Though the words were comprehensible, it had sounded like a cement mixer doing a U-turn in gravel.

Tony looked down the long stairway at Julian, who stood in the shadows below, and waved. Idly, he wondered how long it would take to hit bottom. Julian, grinning the grin of the hopelessly naive, waved back.

Despite the cold, Tony began to sweat. This idea was looking dumber all the time. The man Julian had seen might not have been Clint at all. And, if indeed it was Clint, he might not be too happy with one of his band members, a temporary one at that, bursting in on him. Clint liked his privacy.

His eyes followed the slant of the stairs and Kozol was wondering just how many bones he was going to be breaking on the way down when the thick door creaked open on protesting hinges.

"Come inside," instructed the man.

With a muffled sigh of relief, Tony complied. He was led down the narrow hallway, first right, then left. There was enough light to see by. No more, no less. They paused outside an open doorway and the stout fellow gestured for Tony to go ahead.

Inside, seated around a large, rustic wooden table sat six men holding playing cards. Voices stopped as they all looked up, and one of them grinned at Kozol, though he looked a little surprised to see him.

"Tony," said Clint with a broad smile, "what are you doing here? How in tarnation did you find me? Beaton, am I right?" Clint folded his cards flat on the table and waved. "Come on over, man."

"Hello, Clint. Sorry to interrupt." Tony examined the men seated around the game table. With the exception of Clint, the only other face he recognized belonged to Scott Day, the local deejay he'd been introduced to.

"Nonsense, don't worry about it." Clint addressed his playing partners, "This here is Tony Kozol, gentleman. Plays guitar for me. Of course, you know Scott, right?"

Tony said hi.

"How's it going, Tony?" Scott reached across the table, spilling a stack of red poker chips. He squeezed Kozol's hand. "Good to see you, again."

"You too, Scott."

Everyone exchanged brief hellos. Kozol was beginning to wish he could make like a character from Kafka and "go cockroach," quietly and swiftly disappearing between the cracks in the floorboards.

"So Beaton told you about our little game—prepared to lose some money? Pull up a chair. Boys, make some room."

"Well," began Tony, wanting to do anything other than lose his money at a poker table but seeing no good way out of it, "maybe one hand."

Tony sat. At least he hadn't had to explain what he was doing there. Tony was quite happy to let Clint think Beaton had spilled the beans on the poker game. With luck, Clint would never be any the wiser.

A young woman stood in front of the well-stocked bar on the far wall. She looked like the living model from which the inferior by comparison Barbie Doll might have been created. Her bright pink dress was just short enough and just tight enough to restrict Kozol's breathing and further add to her resemblance to a perfect plaything. She spoke in a high, smooth voice. "Lone Star okay?"

Tony nodded, giving his dry tongue time to work itself free.

"That's a boy," replied Clint. "That Beaton," Clint shook his head, "knows where all the action is and can't keep his mouth shut."

"I hope you won't come down on him for telling me. Maybe we just shouldn't mention it?"

"Sure, you bet."

"Thanks. By the way," Tony couldn't help asking, "how's Grace?"

Clint shrugged. "Sleeping, I suppose. Had her taken back to the Radisson in a cab. She'll be good as new in the morning."

"Sure." Kozol wondered again just whose room Grace was spending the night in, her own or Clint's? And was it really any of his business? This time he'd gotten himself mixed up with a complicated and twisted bunch of folk.

"You playing or jawing?" asked a man as lean as a bamboo shoot, nervously fanning his cards.

"Playing." Clint picked up his cards.

A jovial looking fellow with a double chin and a triple stomach, barely contained in a pale blue polo shirt, spoke up. "Hope you can afford the stakes."

"Don't worry," Clint answered for Tony. "I pay the boys in the band well enough. Don't I, Tony?"

"More than enough," replied Tony diplomatically. He reluctantly opened his wallet and quickly found out how little one hundred dollars bought. A small pile of chips lay before him.

But not for long.

"Sorry," said Clint, scooping a pile of cash—an annoying amount of which was Tony's—into his cowboy hat and popping it onto his head. "Join us again tomorrow night and we'll give you a chance to get even. Right, boys?"

The boys, none with the exception of Clint and Scott, who were under forty and one who had to be on the far side of sixty, nodded and voiced their collective agreement.

"I don't know," Tony said, hoping to beg off, "you've pretty much busted me." Worse yet, if there was something worse than being broke, he hadn't gleaned a shred of valuable information, except how not to play poker.

Clint was grinning. But then Kozol figured the guy didn't have much to frown about. Pockets, and a hat, full of money, a healthy career. Women, including the one Tony wanted.

"Why, look at it this way, Tony." Clint tapped the deck of cards on the table and shuffled. "You get too much in the hole, you can consider it job security. After all, I can't hang you out to dry if you owe me a bundle now, can I?" The playing cards thwacked against the table like gunfire.

"Interesting logic," Tony replied amicably as he could manage. "I'll keep that in mind." He bade goodnight to the remaining players and was escorted back the way he'd come. A little poorer and none the wiser. So much for playing detective.

Tony had almost forgotten about Julian Santana until the kid jumped out of the shadows and spooked him.

"Hey, watch what you're doing!"

"It's only me, Mr. Tony. I didn't want to be seen."

"Well, you scared the daylights out of me."

"Sorry," whispered Julian. "I have been waiting a long time for you. What takes you so long, Mr. Tony? Did you find out something important?"

Kozol's answer was evasive. "These things take time."

"What is going on up there?" Julian glanced up at the closed door. "Did you see Mr. Cash?"

Tony buttoned his shirt up to his neck. The wind had picked up and the temperature had dropped. "Yeah, I saw him."

"And?"

Kozol made a sour face which he expected was wasted on the kid but he had felt compelled to make it anyway. "And he took all my money."

Julian looked puzzled. "What about Claudia. What about my sister?"

Apparently Kozol losing all his money was an insignificant event. "I asked him." Tony watched a small line of cars move as the traffic light changed from red to green.

A scent of what seemed to be Thai food dissolved in the air around him. Maybe it was only his hungry imagination. Kozol was starving again.

"What did he tell you? Does your Mr. Clint know where Claudia is?"

"Yeah," said Tony. "He knows."

The young man's body tensed up like a cornered cat. If he'd

had fur and a tail they would have been sticking straight up. "Where is she?"

"She's dead," Kozol said glumly. "Your sister is dead. I'm sorry, Julian, but Claudia is dead. *Muerte,* you know?"

"But—but how does Clint know this? What does he know about Claudia?"

"Same as you or I. Look, when I asked him about your sister he told me what he'd told us the first time, which was that he'd never seen nor heard of Claudia Santana before you came looking for her. And the police have been talking to everybody they consider even remotely connected with Jack Henderson's murder and word has gotten out about your sister. Claudia was killed in that cave. Let it go already."

"No."

"In it," continued Tony, "or, who knows? Maybe she was left in Bracken Cave after being killed someplace else." Kozol waved his hand like a tour guide explaining the night sky. "Maybe here in Austin. Like I said, the only time Clint ever heard of your sister was first," Tony said, enumerating with his fingers, "when you and I came asking about her the other night at the after show party and second," continued Kozol, "when someone from the police department, probably my friend, Izzie, told him about the body in San Antonio; looking for a connection between her and Jack, I expect."

Tony put a hand on Julian's shoulder and looked him steadily in the eye. "You should make arrangements to go home—to take your sister home."

Julian looked like his mind had abandoned him for higher ground.

"Are you okay?"

"Claudia speaks to me."

Oh, brother. It was all Tony could do to keep from rolling

his eyes like loose marbles. "And my stomach is speaking to me." If sarcasm were edible it would stop. "It's saying you should go home and get some sleep. Because that's exactly what I'm going to do after I get something to eat."

"How can you eat when Claudia needs help? Our help."

Once more, Tony was tempted to spit out some healthy words of mordancy. If that pile of bones hadn't been the kid's sister, he probably would have told him that the only help Claudia needed was an exorcist or Dr. Frankenstein. Maybe even a voodoo witch doctor. He chose a flanking maneuver. "I wish I could help you, Julian. But I can't."

Wordlessly, Julian Santana turned and walked away.

Kozol stuffed his hands in his pockets. "I mean, I've got two dead bandmates already," he said, raising his voice. "I'd like to know who killed them. And I haven't got a clue! Except that my gut tells me that it's related to Clint Cash and the Cowhands somehow. I'd like to find some answers without losing my job—which is precarious enough as it is!"

Julian turned about. "And Claudia disappeared after going to see someone at a Clint Cash and the Cowhands show." Even across the darkness, the young man's eyes glowed with determination. "You say my sister is dead. So? Maybe if you find her killer, you will find the killer of your friends, Mr. Tony."

Seconds passed like hours as the two men stared at one another. Tony didn't like chasing up blind alleys, let alone dead ones. But what could he do?

"Come on," Kozol said. He headed back toward the brightest lights of downtown.

"Where are we going?" asked Julian, running to catch up, his eyes now glittering with expectation. "Are we going to grill a suspect?"

"No," answered Tony, without turning or stopping. "Who knows? Maybe we'll find an all night taco stand open around here. I hope so. Because the only thing I'm in the mood for grilling right now is a *fajita*."

ELEVEN

ELEVEN

IN THE HOPE OF finding something quick, if distasteful, to eat, Tony and Julian hoofed it from the Warehouse District and made their way towards 6th Street. At the intersection of Congress Avenue, Kozol spied two familiar looking figures hopping into a dark sedan.

It looked like Johnnie Beaton and Brian Love, if Tony's weary eyes weren't making a fool of him. After all, how many scrawny little redheaded cowboys with broken arms could there be wandering around Austin in one night anyway?

Then again, how many times had his impish brown eyes made a fool of him in the past? He'd need a calculator to add it up.

Hungry and tired of walking—tired of standing—Tony waved. "Those are friends of mine," he explained to Julian, waving again; the descriptive "friend" being used rather loosely, especially in Brian Love's case.

With a little luck, Tony figured he and Julian could catch a ride back to the hotel and order up some room service. He dreamed of tossing off his shoes, kicking back on the bed and wolfing down some overpriced hotel room service chow.

Beaton and Love hadn't seen him, so Kozol raised his hand and tried again. He shouted.

"Hey—" Tony's call was stifled by a big hand pushed against

his lips and smashing his nose. He couldn't breathe. The taste of cheap steel led an assault on his tongue. Whoever was attacking him had crummy taste in jewelry. Santana was yelling something in Spanish in the background.

Startled eyes looked down at the hand on his face as Tony struggled to push it off. Then he saw them.

Tattoos!

And the fingers were numbered!

Made stronger with indignation, Tony thrust the hand away and turned around. "Rock! What do you think you're doing?"

The bassist yanked Kozol back from the street and the glare of the passing headlights, with an ease that reminded Tony that Rock could toss him around like a Raggedy Andy if he chose.

Rock peeled Julian off his back. The kid had, quite ineffectually, been trying to aid Kozol. And though he'd failed miserably, Tony was grateful for the effort. It showed the guy had some moxie and possibly some loyalty. Maybe the kid was okay after all.

"Shhh," Rock held a slightly moist hand up to his lips. The saliva was Tony's. "Geez, you slobbered all over me." Rock wiped his hand on his black pants, leaving a shiny trail like a passing slug across the blacktop.

"You were smothering me," retorted Tony. "You're lucky I didn't take a bite out of you. Lord knows I'm hungry enough."

Rock cast a worried look down Congress. "They're taking off. Quick, come on!"

The bassist gave Tony and Julian a push in the direction of a small blue Mazda pickup truck which had seen better days. And having once had the displeasure of being a passenger, or pawn, in a moving vehicle of which Rock was in control, Tony knew the little mini-pickup had also seen better drivers.

"Where are we going?" protested Tony.

"I don't know." Rock twisted the key in the ignition. "Wherever those two are going."

Julian squeezed Tony into the center of the little truck, catching him with a bony elbow to the ribs. "Sorry, Mr. Tony."

Even with the two of them countering Rock's weight, Kozol sensed the little truck was leaning dangerously to the driver's side.

They flew away from the curb leaving a line of smelly rubber and headed toward the brightly lit Texas State Capitol.

"Well, where are Beaton and Love going?"

"I don't know." Rock struggled to turn the Mazda against a red light in a dizzying effort to maintain a reasonable distance with the late model sedan that Beaton was driving.

"If you don't mind, Rock," Tony said, as the Mazda hopped on and off the median with a jolt, "I think I'd rather be riding with those guys." Kozol grunted as the Mazda skidded around another curve and Rock slammed into his side.

"Very funny."

"I'm a funny guy." Kozol tried taking shallow breaths in an effort to reduce his horizontal displacement. It wasn't working. "Where'd you get this truck, anyway?"

A bottle of whiskey, which had been pressed into a crevice against the windshield, came loose and slid across the dashboard. Someone had been drinking and, from the smell coming out with every breath, Kozol didn't need a Breathalyzer to know it was Rock.

"I borrowed it from Chico."

"Who is Chico?"

Rock took his eyes off the road and looked at Tony. "From the Chicotones."

"Watch out!" cried Julian. He pointed out the window. "They turned up there!"

Tony gave the kid a look of utter exasperation. "What, you too?"

"Don't worry," pledged Rock, "we won't lose them."

"I'm so glad." Tony's fingers held the dashboard in a death-grip. "Yet again I ask, why are we following Beaton and Love?"

Rock's sweaty palms slid around the tiny wheel. It was like a toy in his hands. "You never asked."

Kozol pounded a fist against his temple. Either it was going to cure his headache or break his skull in two. Either one would do. "Yes, I did."

"No," said Rock, taking his eyes off the road once more, "you asked where we were going. You never asked why we were following those guys."

Through gritted teeth, Tony managed to say, "Well, I'm asking now, Rock." He was doing well. He hadn't exploded and he'd managed to speak with feigned calm. "So, tell me, why are we following Beaton and Love? And keep your eyes on the road!"

Rock kept one eye on the road ahead while he explained, not that it mattered as the little pickup rarely seemed to use the blacktop as a defining surface. Trying to keep Rock on the road was like trying to keep a two year old coloring between the lines. "Those two are up to something."

"Like what?"

Rock was slowing the Mazda down. The other car had twisted off into the darkness. "I don't know for sure. But they sure are acting strange."

"There seems to be a lot of that going around," cracked Kozol. Then, as the Mazda headed up into the utter darkness, Tony realized that Rock was driving with the headlights off. "Hey, you forgot to turn on the—"

Without warning, Rock cut the vehicle sharply to the left and killed the engine. Tony's head bounced off the windshield and he cried out, "What on earth are you stopping for?" Tony could only pray the Mazda was truly dead and not capable of resurrection. "That's the worst driving I have ever seen and—"

In response, Tony got Rock's big, dumb, tattooed hand stuffed in his mouth again, cheap rings and all. "Keep it down, will you?" Rock slowly opened the creaking driver's side door and pounced, whiskey bottle in hand, to the grass. "Come on. I see the rental up ahead. They've stopped."

Tony spat and wiped his mouth. "What rental?" Kozol asked, whispering obligingly. Better to cooperate with the maniac than get a handful of Rock Bottom in his face a third time.

"The rental that Beaton and Love got," said Rock, dripping with exasperation. "Aren't you listening to anything I say, Tony?" Rock tipped a stream of whiskey down his throat and handed the bottle magnanimously to his cohorts.

Tony reached it before Julian could even stretch his arm halfway out and poured about a Niagara Falls' worth down his own hatch before turning the bottle over to the kid.

The cheap whiskey nearly burned a hole out the bottoms of Tony's shoes as it raced heedlessly through his body. Suddenly, the world was looking better, if blurrier.

The three men passed the bottle as Rock briefly explained what he had been up to.

"I saw Johnnie tonight at the Austinland, after the police left. He was talking to some old Mexican geezer outside in the parking lot. Then Johnnie fetched Love and the three of them got cozy in a little bar on Sixth."

"You followed them?"

"Yep."

"And they didn't see you?"

"Nope. Anyway, I watched them in the bar from the outside window," Rock said proudly. "Had a good clear view of them. They talked. Some money changed hands and the old guy gives them something."

"Okay, I'm asking. What?"

"A piece of paper," Rock answered smugly.

Tony scratched his head and passed the whiskey around once more. "So you decided to keep following them."

"That's right, Tony." Rock grinned, looking quite pleased with himself. He also looked halfway to Jupiter using alcohol for fuel. "I told you I was going to help you out."

Tony gingerly touched the growing softball-sized bump on his forehead. "Yeah, thanks, Rock."

Julian moodily looked at the dim stars overhead and pursed his lips over the bottle and its steadily diminishing contents. "Maybe they have my sister, Claudia."

Rock nodded.

Tony groaned.

"Well," said Rock, in his own defense, "why not? They've got shovels. And an axe."

"Shovels?" repeated Tony. Visions of dead bodies and cemeteries filled the space between his ears.

Rock bobbed his head up and down and explained. "After talking to the old man, Johnnie and Brian headed straight for the hotel, checked out a rental car, drove to an all night discount store and picked up a shovel and a pickaxe."

Tony couldn't believe what he was hearing, let alone that he was wasting his time listening. And lying in the cold grass out in the middle of Who-The-Hell-Knows-Where, Texas.

"They came back to town and Love ran into that drugstore on Congress. That's when I saw you guys."

"Claudia!" The word burst forth from Julian's lips with venom. He jumped to attention like a demon at the starting line.

Tony, who'd made himself not comfortable at all amongst the rocks protruding like tiny enemies in the dry grass, rose unsteadily to his feet.

"They have killed my sister and now they are burying her body!" He started to run.

Tony quickly pulled him back. "Wait, Julian." He turned the kid around and pulled him lower. "We don't know that for sure." Not that he wasn't thinking it himself.

"There's only one way to find out," Rock said, tossing the empty whiskey bottle in the direction of the little Mazda.

"They can't have gone far on foot." Kozol groaned and led the way. "Where are we anyway?"

"Who knows?" replied Rock. "I saw a sign back there a bit. Some kind of park, I think."

Julian staggered and blundered into a metal pole. What looked like an inverted Christmas tree made of chain links rattled noisily. "What is this thing?"

Rock and Tony stared at the pole. "Stranger and stranger," muttered Kozol, waving Julian onward.

They stumbled around in the darkness. There was no sight of Beaton and Love. Tony and Rock might have wandered about getting nowhere all night if they hadn't heard the digging.

"Over here," Tony called softly to his companions, who had fanned out across the dark landscape.

They crawled up to where Kozol lay atop a small knoll on his belly and peered down. "See?"

"Yeah," whispered Rock, "I see them." He slithered up to a small boulder.

Love and Beaton were swinging away at the edge of a creek bed. Johnnie with the shovel, while Love was doing the one-armed pickaxe boogie.

Johnnie was singing. No doubt aided on the choruses by a bottle as high octane as the one Rock had brought along for companionship. Beaton and Love's voices carried up the hill.

"Will you keep it down," Love was complaining, his feet

slipping across the mound of loose earth that bordered the hole they had so far excavated. "Somebody's gonna hear us."

"Nonsense," grumbled Johnnie between choruses of *Don't The Girls All Get Prettier At Closing Time,* "who's going to hear us? The stinking coyotes?" He kicked a long chrome-plated flashlight that laid atop the loose earth out of the shovel's way and scooped up another load of soil.

"All the same," griped Love, aiming for the earth with his pickaxe and hitting a stone instead. With a high-pitched *ping!* the rock shot off into the distance.

"Hey, I hit something!"

Love leaned forward. "Is it—"

Johnnie pulled something long and white from the broken ground. "It's a bone! An Indian bone! We're cursed! Cursed!" He threw the bone towards the creek and wiped his hands viciously on his trousers.

"Keep 'yer voice down, Johnnie."

"But it's bad luck to be digging up Indian bones. You heard what the old man said."

"You don't even know it was an Indian bone. Looked like a moose bone to me."

"There aren't any moose in Texas."

"How the hell do you know? You a moose expert or something? It could have been prehistoric."

"A prehistoric moose?"

"Could be."

Johnnie spat. "Sometimes I think your brain is prehistoric."

"Just keep digging so we can get this over with and get out of here without getting caught."

"Yeah, and soon we'll be out of town and no one will ever know."

"It'll be easy street," said Love, striking at the earth with his pickaxe. "Now get busy. There's not much more to go."

"If those guys are burying something," Tony glanced at Julian, whose face was an unreadable mask, "where is it?" He had expected to see a large blanket covered corpse or some such thing. But there was nothing lying about that he could see to fit the bill.

"Could be back in the car," suggested Rock.

"Maybe we should check it out. You want to do it, Julian?" whispered Kozol. He was hoping to get the hot-blooded kid out of the way. It had to hurt to watch those two thugs digging a hole for what could be your sister.

"No," Santana answered forcefully. "I am not moving my eyes from those two men. If they killed my sister, I will make my revenge."

Tony shivered. "If they killed your sister, the police will fix them." He gripped the boy's arm. "Without you winding up in prison yourself."

Rock crouched on his knees. "I'll go." He scuttled backwards. "It won't take me long. Whistle or something if you see them headed my way."

Tony nodded, then turned his attention back to his bandmates. They looked like a couple of grave robbers. Johnnie had jumped down into the ever larger hole and was tossing dirt over his shoulder. Love had given up, at least momentarily, and was using his pickaxe to prop himself up.

Suddenly, Johnnie stopped short, tossed his shovel towards the creek and whooped. "I'VE FOUND HER! I'VE FOUND HER!"

Kozol carefully lifted his head up just a smidgen, not wanting to be seen, but curious to see what all the fuss was about.

But that wasn't going to matter. Not wanting to be seen had become the least of his troubles and a real non-issue.

Julian had leapt to his feet like a frightful wildcat and shouted, "Eiiieeeiiee!" The boy half ran, half fell down the hill like a lunatic boulder come to life and racing straight for Beaton and Love. *"Chingadores!"*

After a moment's shock, Tony came unfrozen, jumped to his feet and followed. "No, Julian! No!" he screamed between dry, aching breaths. "No!"

With Johnnie in the hole, Brian Love became Julian's first target. He charged Love, who tried to defend himself, swinging the pickaxe with his one good arm. Julian dodged the sharp tipped blade and plowed into him. Love dropped the axe as the two men fell into the hole on top of Johnnie.

Tony was shouting, though even he didn't know what he was saying. He stopped short of the pit. The three men, all scared, angry and drunk as sinning sailors on shore leave, were punching, kicking and bellowing wildly.

Love screamed loudest. "My arm! My arm! You've broke my arm!"

"Shut up and help me, you idiot!" urged Johnnie. "This kid's trying to kill me. And your friggin' arm was friggin' broken already. Oof!" Johnnie'd had the air knocked out of him as Julian's fist hit his stomach dead center.

"Well, he's broke it again, the bastard." Love raised his casted arm with what appeared to Tony to be the intention of bouncing it off Julian's face. Beaton had managed to subdue the boy and held his arms behind his back.

"Stop!" Tony thundered.

"Kozol?!" Johnnie cried.

"Lawyer?" Love lowered his arm, but only by half. "What are you doing here? Trying to muscle in?" He spat. "Forget it."

"Let go of him, Johnnie."

"Oh, all right, Tony." Beaton eased his grip.

"Are you nuts? Hold onto him, Johnnie. That little piece of Mexican garbage broke my damn arm!"

"Oh, shut up, Love, will you?" Tony jumped down into the pit and pulled Julian away from Johnnie.

"I kill you! I kill you!" hissed Julian so fiercely that the venom attached to his words shot out of his mouth like aster-oid droppings. "Where is my sister? What did you do to her? I kill you, like you killed her!"

"Hold on, Julian. Let me handle this." Kozol looked over his shoulder, hoping Rock would show up sometime.

Anytime.

Soon. In case he needed some muscle.

Turning his attention to Love, Tony said, "If your arm is bro-ken, which I am not sure it is, it's only because you fell in this stupid hole in the first place. And I," continued Kozol, "would like to know just what the two of you are up to digging a hole out here in the middle of the night, in the middle of nowhere, in the first place?"

"Like you don't know," cracked Love angrily, clutching his good arm with his bad.

Kozol folded his arms. "No, I don't know. Enlighten me."

"Just digging a hole, Tony." Johnnie pulled off his jacket and shook the dirt out of it. He grinned, hands spread out from his side in a gesture of supplication. "What's the big deal? Why are you here? Following us? And what's with this kid and his sister? That all he thinks about?"

Julian took a menacing step in Johnnie's direction. Beaton held him off with the pickaxe.

Tony kept his eyes on Johnnie. With his left foot, his band-mate was trying surreptitiously to cover something dark in the ground with loose dirt he was spreading with his toe. "Maybe he thinks you two are trying to bury her...or dig her up maybe?" He gazed meaningfully at Johnnie's busy foot.

Johnnie smiled. "Is that what this is all about?" His body slipped into a more relaxed posture. "Man, you've got it all wrong, Tony."

"Shut up, Johnnie," ordered Love.

The vibrating sounds of what might have been a brontosaurus out for a midnight jog caught the attention of all four men. Rock stopped inches short of the hole. It was a good thing. There wasn't much more room to go around down there. "Car's clean," he announced with a huff. He looked from man to man. "What's up?"

"What's up?" bellowed Love. "Why, you dumb ox, I—"

Rock's eyes narrowed and he took a step over the precipice. His big foot dangled in the air.

That was enough for Love to lower his voice and change his tone. "That is," the disabled guitarist cleared his throat and backtracked, "these two bums came stumbling in on me and Johnnie for no reason. No reason at all, mind you." He pleaded his case to Rock. "We were minding our own business. There was no call to come crashing down on us like crazy marauders and trying to murder us."

"In the first place," interrupted Tony, carefully lifting a small metal box from under Johnnie's boot, "I don't suppose the City of Austin would be too happy about you digging up one of their fine parks."

"We was just—"

Tony held up his hand and shook the little box. Johnnie and Brian looked nervous. Kozol tried to raise the lid but it was all but cemented shut. He tossed the box up to Rock. "See if you can open that, will you?"

Rock caught the box, grinned, tapped the side against his heel, then pried the lid open with his fingertips.

Love and Beaton leaned towards him. There was a collective silence.

Rock looked inside. "It's empty," he pronounced, tipped the box upside down. "Just a little dirt and some pebbles." With his fingernails, the big guy scraped away the smudge concealing some sort of writing on the cover. "It's an old cigar box."

Love let out a long, mournful groan.

Johnnie, on the other hand, was laughing. "Sonofabitch!"

Tony asked, "What's so funny?"

Johnnie grabbed hold of the flashlight, flitted it along the ground to focus on a broad sheet of thick, wrinkled yellow paper. He handed the document over to Tony against Love's protests. "Old codger tricked us but good. Took us for a couple of back easters and did us good, eh, Brian?"

Love remained, blissfully from Kozol's point of view, silent.

Tony studied the paper, turning it this way and that. Julian was looking over his shoulder.

"Don't you get it, Tony? It's a treasure map." Johnnie whooped again. He pulled a flask from his jacket and took a sip. "Want some?"

Kozol shook his head no. Rock told Johnnie to toss the bottle up, which the guitarist cum treasure seeker obligingly did.

"Treasure-smeasure. Sonofabitch." Johnnie sat down in the dirt. "Damn, I'm tired. That map cost us three hundred dollars apiece." He looked at his wrist and found it empty. "What time is it anyway?"

Tony checked his watch. "Closer to morning than night."

"So," said Johnnie, with a tired grin on his tired face, "what did you think? Think we were burying a body out here or something?"

"Yeah, or something," confessed Tony.

"What ever gave you a dumb idea like that?"

Kozol shot a glance at Rock who was in no hurry to return Beaton's flask. "We got a tip."

Beaton laughed once more and slapped his knees. "Don't that beat all. You got a tip." His head shook from side to side. "We got a tip, too! Looks like yours was as worthless as ours!"

Tony asked, "What made you think you'd actually find a treasure out here?"

"It's out here," Love said, breaking the silence with words of conviction.

"Oh yeah? Rock slumped down to his knees and handed the flask over to Johnnie's outstretched hand.

"We met this old guy, see, who told us all about this here treasure," illuminated Love. "It's been buried out here for a hundred years or so."

Rock nodded. "That sounds like the fella I saw the two of you talking to in that bar up on Sixth earlier."

"Yeah," said Johnnie. "It must've been. What were you doing? Spying on us, Rock?"

"It was something to do," admitted the big guy. "I was trying to help Tony find Jack and Hector's killer or killers. I told him I would."

"Wow," said Johnnie, in awe, "playing detective. That's cool. I always figured it would be neat to be a detective—carry a big old gun, have one of those secretaries with a big rack—"

"Shut up, Johnnie," interrupted Love. "You guys want to hear this or not?"

Tony spoke for the group. "We want to hear it, Love."

"Then everybody shut up and let me tell it. It's like this," Love grabbed the silver flask from his partner in crime, downed its remains, cleared his throat and said, "Pease Park is—"

"Pease Park?" interrupted Rock.

"Didn't I just say not to interrupt me?" He scowled at Rock, but not enough to get the big man's dander up. "Pease Park is where we're sittin'. Don't you even know that much?"

"No," answered Rock. "We were driving with the headlights out, following you two. None of us know where we are—"

"—or what we were doing." Love scratched his unshaven cheeks with his left hand. Apparently the arm wasn't broken at all. What a surprise.

"Don't that beat all. Anyway," Love continued, "Pease Park

is where we are. That is, the area of Shoal Creek—" He turned to Rock again and pointed over the bassist's shoulder. "That's the creek over there, Shoal Creek."

"Got it," clicked Rock, giving Brian the okay symbol with his fingers.

"What has this to do with Claudia?" Julian interjected sullenly. He kicked at the dirt around his feet.

"Nothing," Love said flatly. "Not a goddam thing. What have you got to do with anything? You're not in the band. You don't belong here. You've got nothing to do with nothing. Except, maybe you killed two of my friends? You know," Brian said, standing over Julian with a steely coldness, "they hang wetbacks for murder in these parts. Pick out a big ole tree and—" Love made a slurping noise. "Just toss up a good stiff bit of rope, wrap it around your sorry neck and—"

Tony held Julian back. "You got some kind of problem with Mexico, Love? Is it Mexicans you don't like, or is it just people in general you hate so bad?"

"Mexico," answered Love, insensibly, "is un-American."

"What's that supposed to mean?" Kozol couldn't hide his exasperation.

Rock cut them off. "Tell us about the treasure, Brian." Rock squirmed. He was as excited as a boy at circle time.

"I was just getting to that," Love commented. "If you'd all just keep your traps shut and listen." He crossed his arms, tapped his foot and waited. Apparently satisfied that his demands for shutting up would be met, he continued, "Seems there was a troop of Mexican soldiers back in the 1800s returning from East Texas to San Antonio. The soldiers met up with an Indian ambush." Love spat. "Right about here."

"And?" Tony found the whole thing, while not impossible, implausible to say the least. Buried treasures were the stuff of legends.

"And they were carrying a load of gold." Love spat again. "Those Mexican soldiers managed to beat back the Injuns but they'd lost a lot of their own men. So," Brian pawed the up-turned ground with the toe of his boot, "they lightened their load. Buried a box full of gold right here. Probably worth millions today."

"Yeah," quipped Kozol, "to the old man that sells maps to suckers like you two."

"It's true, Tony," Beaton swore. "Why, people have been looking for that buried Mexican gold for a hundred years. It's famous! Just like Love said."

"Yeah, so laugh it up, lawyer," Love said, angrily. "But that gold's out here. Bet on it. Spanish gold pieces. Been sitting here for over a century just waiting for somebody to scoop 'em up."

"Yeah. Well," Johnnie said with an audible groan as he worked himself slowly up to a semi-standing position, "it ain't gonna be us, is it?" He looked like an early hominid, *homo imbicilis,* "Leastwise, not tonight."

Tony looked at the sky. A trace of light made its way hesitantly up from the horizon. "It's going to be light soon. Maybe we'd all better leave."

Tony could all too well picture the bunch of them sharing a cell for the day in downtown Austin, charged with digging one stupid hole in a public park.

And his old friend, Izzie, would be standing on the other side of the bars, the free to go and have a nice day side, laughing up a summer storm.

And Kozol had no umbrella. "Let's get out of here before somebody sees us."

The five of them headed wearily towards their vehicles. As they did so, the loosely knit band passed another one of those crazy metal poles sticking out of the ground with a chain basket on top. "What on earth are those things?"

Beaton explained. "It's for disc golf. Goofy sport is popular around these parts, I hear."

"Disc golf?" Rock scratched his head.

"Yeah, something to do with throwing Frisbees into those little baskets on top."

Tony paused and gazed at the pole. That made absolutely no sense at all. Yet he had the queer sensation that Johnnie was right.

"Say, Tony," said Beaton, "did you really think we were burying that kid's sister out here?"

"Huh? Oh, yeah. Or digging her up," Kozol confessed, without breaking stride.

"Man, that must've been something. I mean, seeing us out there digging and thinking we were killers." Johnnie snorted. "What a hoot!"

"Yeah, it was something. Who do you think killed Hector and Jack?"

"Man, I don't know. I'm just a guitar picker," was Johnnie's only reply.

"If you ask me—" began Brian.

"Which I didn't," Tony replied sternly.

"If you ask me," Brian continued, nonplussed. After all, he was never one to take anybody's opinion or feelings to heart. They barely warranted consideration. "The person you should be asking that question is your girlie friend."

Tony stopped in his tracks. "My," he hesitated, "girlfriend?"

Love grinned maliciously. "I've got a lousy broken arm, not broken eyes. I know what goes on," he boasted. "Maybe Clint does, too..."

Kozol resumed hiking. The little Mazda's dark hulk was in view. To Tony it represented refuge—such as it was. From the night. From Brian Love. From wakefulness itself.

Love was still spouting off. "Saw your little girlfriend having an argument with Hector just before he disappeared. Next thing you know, the poor bastard's found dead." Love cupped a hand to his ear. "What's that? Where was this, you ask?" chided Love. "Why, right outside the studmobile!"

Kozol kept walking. Left foot, right foot. Left foot, right foot.

"That's where!"

Tony bit his cheek so hard he tasted blood.

TWELVE

"GET SOME SLEEP," Rock called to Kozol's backside as Tony limped out of the little Mazda. "I got to get Chico his truck back. I'll drop the kid off on the way," he added, nodding toward Julian who slept in the truck's cold, hard bed.

The hotel doorman waved Tony a good morning. Kozol merely grumbled back a mutual wish. After all, the doorman was paid to be chipper at this hour. He wasn't.

It was after nine. He'd been up all night. A breakfast of watery *huevos rancheros* at a dive Rock had selected near the university had sealed the deal.

Sleep beckoned.

Sleep insisted.

Take off your shoes, lie down...close dry, tired eyes and drop dead. Tony was planning on coming as close to death as he could resemble without crossing the line. No need to go that far. Just a long, dull dormancy. Hibernate with the bears.

Tony spun through the spinning lobby door and fell in the direction of the elevators. He pushed the button. It had taken the last scrap of his energy.

With a *pong!*, the elevator doors slowly opened. Kozol caught a glimpse of a familiar black hat and spun around, sticking his nose up against the humongous aquarium that blocked the elevators off from the main lobby. "Hello, little fishies," he whispered to the brightly colored, flitting water dwellers. "Now, don't give me away."

A fat, black one attempted a nibble at Tony's nose but got only a mouthful of wet glass. Tony grinned. The black fish gave him a dirty look.

"Kozol!"

"Oh, great," Tony said softly to a nearby clownfish who really seemed to be listening. "I was hoping it wasn't Murdock. I was hoping he wouldn't see me."

Suddenly, Kozol wished he could make like Don Knotts in *The Incredible Mister Limpet*. Wish himself into the aquarium. He'd even be willing to chase down enemy submarines for the Navy. Anything to get out of his current predicament.

"I wish, I wish I was a fish. I wish I was a fish..."

Wasn't that how it went?

"Glad to see you're up and about already."

Kozol turned about. Apparently he'd gotten the incantation wrong. Maybe he'd rent the video when he got home to Florida. "Morning, Granger." Study up. Take magic incantation lessons. "You're looking good." He stuck a grin on his face and straightened up.

"You look like hell."

Tony wanted to tell Clint's abrasive manager the same, but, even in a sleepless, giddy state, thought better of it. "I had a tough night."

Granger's cologne smelled expensive. Lousy, but expensive. His clothes were clean and looked fresh pressed. His boots shone like black Texas stars.

For once, Tony found himself jealous of the man. Kozol himself looked and felt about as elegant and fresh-scented as Bourbon Street the night after Mardi Gras when all the cigarette butts, spilled beer and crawfish remnants had turned into a reeking, inescapable post-Mardi Gras soup.

"Yeah, well, glad to see you up and about anyway. It's about time you started taking this business, and me, serious."

"I'm doing my best," Kozol said, fighting back a yawn.

"You have breakfast yet?"

"Eggs."

"Good. Come on. We'll walk on over to the convention center."

"Walk to the convention center?"

"Yeah, the Austin Convention Center. Let's go. It's not far."

"That's okay. You go on ahead. I'll meet you there. I was just going up to...a..."

"To what?" Granger had one of those suspicious minds Elvis liked to sing about.

"Nothing," replied a suddenly defeated Kozol. And, unlike Napoleon, he knew it. "Let's go."

"Tell you the truth," Murdock said to the rhythm of his gangly strides, "I half-figured you wouldn't show up for Clint's panel this morning. Even though I specifically told you to be there."

"You kidding?" Tony said, finally understanding what Granger was going on about. The truth was, he'd forgotten all about Clint's talk. "I wouldn't miss it."

"That's good." Murdock's nostrils flared. "You shower this morning?"

"Well—"

"Never mind." Granger shook his head in disgust. He handed Kozol a stick of gum and guided him up the steps of the convention hall where a blockade of young people sat in folding chairs at folding tables distributing name tags on slender ropes reminiscent of bolo ties.

Tony wondered whether Granger was expecting him to use

the stick of minty scented gum as a washcloth. Should he rub it over his grungy arms and legs or chew it and try to make a bubble?

He opted for chewing. Probably the more socially acceptable of the two options. Though that rubbing idea was something to consider. Perhaps he was on to something...

"I've got some meetings." Murdock thumbed through a pocket schedule of the day's events. "Clint's speaking at eleven in Room 212. I'll see you there, right?"

"Absolutely," promised Tony.

"In the meantime, go get your goodie bag and take a look at the trade show, why don't you?"

"Good idea." Kozol was being his agreeable old self. Assuming he'd ever had an agreeable old self to be. Maybe it was his new agreeable old self.

"By the way," Granger asked, "your friend on the force, that Izzie guy—"

"Yes?"

"Did he tell you anything more about the murder?"

"You mean Hector?"

Granger tipped his head. "Or Jack."

"No. Nothing."

"Hmm." Granger pulled a toothpick from his front shirt pocket and began chewing. "You let me know right away if you hear anything, will you, Kozol?"

Tony agreed. "Yeah, sure. But why the special interest?"

"No special interest. Those two guys were employees of Clint's. I'm his manager. It's my job to know what's going on. I'm asking you to keep me informed. Specially seeing how you've got a friend on the local force."

Once more, Tony agreed. He seemed to have discovered a wonderful new elixir. It was both a stress reliever and releaser. Be agreeable.

It was so simple that he was finding it painful. Especially when it came to agreeing with Granger Murdock. The true test would come when he tried it on Brian Love. Kozol shivered at the thought. Would it work?

Be agreeable with Love? Tony couldn't believe he was even considering it. He figured it was a sign of how exhausted he was. He really needed some rest.

Tony left Granger and worked his way to the back of the large trade room. Stretching from 1st Street to 3rd Street one way and Trinity and Red River the other, the City of Austin Convention Center was enormous. According to the burnished placard he scanned, it was over four hundred thousand square feet under one roof with plans to double its size in the offing. The current center had been built of native limestone and polished granite in 1992.

After asking directions, Tony found his next destination. A conference favorite. The goodie bag giveaway spot. A small line in front of him quickly dissipated and a young girl checked his badge then forked over a sack bigger than a week's supply of Kozol's groceries. It was heavier, too. Heavier than Tony was expecting. The bag dropped to his feet in freefall. He grunted and pulled his shoes out from under. He would just about need a forklift to haul it around.

Tony looked at the girl who'd given him his goodie bag. She was lightly tossing another cloth sack up to the next fellow in line behind him. She didn't look like she particularly worked out. At least, Tony didn't peg her for one of those "I go to the gym six days a week" types. Kozol put her skill with the bags down to several days of constant lifting. No way she was stronger than he was.

No way.

He dragged his bag and feet up and down the crowded aisles. Smiling faces smiled and handy hands reached out to offer sample merchandise and brightly covered brochures and free papers.

Tony dutifully smiled back and took all proffered gifts, not wishing to hurt anyone's feelings. His shoulders grew numb. One helpful booth attendant handed him a second bag, a plastic one with handles. It had the name and logo of a major CD manufacturer on its side.

Quickly, it too was half full and full of holes. If things kept up, he was going to be needing another bag soon.

Arms aching, Tony shuffled over to the far corner of the trade hall which had been set up as a dining area. There was a line of self serve beverages, tea, soda, juice, along with light fare such as deli sandwiches, muffins and the like. Help yourself and pay the cashier at the end of the line. Sort of a good analog of life if you thought about it. Tony didn't much.

The line was long and Kozol's patience short.

Tony wove his way through the round tables. Despite the crowds, he found a spot near the back. He dropped his bags on the floor and his butt in the seat.

In the corner across the way, a small stage had been erected. At the moment, a pretty but frail looking, twenty-odd years old woman with clipped blonde hair, shorter than Tony's own, was doing her solo act. The young lady had dangling gold hoops hanging from her ears. She was sitting on a slender wooden stool, singing songs and strumming a Gibson Hummingbird model guitar for the half-interested crowd. The songs were probably originals. At least, Tony didn't recognize the song she was doing and it wasn't bad.

Kozol closed his eyes and caught his breath. A bottle of Radam's Microbe Killer might just be the thing. Tony had read about the goofy stuff in an Austin guide book he'd been flipping through back in his hotel room. Beaton had picked the book up in a local bookshop. Probably because he was researching his Mexican treasure, Tony now realized, and not because he was interested in local Austin color. Beaton wasn't—no shattered illusion—boning up on his American history for the joy of learning.

On the label of Radam's Microbe Killer there had been a picture of a man, who for all intents and purposes, seemed to be beating Death to death. Back in the late 1800s, around the time that Love's treasure was purportedly being lost or buried, Microbe Killer was touted as a cure to everything and everybody. The magic brew had contained sulfuric acid, hydrochloric acid, a little bit of red wine and ninety-nine percent water.

It had certainly cured its inventor of poverty as the guy had ended up with a spiffy mansion in New York City overlooking Central Park.

Such a miracle cure ought to perk Kozol up at least as much as the jolt of java he was yearning for but didn't have the energy to seek out.

Tony raised his head and his rock heavy eyelids when a familiar name hit his ears. The girl on the stool with the Gibson had risen to introduce a friend who was about to come up, with the audience's encouragement, to join her in a number.

A dozen tables in front of him, Grace Burns, dressed in a snug pair of jeans and a Southwest Music Conference t-shirt, rose, tipped her head to the audience and joined her blonde friend at the tiny makeshift stage.

The two ladies launched into a startlingly good rendition of Neil Young's *Lotta Love*. Kozol hadn't realized until then just how like Nicolette Larson, one of Tony's favorite singers, Grace sounded.

Tony applauded loudest and rushed over as Grace humbly thanked the audience for listening and started to slip into the swirling stream of attendees swimming up and down the aisles of the music trade show. "Grace!"

He caught her arm and she turned.

"What do you want?"

Things were off to a bad start.

But Tony was undeterred. Seemed he was always off to a bad start. Often a not so good middle. And those endings could be pretty shaky.

Nonetheless, he went on. "I wanted to see how you were doing." He took a step back and studied the young woman. The one he'd recently made love to, though you'd never know it by her body language. "Are you okay?"

She crossed her arms. "I'm fine."

"Good."

"If there's nothing else?" Grace made to leave.

"Wait."

"What, Tony?"

"Did you get back to the hotel okay last night?" What a stupid question. "No, I was run over by a truck and won't be out of intensive care for a week," he expected her to say. After all, he probably would have.

Instead, Grace's eyes turned chilly as dry ice giving off the vapors. "Why do you ask, Tony? You don't care." She turned on her heels and stepped quickly away.

Ouch, that hurt. Kozol darted after her. "What do you mean, I don't care?" He glared at an onlooker who quickly dropped her eyes and then swiftly moved on, soon to be lost in the safety of the crowd.

"You said you were going to come back last night. I thought you were going to take me home after you got done talking to that friend of yours. That Izzie."

"But I did come back," Tony replied, not above groveling and pleading. "You were asleep."

"You could have woke me."

"But you took a sleeping pill."

"I did no such thing."

"Yes, you did. Tanya told me. Ask her."

"I did?" Grace looked unsure of herself. "The last thing I remember," she said slowly, "is asking Tanya if she'd found her shawl."

"Believe me, you were out cold."

She shook her head as if trying to clear her thoughts. "I don't remember. And that doesn't matter. Because I did wake up and Clint and Scott told me you'd gone off with your friends." Her icy eyes looked on the verge of melting. Grace held a finger up to her eye and wiped away a small tear.

"I didn't go with my friends. I mean, she is a friend, but I was with—"

"He took me back to his room."

"Who, Clint?"

"No, Scott. The DJ, you know."

Scott hadn't mentioned that he'd been in the cab taking Grace back to the hotel. Tony glowered. "Yeah, I know."

Tony wasn't going to mention that he'd played poker with Clint and Scott Day that night. He figured Grace would only take it the wrong way—like she seemed to be taking everything else—and he'd look like an even bigger heel. One of those four inch spike jobs he saw the girls teetering on across the runways on TV. Why did she have it in for him?

"So why did Scott take you back to his room?" And what was he doing with a hotel room? Kozol wanted to scream. After all, Scott Day was a local Austinite. If he had a hotel room, it could only mean he was looking for trouble.

"Not his room, Clint's. I didn't have my key. And I was tired and it just seemed easier. Clint's valet let us in."

"Sorry," said Tony. "I guess I ask too many questions."

Grace made no reply.

"Look, about you and Clint—"

"Clint!" Grace looked at her watch and her eyes doubled in size. "He's speaking right now and I promised Clint and Granger I'd attend. I'm sorry, Tony, but I have to go!"

Tony's face contorted. "Don't tell me it's eleven already?" His heart jumped into second gear.

Grace tapped her watch glass. "It's nearly quarter past."

"Oh, sh—" Tony grabbed Grace's hand and raced across the trade floor, making friends and enemies with every bump depending on where he struck them and how much they did or didn't like it. "I promised Granger I'd be there, too!"

They ran up the escalator, found the door to Room 212 closed, caught a breath and entered.

The room was full.

But that didn't keep Granger Murdock, seated up in the front row, at the end of the center aisle, from turning and noticing Tony and Grace's late entrance and glaring like an angry bull with headlight-sized eyeballs.

Ignoring the evil eye of Clint's manager, Tony pulled Grace to the back wall where they squeezed in amongst the others who couldn't find seats. Clint was SRO. Standing room only.

Clint was up at the elevated platform at the far end of the big room, sitting next to Scott Day, who was moderating and was seated in the middle. On Scott's opposite side sat the head of AWE Records, Arthur Levine, and on Clint's side, Peter Magnuson, A&R chief, filled out the panel.

"That was a great question. And I think Clint gave a good explanation of his songwriting process. Peter, do you have anything to add?"

Kozol noted that Scott Day was at his shmooziest. Seemed to be his specialty. Grace had let go of Tony's hand but hung close by.

"No, just keep writing great songs, guys."

There was a polite sprinkling of laughter.

"Next question?" Scott surveyed the audience and selected a raised hand near the front.

"Is it true you were playing open mic nights on 6th Street only a few years ago?"

Clint laughed and stroked his chin. "Oh, man. You bet. Every one of them. And for tips only. Most nights, the buskers—you know, those guys and girls you see out on the sidewalks here putting on a show, singing, dancing, reading fortunes and whatever—well, they were pulling down more greenbacks than I was. That's when I decided to try my luck in Nashville."

"Lucky for us," added Peter Magnuson. He ran AWE Records Nashville A&R Department and had taken credit for "discovering" Clint.

"See," Scott said to the audience, "you can all do it. Who else has a question?" A dozen hands went up and Scott called on a waifish looking girl in a jade dress. "Yes?"

In a small voice, she said, "I'd like to know how a keyboard player, or any musician for that matter, gets a job with a band like Clint Cash and the Cowhands. Is it strictly who you know?"

"What do you say, Clint? We're buddies. Can I get a job with the Cowhands?" gibed Scott Day. "I can whistle."

The audience laughed appreciatively and Clint tipped his hat. "Well, you'll have to call my manager. But seriously," he drawled, "it really is about musicianship and fitting in. After all, being in a full-time band is a job as well as a relationship. We all gotta get along. It takes a lot of hard work too, of course. And a little lady luck doesn't hurt none."

Kozol thought that a rather odd statement considering two of Clint's crew were recently expired and most of the others were as unpleasant as a bottle full of hungry rattlesnakes and scorpions.

"In fact," Clint said, his eyes scanning, focusing and locking in on Kozol, "one of my bandmates, the most recent one, is right here in the audience. In the back there." Clint's hand stretched over the table.

"Please don't let him be pointing at me. Please don't let him be pointing at me." Tony pretended to be staring at a distant light fixture—a rather repulsive piece of glass trash that hung from similar conference rooms across the country, he supposed; or maybe an elite chandelier team shuttled the same fixture cross-continentally from hotel to hotel.

"Tony!"

Grace elbowed him.

He looked at the podium.

"Oh, me?" he said.

Clint grinned. "Come on up here."

Tony waved his hands no.

"Oh, come on, now, Tony," Scott said. "As the latest member of the Cowhands we're all sure you have a lot of insight to offer. And we all want to hear it, don't we audience?"

Oh good, the old get the audience against him trick. Tony snuck a peek at Murdock who was glaring in his direction. At least there was somebody on his side.

But the audience insisted. And so did Clint.

Tony walked to the dais with all the hurry of a man on his way to the hangman's noose. He hopped up the left side of the platform.

"Tony Kozol, ladies and gentlemen," announced Scott Day.

A room attendant shoved another chair between Clint and Arthur Levine. Clint patted Tony on the back.

"So," said Scott, "why don't you tell us how you got the gig with Clint Cash and the Cowhands? You two related?"

"No," said a red-faced Kozol. "Nothing like that. In fact," he said, turning to his boss, "I've never seen this guy before. Who did you say he was?"

The audience howled.

And Tony Kozol realized this wasn't so bad after all.

"As you can tell," replied Clint, "Tony is the newest member of the band. And he hasn't learnt his manners yet. But I'm from Texas. I'll break him."

The audience roared again.

Kozol said, "I don't even know what that means and I don't want to."

"Okay, okay," interrupted Scott Day. "Before this gets any uglier, let's get back to the question. Tell us how you got the gig, number one. And secondly, tell us what it's like to be on the road with Clint Cash and the Cowhands."

"Well, truth is it was a fluke of sorts. Lady luck, like Clint says. I'd been doing some freelance work as a musician but had nothing on the burner at the time when I got a call from a promoter friend of mine. I live in Ocean Palm, Florida, by the way, which is between West Palm Beach and Fort Lauderdale. Anyway, it turns out that Clint Cash and the Cowhands were in town for a few days leading up to a show they were going to do later that week."

"My friend, the promoter calls me, all frantic telling me that Clint's canceling a sold out show and how he's going to lose his house all because their regular rhythm guitar player, Brian Love, broke his arm."

Someone in the crowd interjected. "How'd he break his arm?"

"I heard it was a Jet Ski accident," Tony said. "But if you catch me later," he quipped, "I'll tell you what else I heard."

The laughter died down and Kozol continued, growing more comfortable by the minute. This speaking in public was a piece of cake after all. He even shot a grin Murdock's way but Granger only folded his arms and stared. "So, anyway, my friend, Michael, asks me if I can fill in. Do a couple of rehearsals and fake my way through the show. He offered me a fair amount of money, which, being musicians, I'm sure all of us here know how scarce a commodity that is, so I accepted. Gladly.

"Michael said he'd call Clint's manager, Granger Murdock and try and convince him. Which obviously he did. We had a rehearsal that afternoon. It was a Tuesday, I think," he said, testing his memory. "I stayed up for the next forty-eight hours rehearsing, woodshedding on my own with Clint's latest CD, trying to memorize the set list. And here I am."

"And how's life on the road with this guy?" Day said, pointing at Clint.

Clint raised an eyebrow and assumed a mean posture.

"Terrific," answered Kozol. "I mean, it's everything that you'd imagine it would be. Playing great music with great musicians, out on the road. It's just incredible." What's incredible, Tony thought, is how easily I can shovel out this stuff. But the audience loved it and so did Clint who'd broken into a grin.

Even Murdock wouldn't be able to razz him anymore after today's performance. Clint gave Tony another slap on the back. This was a day big on slaps. The boss was in a generous mood.

A hand went up in the middle of the room.

And Tony tried to burn a hole through the floor. He tucked his head between his shoulders, slid down in his slippery seat and thought about hiding under the draped table. "Please don't let it be him," he mouthed. "Please don't let it be Mr. Paisley Curtains."

It was Mr. Paisley Curtains. "Roger Daring, KKAU." He held a notepad in one hand, a pencil in the other. It may as well have been a knife. He might as well have stuck it in Tony's back.

Kozol watched him in horrible fascination, like the about to be executed watches the executioner. As large as he was, Daring's khaki pants were bigger. Today's choice of curtains was a mess of purple paisley.

"Yes, your question please," replied Scott.

Daring pushed Tony's mother's eyeglasses up his nose and cleared his throat. "It's a follow-up question, really, for Mr. Kozol." His pasty face twisted in Tony's direction.

Tony stared straight ahead at the reporter. It was time to face the inevitable. There was nowhere to run.

"I was wondering if you could add anything further to your comment yesterday—"

Kozol saw Murdock out of the corner of his eye. Clint's manager's head was going back and forth quickly, from Kozol to Daring and back again. Like the guy was watching a high stakes ping-pong match. Tony had a feeling he was losing.

"—about Clint Cash killing Jack Henderson and—"

Murdock jumped up.

Clint pushed his chair back and leapt to his feet. Scott Day grabbed the microphone.

"Well, I see our time is—"

"I never said that!" shouted Kozol. "Hector said that. I mean, he didn't say that, he was drunk and he only said that Clint was responsible—"

"Shut up, Kozol," warned Murdock.

"—about up," continued Scott. "Thank you all for coming. And don't forget the show tonight."

"And I don't think he meant that Clint really killed Jack. He only meant—" Tony's time was up.

Murdock reached the platform and gripped the table. His face, uglier and bigger than he'd ever seen it, stopped inches from Tony's. "You're fired!"

THIRTEEN

KOZOL TURNED ON the spout and pushed his hands beneath the running water. He didn't care if it was hot or cold. The odd thing was that in a convention of six thousand or so people, the men's room was empty. Just him and a toilet filled with lime scented disinfectant.

Apparently nobody even wanted to be seen with him in the restroom and they'd all deserted him. Like Grace had done.

As the crowd had emptied the ballroom, home of his unexpected victory and defeat, Tony's eyes had searched out Grace at the back of the room. Delightful, wonderful, sings like an angel, makes love like a devil, Grace.

She was gone.

And Tony's career was over. Once again.

Kozol was about to stick his head under the faucet when a voice caught him.

"Tough break, Kozol."

Tony turned. "Hi, Scott. Fancy meeting you here."

"You come here because you're pissed or to take a piss?"

Kozol looked at Scott Day's reflection in the sink to ceiling mirror. He was dressed in skintight jeans and wore a crisp white t-shirt with his radio station's call letters in four inch tall red stencil across the front, KAUS. His well tanned face made the whiteness of his teeth seem even more intense. Quite a contrast to the sallow, unkempt face with the dark circles under swollen eyes that Tony saw up close in the mirror. His own bone tired face.

Tony shut off the water and reached for a paper towel. He twisted the little handle on the side of the paper dispenser and was rewarded with about a quarter inch of rough brown paper. The machine was empty. "Great." He wiped his hands on his shirt.

When Kozol turned back, Scott Day was still standing there. "You got something to say?"

Scott stuck his thumbs in his pockets. "Hey man, I know it was a tough break back there but don't sweat it. I mean, I know this Roger Daring guy. At least, I've heard of him. Some little piece of trash reporter out to make a name for himself. I hear his last job was covering high school sports and fine dining."

Scott walked toward the stalls and looked under the doors. Tony didn't ask why. You didn't ask too many questions in a bathroom.

Softly Scott said, "I've already made a few calls. I don't think we're going to have to worry about that piece of dogmeat, if you know what I mean."

"No," replied Tony, "I don't think I do. You put out a contract on him or something? Dial 1-800-HITMAN and place an order all because that louse is spreading rumors about Clint?"

Scott grinned.

It wasn't a pretty sight. At least not from Kozol's perspective. He'd been fired and wouldn't be likely to get much of a recommendation from Clint Cash after today's debacle. Looked like he'd have some time to do some fishing with Izzie after all, if the man had the time. After all, he had a job.

"Nah, nothing like that. But this is a small town. We take care of each other."

"So why go to all this trouble for Clint?"

"We're friends. Friends take care of friends."

"Well, isn't that nice. I'll be sure to tell all my friends in the unemployment line you said that." Tony made for the door.

"Hold on, Tony." Scott caught Kozol's arm. "You don't make it easy for anybody to help you, do you?"

"Help me? Just what do you mean by that?"

Day glanced down the row of empty stalls again. "Look," he said in low tones, "I feel kind of bad about what happened. I mean, Murdock shouldn't have fired you. What he should have done was go after that reporter with a shotgun and stick it up his rear end." Scott leaned a hand against the wall. "And I feel kind of bad about you getting hassled by the police."

"How's that?" Kozol didn't like where any of this was going.

"You know, about the drugs and all."

"The drugs? What do you know about that?"

The bathroom door opened and a beanpole of a man with a longish, fuzzy blonde ponytail and a mustache sauntered in. He glanced at the two men then occupied an empty stall.

"Well?" Tony asked again.

Scott motioned at the closed stall and pressed a finger to his lips.

Tony waited awkwardly until the third man in this senseless triangle washed his hands and left. Scott put his back up to the door. "This will keep the riffraff out."

Kozol felt sorry for any riffraff who might need a bathroom in a hurry. "You know, Scott, even though I don't have a job and time is pretty much all I've got, I would like to get back to the hotel and pack my bags. Because the sooner I get out of here the better. And I don't just mean this men's room."

"But that's what I'm trying to tell you. Forget about being fired."

"Tell that to Murdock."

"The hell with Murdock. I'll talk to Clint and straighten this out. Trust me. You've got my word."

Kozol wasn't sure what the blue book value on that might be and instead he asked, "Why are you doing this for me?"

"I told you. I feel bad about you getting hassled by the police over a little coke."

"That little bag of coke could have gotten me locked up for life. I hear they're tough as anything on drugs in this state. And as much as I like Texas, I don't feel like spending the next twenty years of my life seeing it from between the bars. If I hadn't had a friend on the force, I'd probably be sitting in a cell somewhere downtown now."

"I know," said Scott. "It's a sin, ain't it? I mean, if a person is doing a little recreational drug use, why does the government have to butt in and make it a crime?"

"I'm more interested in protecting my skin than having a philosophical discussion about the legalization of drugs."

"I gotcha." Scott Day came closer. "All I'm saying is, it's nobody's business. What a man does for himself. Sex, drugs. Whatever. Putting on fishnet stockings and doing the rumba with a plastic chicken. To each his own."

"Just what do you know about these drugs, anyway?" And why did the sight of Scott Day in fishnet stockings doing the rumba with a plastic chicken seem so easy to picture?

Scott held a hand up to his heart. "Personally," he said, "I know nothing." He placed a limp hand on Tony's shoulder. "But who knows? Maybe somebody, like Jack, was doing a little coke? Maybe somebody else in the band, or one of the crew, or one of the dozens of people wandering around backstage at the Austinland. You know what it's like."

Scott continued, "Maybe somebody had a little bag of coke on him or her and when Henderson's body was found and the police started swarming all over the place, that somebody stashed the bag the first place he or she could think of ..."

"My guitar case."

"Yeah, why not?"

"That still doesn't explain how an identical bag ended up in Henderson's shirt pocket."

"No." Scott scratched his chin. "But that's just one explanation. Maybe Henderson was dealing and had stuck the coke in your guitar case figuring he'd get it out later."

"Only he didn't live that long."

Scott rolled his eyes. "Life is full of risks."

"I heard Henderson was gay."

The DJ shrugged. "I heard you were a disbarred attorney."

Tony could see this conversation was going nowhere and back again. "You're a bright guy, lots of ideas. Tell me, Scott, who do you think murdered Hector Orlando then?"

"Good question. Maybe Henderson and Hector Orlando were partners in the drug business. Or Hector found out something he shouldn't have. Then again," he mused, "it could have been some lunatic fan. A groupie, you know?"

"A groupie? That's what Tanya said."

"Sure, you see? Maybe some groupie went for him. Wanted to have sex in Clint's bus, then strangled the poor guy. There are a lot of screwed up people out there."

Tony agreed. He was looking at one. He reached for the door and Scott stepped back. "I've got to go." Funny, he thought as he left, most people said that on their way into the bathroom, not on the way out.

"Just don't pack your bags until you hear from me!" called Scott.

TONY TURNED HIS HEAD to see where all the banging was coming from. But it was no use. The banging was coming from his head. "Let me get this straight," he said, leaning back in the wooden chair across from Izzie's desk. "You're telling me that Claudia Santana is not dead after all?"

"No," said Izzie, "that's not what I'm telling you." He wore his Clint Cash and the Cowhands complimentary tour jacket rolled up at the sleeves. A fast food burrito gave off an intoxicating smell of burnt rubber. His desk looked less cluttered than the last time Kozol had seen it, but then that was only because most of what had been on the desk was now on the floor at his feet.

"So, what are you telling me exactly?"

"I'm telling you that the forensics report came up on the Jane Doe in Bracken Cave and it is not Claudia Santana."

"And they're certain it's not her?"

"Yep. The dead girl had a left foot deformity from birth. I forget what they call it."

"So Claudia Santana isn't dead."

Izzie grinned evilly. "We don't know that. Maybe she is, maybe she isn't. She just isn't the girl that was found in Bracken Cave."

"This stinks," said Tony, "and I don't just mean your lunch."

"Breakfast," said Izzie.

"Whatever," replied Kozol. "I mean, I only came up here to tell you that I suddenly have come into some leisure time and that I'd take you up on your offer to go fishing and you tell me this."

Tony beat out a nervous rhythm atop Izzie's desk. "Couldn't you have kept your mouth shut? This isn't any of my business, after all. You're with the police, for chrissake, aren't you supposed to keep this sort of stuff confidential?"

"Hey, it's not my case and why should I suffer alone?" Izzie chomped an end off his burrito. He spoke and chewed at the same time. "Besides, you know all the players, I figured you'd be interested."

"Yeah, well, you figured wrong. Since being fired an hour ago my priorities have changed."

"Sure." Izzie thumbed a folder. "You wanna know who she is?"

"Nope."

"Name's Margarita Buenel. Such a shame." Izzie made tsk-tsking noises. Whether it was from the food or the mood, Kozol couldn't tell.

"What's a shame?" Rats, he'd bitten.

"Margarita was only a child. Barely seventeen years old."

Tony sighed. "That is too bad."

"You know where she is from?"

"No, but I suppose you'd like to tell me."

"San Miguel de Allende. Mean anything to you? A small town up in the mountains above Mexico City."

"Means nothing. Should it?" Tony had a feeling it should.

"It so happens that is the same town that Julian and Claudia Santana come from." Izzie slapped the folder down on his desk. "Quite a coincidence, no?"

"Yeah," agreed Tony, "if you believe in coincidences."

"Bumping into you was a coincidence. A group of researchers finding Margarita Buenel's bones in Bracken Cave was a coincidence."

"But the dead girl wearing the missing girl's bracelet, and both from the same town, that'd be one heck of a coincidence, wouldn't it?" Kozol said.

"You see the problems."

"And how does any of this relate to Jack Henderson and Hector Orlando?"

"You tell me. I checked your schedule. Clint Cash and the Cowhands were in San Antonio before coming up to Austin."

"That's true, too. But we've been lots of places and as far as I know we haven't been leaving a string of dead bodies in our wake."

"So why start now?"

Tony rubbed his sagging face. "Damned if I know. Have you asked Julian Santana?"

"Haven't been able to find him. But we will."

Kozol thought about what Scott Day had said. Maybe there was something to all this, something drug related. "Any leads on the coke you found in my guitar case?"

"Nothing. You hear any whispers?"

"Not really. I mean, you always hear talk about drugs but nothing specific. But let's say that Julian and his sister were dealing. That could explain the baggie in my guitar case."

"And in Jack Henderson's pocket," added Izzie.

"Yeah, Claudia went in and certainly had access. Maybe Jack was her connection."

"Maybe. And maybe she killed him and disappeared."

"I hope not. Because then what is Julian's connection in all this? Was he really looking for his sister or did he or his sister leave something incriminating behind at the Austinland after killing Henderson that he wanted to retrieve?"

"You're becoming twisted, Tony. You could be a cop."

"No, thanks. What about Hector Gonzalez? Anything come up on his murderer?"

"Nothing. The guy was asphyxiated. So all I can tell you is somebody strong did the deed. There were a lot of loose hairs around the bed. But Clint is known for bopping with the ladies so I don't know that we'll get very far with the investigation in that direction. You got any angles on it?"

Tony wondered just how many of Grace's short hairs they'd found. But refrained from asking for the police report. "There is one thing I forgot to mention." He squirmed.

"Forgot to mention?" Izzie groaned.

"Well, okay, should have mentioned."

"Let's hear it," Izzie said tersely.

"The night Hector was killed I saw Julian standing outside Clint's bus."

Izzie leaned forward. "What time was this?"

"Uh, right before I found Hector's body."

Izzie pulled his hair. Not a pleasant sight. "If I didn't need a fishing buddy, I'd lock you up and throw the key in Lake Travis. Is there anything else you're keeping from me, Kozol?"

Well, there was that little matter of a deep hole in Pease Park, but in spite of Izzie's threats, Tony saw no point in stirring the pot. "No, that's it."

"Seems like I got all the more reason to locate that Santana kid now, and his sister."

"If she's alive," taunted Tony, throwing Izzie's earlier words back in his face.

Izzie replied by throwing half a black bean burrito at Tony's face. Tony made the mistake of catching it in one hand where it oozed slowly while Izzie chuckled loudly.

"Serves you right," said Izzie. He scratched an address on the back of a business card.

Tony scraped the burrito off his hand and took the card. It wasn't Izzie's. It was for some local carpet cleaning outfit. "Thanks," said Tony. "But I think if I just wash my hands I'll be okay."

"Turn it over, wiseguy."

Tony read the address.

"That's my place. After you finish packing just dump your stuff at my house. Marta should be there to let you in. She's painting a mural on the living room wall."

"You don't have to do this."

"I know. And you didn't ask. But you've got to stay someplace. What are you going to do? Check into another hotel? Forget about it," Izzie said, before Tony could reply. "I've got lots of room."

Tony shoved the card in his pocket. "You know, you could get some business cards printed up, professional like."

"What for?" Izzie looked offended. "People are always giving cards out to me. I'm recycling."

"Right." Tony remembered how cheap Izzie had been in college. Some things didn't change. Tony said thanks and forced Izzie to shake hands; further ridding himself of glue-like burrito.

"DOOR'S OPEN!" shouted Kozol, scooping up his share of the toiletries from the bathroom. At least Beaton wasn't around. Tony wanted to pack up and be gone without having to face his now former bandmates.

He pulled the door open and reached for his suitcase in the narrow closet. "I'm just packing up. Could you come back and clean the room in about an hour, please?"

"Why, certainly, sir."

Kozol turned. "Clint!"

"Howdy, you need clean sheets today, mister?" He held a denim jacket by the fingertips. "I hear this is yours." He dropped the jacket on the bed when Tony failed to take it. "Grace left it in my room. Said to tell you thanks."

"Tell her she's welcome. So, is that all?"

"No."

"Don't tell me, you've come to give me a going away present. How thoughtful." Kozol's suitcase banged against his knees and he threw it down on the bed. "What is it? A free CD? An autographed picture?" How nice, Tony thought, not to have to be sickeningly pleasant to the man now that he wasn't signing Tony's paychecks. Thinking of which, Kozol asked, "Did you bring my final paycheck?"

"Got it right here." Clint patted his jeans. The man rarely went anywhere in other than blues, the only sure exception being awards shows. Country folk took their award ceremonies seriously. Clint wore a black leather vest over a white shirt.

"Great, just drop it on the dresser, will you, I'm in kind of a hurry."

"Man you are full of vinegar today. What's got the twist in your shorts?"

Tony turned and faced his ex-boss. "Let's see," he began, "I've been up all night. I've had drugs planted in my guitar case. Two guys I know are dead and," he said snapping his fingers, "oh, yeah, I've just been fired."

Clint grinned and took off his hat. "Aw, shucks, calm down, Tony. You aren't fired."

Tony dropped the shirt he was balling up in his hands. "What?"

"I said you aren't fired."

"Tell that to Granger."

A flash of fury crossed Clint's face like a quick shadow. "I tell Granger anything I want to. I'm the boss of this here outfit. Murdock works for me." His voice was rising. "I didn't say you were fired. Did you hear me tell you you were fired?"

Tony remained transfixed.

"No, I never said no such thing. If I want to kick your ass out, I'll tell you so myself. Murdock may write the paychecks but it's my money!"

Kozol had never seen Clint get this worked up before. "Thanks, Clint, but I think it's best if I move on."

"What do you mean?" Clint walked to the window and turned back.

"I mean too much B.S. and too many corpses. I don't feel like dealing with anymore of either."

"So who does? But we're a band. We've got to stick together."

"Did Scott Day talk to you?"

"Sure, so what?"

"I don't know. I just can't figure out why everybody suddenly wants to keep me around."

"What? You got low self esteem or something? Look, you're a good player and a decent guy. Let's not rock the boat."

"I'd say the boat is rocking enough to capsize at this point."

"My point exactly. I mean, take all this murder trouble. I got a dead body in my friggin' bus!"

"Any ideas how it got there?"

Clint rubbed his cowboy hat against his head. "Nope. Do you? After all, you're the one who found Hector."

"What do you know about coke?"

"I know I prefer Pepsi," Clint replied. "But let's keep it between ourselves. I wouldn't want to spoil any sponsor relationships."

"You know what I mean, Clint."

"I know that I don't tolerate any drugs. If you know something or heard something about anybody dealing in my band, I want to know."

Kozol threw another shirt in the suitcase. "I don't get it, Clint. That was quite a little scene back there at the convention center today. I all but accused you of murder. And you tell me you don't mind?"

"No hard feelings, Tony. I didn't kill anybody and Scott and Granger are already handling the press."

Tony wondered just how they were handling it. Would the press corp soon be the press corpse?

"So, what do you say? Stick around? We've got a show scheduled for tonight. Think about all those people who are going to be let down if we cancel another show."

"I don't know..."

"Come on, I'll even give you a chance to win back some of your money at the poker table. In fact, I think a little bonus is in order after all you've been through."

"I tell you what," Tony said. "I'll stick around and do tonight's show. After that, I don't know."

Clint went to the door and laid his hand on the knob. "Finish out the tour. I'll make it worth your while, Tony." He opened the door and stepped into the hall, holding the door open with his foot. "How does a new car sound?"

"What, and give up my seventeen year old Saab? I'm still breaking it in."

Clint draped a slippery arm over Tony's shoulder. Tony felt like that kid in *The Jungle Book* being mesmerized by that snake, whatsisname, Kaa? Kaa was Clint's long, slimy arm curling around his neck, hypnotizing his mind before devouring his flesh.

"How's about a pickup? What color you like, red?"

"It's a deal," Tony answered. What the heck, it beat unemployment.

"You know," Clint said, with a satisfied grin on his face, "I'd like you to stay on permanent with the Cowhands. Even after the tour."

"How's that?"

"You know, I'll put you on a regular salary. Of course, you'd have to move up to Nashville. Can't have you living down in Florida. Nashville's great, you'll love it."

"I'm not sure I'm ready to pick up and move, Clint. Besides, what about Brian Love? How's he going to take it?"

"Don't worry about Brian," Clint said. "I'll handle him. Maybe we'll have two rhythm guitarists. Or I'll move Brian over to pedal steel. He plays a little, you know."

"No, I didn't know." Actually, putting Love out of work was more than enough reason to accept the job on a permanent basis.

"Come on board regular like and you get a share of the royalties, plus salary, and a year-to-year contract."

"How can I say no?"

Clint undraped his arm and offered his hand to Tony. They shook. "Well," exclaimed Clint, "I've got to go. Meeting some interviewer downstairs from one of the local rags. There's a rehearsal in ninety minutes. Don't be late!"

Tony shook his head as Clint galloped off. Other pastures and all that.

As he turned to go back to his room, a hand caught him roughly at the shoulder. Tony twisted his head back and pulled away. "Love! What do you want?" Kozol pushed the little man away. "I'm getting tired of people blindsiding me. So clear out."

"You're mistaken if you think you're going to get away with it, lawyer," Love said menacingly. His hands were balled into tight little fists. His lips quivered.

"I don't know what you're talking about."

"I'm talking about you trying to replace me. It will never happen. Murdock fired your sorry butt. If I was you, I'd finish packing and get out."

"What are you doing? Listening to my private conversations?"

"There's only one permanent rhythm guitar player in this outfit." Love pounded a thumb against his chest. "That's me."

"Maybe yes, maybe no."

Love grabbed Kozol by the collar. "I'll kill you before I let you take *my* job, lawyer."

FOURTEEN

"WILL SOMEBODY PLEASE get those lights up?!" Owen Otto shouted toward the back of the hall and a bank of lights came on overhead. "Thank you," he said, muttering insults under his breath.

Tony threaded his way across a tangle of cables stretched out on the floor. Clint, Murdock and Peter Magnuson sat in the front row. None of them looked up as he crossed the stage.

Kirk ran through carrying a boom stand. Some guy in a Pyrat Rum tank-top with floppy jeans and cowboy boots sat at the drums. Tony had never seen him before.

"You're on mic two, to the left of Clint, Tony," Otto said.

"Right." Tony picked up his guitar and checked the tuning. Rock sat behind him, his bass across his lap, a beer in his hand. Tony waved but Rock ignored him. Then again, he had his Walkman on.

Across the stage, Grace and Tanya sat on the floor, at the edge of the drum riser, whispering quietly. Beaton and Love were nowhere in sight.

"Hey, Kirk," called Otto, waving his muscled arms, "you wanna get this floor monitor in position?" Kirk sauntered over. "Look at the placement of this thing? You want Clint to fall off the stage or something? Move it back another eight inches."

Kirk kicked the monitor with his foot several times until it balanced at the edge of the stairs.

"I'm going up to the booth." Owen called over to Clint, "We're ready whenever you are, boss!"

Clint nodded, finished his conversation and ambled up on stage. "Where's Beaton?" he hollered.

"Right here, Clint!" Beaton came jogging up stage left and scooped up his Telecaster. "Sorry."

"Everybody know Doug Wills?" Clint asked.

The man at the drums waved a stick.

"Doug's with the Texas Hurricanes and has kindly agreed to help us out tonight. So let's make this easy for him and us and do it right the first time. Got it?"

Everybody muttered their agreement.

"Alright then, top of the A set list, if you please, ladies and gentlemen." Clint gripped the microphone, "And a one, and a two, and—"

Rock pulled up to his microphone and Tony stepped back to keep from getting impaled by his bass. The two men did the *pas-de-deux* but made it through the first number, *Two Boots On The Run*.

"What are you two dancing around for?" griped Murdock from the front row.

"Our microphones are too close," complained Rock and I'm a lefty. If anybody would bother to remember on the setup."

"Alright, alright. One second," came the voice over the monitors. It was attached upstairs to Owen Otto. "Kirk, move Tony's mic over a couple of steps. Clint's got plenty of room in the middle."

"Oh, shit," complained Clint, "can't we get through the set list just once, people, without a screw-up?" He kicked the floor. "And where's Kirk?"

A voice carried over the wall of speakers in the back. "Hold on, I'm coming!"

"Never mind," said Tony, pushing his guitar around to his back where it flapped on its leather strap. "I'll move it my—"

Tony grabbed the microphone stand by the neck. Quick as a tap on the shoulder from Death, Kozol felt as if a lightning bolt had come shooting down from Heaven and struck him in the neck. If this is a heart attack, he thought, in those nanoseconds he had before he hit the floor, I'm too young to die.

Tony hit the floor face up.

The microphone stand fell at his side.

The last thing he heard before passing out was Clint muttering, "Oh, shit," once again.

WHEN TONY OPENED his eyes it was to the worried faces of his bandmates and a number of the crew. Tanya was holding his hand and weeping. "You okay, Tone, baby?"

"Give him some room," bellowed Rock. "You people are sucking up all his air."

Owen held a fried cable up with contempt. "Look at this thing," he said. "Whoever used this frayed cable is an idiot! Somebody could have been killed."

Tony groaned. That somebody was him.

Rock thrust out a beefy arm and Tony grabbed it. He managed a sitting position with the help of his arms as back supports.

"Take it easy, Tone."

"Thanks, Tanya. I'm okay." Though he felt like a million bees were racing up and down his arteries and veins. "Who hit me?"

"Faulty cable," said Otto. "Don't worry. It's been taken care of."

Clint looked down at him. "You gonna be okay?"

"Yeah, just give me a minute."

Clint turned his head. "Hey, Grace!"

Grace looked up. Tony noticed she had been conspicuously absent from his little gang of well-wishers.

"Come here, would you?"

Grace rose and slowly crossed the stage.

"Take Tony back to his dressing room and sit with him a bit. Get him some water or something." He looked back down at Tony. "Can you walk?"

"Yeah. I think so." Tony wobbled but managed to keep his feet under him and reasonably straight.

"Go ahead, Grace."

"But, Clint—"

"Come on, doll. The man needs some TLC."

"That's okay, Clint. I can manage on my own." Tony took a faltering step and nearly keeled over.

Rock and Johnnie caught him.

Clint gave Grace a look that Tony knew meant "no more talking, do it." She did. Putting Tony's arm over her shoulder she led him back down the steps and to his dressing room.

She pushed the door open with one hand and Tony fell onto the nearest chair.

"Thanks. I'll be okay now."

Grace snatched a bottle of water from a stash on the dressing table and twisted off the top. "Clint said to give you some water."

"You always do what Clint tells you?" Tony wondered if those hands could have twisted the life out of Hector Orlando.

"Yes," she said, her voice hard, "I do."

She thrust the open bottle into Tony's hands. "Drink."

Tony gripped the bottle far from his body. The sudden, irrational fear welled over him that if he drank the water he'd be electrocuted. After all, water was an excellent conductor. What if his body was full of pent-up electrical charge and a mouthful of water sent another shock surging through his guts?

Grace turned her back to him, fussing with her hair in the mirror.

"Okay, you've done your good deed. You can leave now."

"Clint told me to keep you company."

"Oh, that's right. And you always do what Clint tells you to do."

Grace glared at him.

But he went on anyway. "Does that include sleeping with me?"

There was a pause.

"Yes, it does."

Tony had only meant the statement to be hurtful, not truthful. Her answer hit him harder than the jolt of electricity he'd taken. "What?"

"That's right. I slept with you because Clint asked me to."

"You're lying."

"No."

"Why on earth would he ask you to go to bed with me?"

"He wanted to know what you knew about Henderson's murder. Maybe he thought you knew who did it or had some clues. Maybe had some inside information from that friend of yours on the force."

Kozol thought about her answers. "But you never even asked me about that."

Grace laughed a cheerless laugh. "That's the funny part, isn't it?"

"Meaning what?"

"Meaning I was able to go to bed with you, like Clint wanted, but I wasn't able to grill you like he wanted. Pretty pathetic, isn't it?"

Tony didn't even nod his head. It was pathetic, but for who? He said, "I'm sorry."

"Don't be," Grace said, looking him in the eye. "We all make choices."

He wasn't about to ask her whether they were the right ones. After all, what did he know about that?

"I guess that's enough TLC," Grace said, making for the door.

"Wait," called Tony. "I heard you were the last one to see Hector Orlando before he was killed."

Grace frowned. "Who told you that?"

"Does it matter?"

"No." She returned to the center of the room and stamped her foot. "People are such gossips around here. Yes, I did see Hector. So what?"

"So it was right outside Clint's bus and then he ended up dead inside. Quite a coincidence, wouldn't you say?" He drove the needle home, "Since you always do what Clint asks you to do, did you kill Hector for him?"

Grace swung an arm through the air. "That's crazy! I ran into Hector out in the parking lot. He was drunk. He was sad and he was lonely. He wanted to talk. All I wanted to do was get away."

"What did he want to talk about?"

She shrugged. "The band. Going home. Quitting."

"He was thinking of quitting?"

"Hector was always thinking of quitting. He's got a family. A wife and kids. Had a wife and kids, poor things. He was tired of being on the road. And he didn't like what happened to Jack."

"Why do you think he said that Clint Cash kills everybody?"

"Oh, come on, Tony," Grace said easily. "You know how it is. He meant being on the road mostly. It's hard on the people on the road and harder still maybe for the people they leave behind. That and one other thing."

"What other thing?"

"Oh, nothing. A girl died a couple of years ago. A backup singer. The one I replaced actually."

"What happened to her?"

"I'm not sure. I heard it was an overdose."

"Drugs?"

"I don't mean cotton candy." She stood in the doorway. "I'd better get back before Clint misses me."

"Right, we wouldn't want to let Clint down."

"Clint's the star of this show. Me, I'm just a girl singer."

"You're very good at what you do."

"What's that supposed to mean?"

"Nothing. Tell me, do you think Clint could've killed Henderson and Orlando?"

"Clint would never do anything to jeopardize his career."

Tony nodded.

Grace smiled, then disappeared, like the Cheshire Cat. But Tony had a feeling her life was no Wonderland.

And Grace's answer had been no answer at all. Clint may not do anything to jeopardize his career, but would he do everything to save it?

FIFTEEN

"YOU COME TO finish me off?"

"Very funny." Rock squeezed into the room. Everywhere he went he seemed to have to cram himself in. "If I wanted to kill you, I'd wring your scrawny neck." He made convincing twisting motions with his hands.

Kozol gulped. He had no doubt Rock could do it. "Like you did Hector?"

"Screw you. Hector was my friend." Rock turned to the door. "Look, I only came to see if you were okay. But if you don't like it, then excuse me."

"Yeah, well, when I came on stage you barely looked my way. You were sitting there like some big oaf on your rear end. Like you were just waiting for something to happen."

"I was waiting for something to happen alright." Rock loomed over him casting a shadow as big as a century old oak. "I was waiting for laggards like you to show up so we could rehearse. Clint ought to impose a money penalty on players who don't show up on time. A lot of outfits do that."

"Maybe you were just waiting for me to take my mic so you could watch me dance?"

"You ever think I might have grabbed your stupid mic to move it out of my way? I'm out of here." Rock stepped out.

"Wait—" Kozol rose from the chair and held out his right hand. "Sorry."

Rock slowly stepped up, grabbed Tony's hand and pressed.

Tony sucked in a breath and let his hand fall to his side. He had a feeling his right hand would be an inoperable ball of mush for some time. "What's going on out there?" Kozol motioned toward the stage.

"They're resetting everything. Checking out all the wiring. Don't want any more accidents."

"Accident, right."

"You think otherwise?"

"I don't know what to think anymore. Somebody might have tried to kill me and I can't figure out why anymore than I can figure out why anybody would want Jack or Hector dead."

"It still could have been an accident," Rock replied.

"Yeah, in my case, but not Jack and Hector. How well did you know Jack?"

"Now you saying I killed him?"

"No, but maybe you know something about the drugs?" It might have been unfair, but Rock with his tattoos and his earrings, and his wild eyes, certainly looked like he might have done a little experimenting at one time or another. Maybe still.

"I know a user when I see one." Rock mashed one hand into the other like he was grinding cornmeal.

"What's that supposed to mean?"

Rock bit his lip. "I probably shouldn't say anything, but I'd bet Clint uses the stuff."

"Clint? Are you kidding?" Kozol paced. "He and Murdock are vehemently opposed to the stuff. Always threatening to toss anybody out who is caught dealing or using."

Rock shrugged. "I'm only telling you what I think. You're free to think different."

"You know," said Tony, "I saw Julian Santana coming out

of Clint's bus the night of the murder. And there is some circumstantial evidence," he thought back to his conversation with Izzie and the suspicion that the Santanas could be part of a drug ring, "that he and his sister were selling coke."

"You believe it?"

"I don't know. It's possible that Claudia Santana or even Julian killed Jack Henderson. It could have been a drug deal gone bad. And I found out today that the girl in Bracken Cave is not Claudia Santana."

"So she's alive?"

"Maybe. And maybe she was never really missing. Julian could have been conning us all along."

It was Rock's turn to pace. "That could fit with something I found out today."

"What's that?"

"Well, I went by Julian's place to see how he was doing this afternoon."

"And?"

"And that's just it. He wasn't there."

Kozol waited for the other shoe to drop. When it didn't, he prodded the big guy. "What's the significance of that? He could have been out taking a walk, shopping, looking for his sister, anything..."

Rock shook his head. "I talked to his landlady. Nice woman. You should meet her sometime. Wearing a big, old blue robe that could have swallowed her up and you'd never know it, but nice as anything. She had this—"

"Whoa." Tony held up a hand. "What's the point here, Rock?"

"She said that Julian had taken off. Moved out. Said that his sister had come by—"

"His sister?!"

Rock nodded. "That's right. Said she'd come by and Julian

packed up his things and the two of them had gone off together."

"Did she say where they went? Did they leave a forwarding address?"

"Landlady didn't say. Or didn't know."

Kozol raced to the door. "Come on, Rock. We've got to get down there and talk to this landlady. We need to know where those two went and what they're up to."

Rock took a small step, then exclaimed, "But what about rehearsal? Clint's going to have a fit."

"There's no time for rehearsal now. This is important!"

Tony turned the corner of the hall, Rock coming up quickly behind him, and slammed into Granger Murdock.

"Going somewhere, boys?" If acid could talk it would have sounded like Murdock at that moment.

"We, uh," Kozol's gears turned. "I'm feeling a little funny yet. Bad, you know? Thought I'd go to one of those emergency medical clinics." Tony was sure he'd started sweating. "You know where there might be one around here?"

Rock nodded. Great support.

"Don't bullshit me. I heard you talking about looking for that stupid Mexican kid."

"You were eavesdropping!"

"Yeah," spat Murdock. "So?"

Granger, Tony knew, considered listening in on others' conversations a God-given right.

"I know that Clint's waiting for you men on stage. You planning on keeping him waiting?"

Tony looked from Granger's face to his boots. Very fancy. Somewhere a snake was missing its skin. That had to hurt.

"You planning on looking for a new job? You think Clint's going to go easy on you? Again?"

"No," answered Tony.

"What about you, Rock?"

"I'll be there." Rock looked at Kozol and shrugged helplessly.

Kozol said, "I guess we can take care of that little errand after rehearsal."

Murdock leaned into his face. "I'm not letting you two boys out of my sight. Right now we're rehearsing. After that, we've got dinner at Rudy's Steakhouse with one of the sponsors. After that, back here to the Austinland. And I don't care if I have to lock you in your dressing room until showtime. You will be here."

"But Granger, I've just got to—"

"If you've got something more important to do than your job, then I suggest you take it up with Clint."

The sound of a drum roll and Beaton tuning up his electric guitar echoed in the corridor.

Footsteps followed.

It was Brian Love. "What are you guys doing back here anyway? A supernatural Bermuda Triangle suck you all up? Clint says get your behinds up there. Now!"

REHEARSAL WENT WELL. That is, nobody died. From now on, Tony was using that as his benchmark. And true to his word, Murdock led Tony and Rock around on a short leash, even following Kozol to the men's room at Rudy's.

The concert went just as smoothly. The opening act was a couple of local Austinite singer-songwriters with acoustic guitars, Grieger and Cone. They were an act that AWE Records was developing. Tony was so far impressed.

After a quick equipment setup change the Cowhands were on stage. Clint ran out to a thunderous crack of applause and when the concert was over an hour and a half later the applause was equally vigorous.

Beaton jostled Rock as he clambered down the back steps of the stage. Tony was right behind him.

"Nice playing, boys," said Beaton.

"You, too. Doug did a great job out there on the skins," Rock said generously.

"Yeah, smokin'. Let's go grab a beer," suggested Beaton.

Rock swiped a line of sweat from his forehead with the back of his arm. "Right behind you."

"Wait." Tony pulled Rock aside. "Are you forgetting? We've got to go see Julian Santana's landlady."

"I don't know, Tony...it's awfully late." Rock tapped his watch.

"I know," said Tony, "but every minute counts. Julian and his sister could be out of the country by now."

"Then what difference is one little beer going to make?"

Beaton called, "You guys coming or what?"

"Alright," Tony said. "One beer."

"Just one," agreed Rock. "Gotta keep my strength up."

"Okay then." Beaton raced down the corridor. "There's beer to be drunk and women to be hustled."

The three men plunged into Clint's big dressing room, made smaller by the dozens of sweaty bodies swirling about in search of a good time on Clint's nickel. Rock plunged a hand into a cooler of ice on the floor and came up with three longnecks. He handed one to Kozol and another to Beaton.

"See 'ya, boys," said the lead guitarist, popping the cap, downing a third and heading for the blonde Tony had seen him with up in their hotel room. A young Texas stud was making moves on her and Johnnie was about to go stake his claim.

Rock had finished off his first beer and was plucking another from the ice chest before Tony had even managed to wet his lips.

"Let's get out of here," Tony said. "The deal was one."

"Yeah, but you haven't finished yours yet."

"I can live without it."

"Besides," said Rock, "Clint's calling us over."

Tony looked across the room. Clint stood near the middle, the king in his kingdom. Murdock and Love were hovering nearby. Scott Day was talking to Peter Magnuson in the corner. "Let's pretend we didn't see him."

"He's waving. We gotta go."

Tony waved back and called, "Great show, Clint. See you tomorrow."

"Now, now. Get your butts over here, boys."

Rock and Tony pushed their way past the throng.

"Get a load of those girls," Clint drooled. "I get the one in the middle and you two have your choice of the rest."

"Thanks, Clint," Tony replied, "but we're in kind of a hurry."

"Hurry? Who hurries at a party? Get drunk, get laid, get some sleep," explained Clint. "That's the motto!"

Kozol could see that Clint had already reached stage one. "Sorry, but we've really got to go."

"Is this about the Julian character?" Clint waved at the girls.

"How did you know?"

"Granger told me. Said you were going to see his landlady." He motioned for the girls to come over. They started forward. "Don't tell me that's more important than partying?"

"We would like to know what happened. Julian and his sister, Claudia, could be drug dealers. They could be killers."

"So why not let the police handle it?"

"They're looking for the pair. It doesn't mean we can't go do a little poking around ourselves. After all, it would be nice to know who killed Jack and Hector, wouldn't it?"

"Of course it would," replied Clint, after what Tony perceived as a moment's hesitation.

"You got any ideas?"

"No." Clint sipped his drink. "Being Clint Cash is a full-time occupation, if you get my drift."

Tony nodded.

"I ain't got time for anything else. No drugs, no nothing."

"It's a shame you've been having such bad luck."

"What's that supposed to mean? Things are going pretty good."

"Tell that to Jack and Hector's families."

Clint shrugged.

Tony went on, "I also heard about that backup singer that died of an overdose a couple years back."

"So?"

"Is that why you're so dead set against drugs?"

"Maybe. Why do you care all of a sudden? You vying for sainthood?"

"No, I just want to know what's going on. Somebody tried to kill me tonight."

"Again, maybe. As far as I know, it was a faulty cord. If I didn't want you around, I wouldn't have asked you to stay, would I?" Clint grinned. The three girls were getting closer.

"What's going on?" Scott Day showed up and draped his arms over Clint and Tony. "Hi'ya, Rock. Got enough beer?"

"This will do for a start," Rock said, killing off his second bottle.

"We playing poker later?" Scott asked.

Tony pulled loose from Scott and motioned for Rock to back off. "Let's get out of here," he whispered.

"What?" bellowed Rock.

The din of the crowd was so overwhelming Tony had to shout. "I said, let's go!"

Tony pushed his way back upstream. When the crowd failed to move aside, he shoved the big guy ahead of him. Rock cleared the path and Kozol sailed on in his wake.

They waved their way out past the security guard at the back door and stepped out into the balmy night.

"You sure you want to do this now?" asked Rock. "Like I said, it's awfully late."

"You said before you wanted to help. But if you don't want to come, that's okay. I'm going."

"Yeah, me too. After all, I've been there. You don't even know where the kid was living. But you're forgetting one thing."

"What's that?"

"How are we going to get there? We'll be lucky to find a cab out here."

Tony's eyes surveyed the parking lot. He snapped his fingers. Beaton's rental from his treasure seeking days, was parked beside the semi that hauled around the band's gear. "I'll be right back."

Kozol returned dangling a key. "We've got wheels."

Rock pulled open the driver's side door. "Oh, no you don't." Kozol gave him a shove, a friendly shove, but a shove. "I'll drive."

"But I'm the one who knows how to get there."

"Yeah," said Tony, climbing behind the wheel, "but I've been a victim of your driving more than once before." He rubbed his forehead. "And I've still got the bruises. The difference between me and you," said Kozol, pulling out of the parking lot and bouncing up the alley and out onto the street, "is that I drive with the headlights on."

"That may be," Rock said, "but I do know which way to go on a one way street."

"What?"

The light up ahead changed from red to green and the traffic surged. Right in Kozol's direction. He slammed on the brake pedal, performed an awkward U-turn to the symphony of multiple cars honking, being deftly conducted by multiple fingers pointing, and followed the herd. "Thanks for telling me."

"You're welcome," smirked Rock.

With Rock navigating they made their way up Trinity to Martin Luther King Boulevard, past the University of Texas main campus. Tony caught a glimpse of the UT Clock Tower as they drove past. It had been a fixture in the Austin skyline since its completion in 1937. At twenty-seven stories tall, with a three and a half ton bell atop, it was impossible to miss. Especially after a Texas sports victory when the whole thing was lit up a burnt orange.

"Turn here!" shouted Rock sticking a hand out the window and pointing to the right. "I think this is it."

Tony quickly turned the wheel and headed up a narrow, upward sloping residential street filled with older, well kept homes. "Which house is it?"

"I think it's just ahead. On your side." Rock lowered himself in the seat to try to get a better look out Tony's window. "That's the one."

Tony rolled to a stop. The house was dark. It was a three story, Victorian styled home, white with pink trim. A broad, elevated porch stuck off the front with a short flight of steps up. A lone, opaque light kept vigil.

A sign outside proclaimed "Rooms Available. Inquire #101."

"You sure?"

"Positive. Come on."

"I'll go," said Tony as he pulled the car up between two others on the street. "You stay here. If this landlady comes face to face with the two of us," Tony was thinking of the giant, punk-looking Rock actually, "at her door, at this hour, she might panic."

Rock opened his car door. "You're forgetting. She's seen me before. I talked to her. You're the one who might spook her."

"Fine," Tony agreed, as they swiftly crossed the street. "But let me do the talking." Their footsteps echoed up the hollow wooden porch steps. Somewhere in the distance a dog barked.

"Are you sure this is the right place?" Tony stopped with his knuckles inches from the door.

"Yeah, will you knock already—"

Tony pulled open the screen door and tapped lightly on the front door. There was no response.

"That's no way to knock," complained Rock. "Out of my way." He pushed past Tony, balled up his fist and struck the door with a burst of a good half dozen right hooks. If that door had been a contender, it would have been down for the count.

It wasn't and it didn't.

A light, visible from the front windows, popped on. The front door opened. A women with hair as white and fine as a spider's web, wearing a thick blue robe which was billowy enough that she could have hidden a three year old elephant calf inside and still had room left over for a cat, peered out at them.

There were about a bazillion tiny wrinkles on her face and a bajillion deeper ones. Her eyes were blue as the night sky. And she didn't look the least bit nervous or frightened. But then again, why should she? figured Kozol, since she was holding a double barreled shotgun level with his chest.

"Good evening, I'm sorry to bother you so late, ma'am," began Kozol, who was inching ever so slowly backwards. "But we were looking for a friend of ours." He waved a hand at Rock who stepped forward and grinned.

The landlady/executioner smiled back. "Why, it's you," she exclaimed, "the nice young man who was by this afternoon." She propped the shotgun against her hip and held it suspended with one hand. "Why didn't you say so?" She pushed the door open. "Come on in."

Tony hesitated. Something about entering the houses of crazed old ladies with shotguns.

Rock stepped forward. "Come on, Tony. What are you waiting for?"

Tony refrained from saying "being blown to bits by a nervous old woman with an elephant in her robe" and followed his overly trusting friend inside.

Tony stepped through the entryway and was immediately blasted. Not with shotgun pellets, but color. Most everything was pink. There was a pink satin sofa with light pink throw pillows. Pink lampshades on the floor lamps and bright pink, low shag, carpet colored the floor. The walls were papered with pink geraniums trimmed up at the ceiling with a six inch wide swath of bluebonnets.

Behind the sofa was about a fifty gallon aquarium. The gravel on the bottom was pink. So were the fluorescent lights in the hood overtop. A lone diver tossed off bubbles that fled to the surface. The poor guy was probably squirming in all that pink. Tony would have suggested a Barbie aerator for the job.

Peering inside the water, Kozol expected to see little pink fishies swimming about. Instead he saw seahorses.

"Nice to see you again. Rock Bottom, isn't it? I was hoping you'd drop by again and pay me a visit."

"Yes, ma'am," replied the big guy.

"And you are?"

Tony cleared his throat. Even her skin was pink. Maybe it was a trick of the light. "Tony Kozol, ma'am."

She had a surprisingly strong grip. "Well, I'm Mrs. Clay, Emma Clay. Call me Em, if you like. Most folk do, except for my Ned who liked to call me his little bluebonnet."

"Thanks, nice to meet you. We're sorry to barge in on you at this hour—" began Tony.

"It's about Julian Santana," Rock interjected.

"Oh, the nice, young boarder you were asking me about this afternoon, Rock. I don't know what else I can tell you, but please, have a seat, boys."

Tony and Rock dropped down onto the sofa. A scent of flowers filled the air. Something sweet.

"Sure thing, Mrs. Clay," answered Rock.

She shuffled off on slippered feet to the kitchen which opened up in the far corner.

"Care for a scotch and a cookie?"

"Scotch and a cookie?" whispered Tony. He mentally ticked off how long it would take to get out the front door if the old lady got drunk and started firing. He wondered if there was a Mr. Clay or if he'd been pinked to death.

"It's great," said Rock. "Had the same thing this afternoon. Wait till you try it."

Mrs. Clay was making noises in the kitchen and, when she returned, she was bearing a silver serving tray loaded up with a decanter of scotch, three glasses and a plateful of cookies that could have fed a Third World army. She offered up drinks and cookies to each then helped herself.

Pulling her feet up beside her and resting the shotgun precariously face-up and aiming at her own face, at the side of the chair she nested in, Mrs. Clay bit into a cookie and washed it down with a healthy mouthful of scotch.

"Delicious," Rock commented.

Tony bit into his cookie and got a rush of sweet.

"They're sugar cookies. That's all I make. They were Ned's favorite, God rest his soul." She'd said the words quickly, as if she'd said them a couple thousand times a day and they came out as "grestisoul."

"Ned was your husband, Mrs. Clay?" asked Tony.

"Yes, gone all these years, grestisoul. Know why he called me his little bluebonnet?"

Tony and Rock shook their heads.

She raised her left index finger to her face. "It's my eyes. The color of bluebonnets, Ned said, grestisoul." She laughed.

"Not that I put much store in his words. Bluebonnet is the state flower of Texas, you know. Grow well up in the Hill Country. You can see them for miles and miles out along the highways. So beautiful."

Emma Clay's eyes glazed over. Whether it was from the scotch or her memories of days gone past, Tony couldn't know.

So that explained the bluebonnet wall trim and blue slippers. There were even bluebonnets planted against the outside of the house.

"Ned worked the granite mine. Have you been out to see our Granite Mountain?"

Tony shook his head no. He glanced at Rock who had broken up part of a cookie into tiny crumbs which he dropped into the aquarium. The seahorses didn't seem to know what to make of it.

"You really should try to get out there. There's nothing like it in all the world. Eight-hundred and sixty-six feet tall. The most beautiful pink granite you ever did see. Made the dome to the State Capitol out of it, they did. From one dome to another, you might say." She sighed and stared off into space again. "Then poor Ned died, grestisoul. Tuberculosis did it."

Okay, so now Tony understood where the woman's love of pink came from.

"That's a shame, Mrs. Clay," Rock said, dusting the surface of the water with sugar. Seahorses pecked nervously at the particles.

She rocked in her chair. "Yes. The most beautiful country on earth, the Hill Country. You know the composer, Oscar J. Fox was so inspired by the view overlooking Lake Marble Falls that he wrote his song, *The Hills Of Home.*

"Wow," said Rock.

Tony shot Rock a look. Had Rock even heard of Oscar J. Fox?

Mrs. Clay must have caught his look because she said, "Oscar J. Fox wrote *Home On The Range* and *Get Along Little Doggie.*"

Tony was impressed. "So why did you move back here, Mrs. Clay?"

The muzzle of the shotgun slid back and caught at the edge of the back cushion of the landlady's chair. Kozol prayed the gun had a safety and that it was on.

"Like I said, Ned died, grestisoul. After that, I just couldn't bear to be alone out there in the country. All my other family was gone, dead or moved away. So I bought this boarding house. Been here ever since."

Rock said, "That's a shame."

"Ned loved his horses, you know. Raised palominos. Beautiful animals, color of gold with long flaxen tails and matching manes."

Tony sipped his whiskey. Seahorses peeked over his shoulder, making him nervous.

Mrs. Clay caught his glance again. She was sharp. "No room for horses here, of course. That's why I keep the seahorses. They remind me of my Ned, grestisoul."

Tony muttered, "Grestisoul," in unison with her. Then quickly cleared his throat in case he'd offended the widow. "What we wanted to ask you about, like Rock said before, was one of your boarders, Julian Santana."

Mrs. Clay polished off her cookie and her drink. "Refill, boys?" Only Rock nodded yes but she topped off both their glasses. "And please, help yourselves to some more cookies."

Rock scooped up two. He waved one of them in front of the glass.

Oh great, thought Kozol, now he's teasing the poor things. And for all he knew, Mrs. Clay, Em, considered one of them to be the reincarnation of Ned, grestisoul.

"He was a nice young man," said Mrs. Clay, sinking back into her chair. "Wasn't here long, but I'm sorry to see him go."

"That's just it, Mrs. Clay," said Kozol. "Do you know where he went?"

Mrs. Clay stared across the room, through the walls and apparently out into the *Twilight Zone*. "No," she said after a moment, "I'm afraid not."

"Can you tell us exactly what happened, Mrs. Clay?"

"Only if you start calling me Em, Tony."

"Okay, Em, could you please tell me what you remember?"

"Surely." She folded her hands in her lap. "Round about noon or so, I suppose, I get a knock on the door. Pretty young thing says she's looking for her brother, Julian."

"Mexican?" asked Tony.

"I'd say so. Spoke English with an accent."

"Did she say her name?"

"Not right away. Knocked on the door. Asked what room Julian was in. I told her 303 upstairs. She came back down a minute later saying there was no answer. Of course, I could have told her that, I'd seen Julian go out a little earlier. Police had been by looking for him, too. I can't imagine why. Such a well-mannered young man."

"Did she leave then?"

"No I told her to come on in and wait a spell, You see, Julian liked to walk down to the market on the corner. I knew he wouldn't be long. Nice girl. But fidgety."

"How's that?"

"Well, I asked her to come on in and sit a spell. But she just stood over there," pointed Em, "next to that bookcase by the front door, looking like one of those flamencos in the zoo."

Tony leaned forward. "Flamencos?"

"Yes, you know, those pink birds with the long legs."

"Flamingos. You mean, flamingos, Em."

"That's what I said, Tony, flamingos. Standing there on one leg, the other tucked up inside her thigh."

Tony nodded. "Of course. I must have heard you wrong." And she still was within arm's reach of that well-polished shotgun. The girl Grace and Tanya had described also stood like that. On one leg.

Mrs. Clay continued, "Then Julian came back. And they left together."

"Did you hear what they said to each other? What did Julian do when he first saw her?"

Mrs. Clay scratched her hand. "Well, that's the funny thing, now that you mention it. His sister runs out and says something to him, I couldn't hear what. I'm not a snoop after all and they were out on the porch. Julian went upstairs alone, packed up his little suitcase and came back down. Julian said goodbye to me, nice boy. And then they left together."

"What's so funny about that, Mrs. Clay?" asked Rock.

"Well, I mean, I knew Julian was looking for his sister, he told me all about it. Then his sister shows up and he leaves with her."

Both men looked puzzled.

"Don't you see? Julian gave me a hug when he left. But I never did see the boy and his sister hug. Seems to me that if you've been looking for each other a long time, the least you do is hug."

"Yeah," said Rock. Plunk! He dropped a chunk of cookie into the aquarium. It sank to the pink gravel bottom and fell apart.

"That is odd," Tony agreed. "Did either of them say where they were going?"

"No, and I didn't ask."

Rock said, "What kind of car was she driving?"

"She wasn't."

"You mean they walked?" Tony said.

"No, they got into a van that was parked right across the street."

"So, she had a van."

"Maybe. But another fellow was driving."

"What did he look like?" Tony asked.

Mrs. Clay's eyes glazed over. "Didn't get a good look at him."

"How about the van, Em? Did you notice the make or the color?"

She appeared to give this some thought. "I don't know much about no makes. It does seem that it was a light color, white maybe. Of course, it could have been dirty. Maybe beige. Had a big dent in the back side, I remember that."

"That sounds like Rick's van," Rock put in.

"Rick?" asked Tony.

"Yeah, the security guard from over at the Austinland. I've seen him getting in and out of a van like that a couple of times. Come to think of it, I haven't seen him around much lately though."

"Neither have I," Tony said thoughtfully. He rose. "Well, we'd better be going."

"So soon?" Mrs. Clay pushed herself up from the chair.

"Yes, it's late. Come on, Rock."

Rock stood and brushed cookie crumbs off his black jeans. "Nice to see you again, Mrs. Clay."

Mrs. Clay held open the front door. "You boys come again. Anytime now, you hear?"

Tony and Rock promised they would try.

Tony spotted a Porsche Boxster convertible nestled up against the curb that he hadn't noticed earlier. It was pink. The color of granite? The top was up, but Kozol had no trouble making out the interior. The seats were blue. Bluebonnet? It couldn't be...but it had to be. The custom plate affixed to the back read *NED*.

"Nice lady, huh?" Rock remarked.

"Yeah," said Tony, starting up the rental car's engine. "So why were you trying to kill her fish back there?"

"What are you talking about?"

"I'm talking about you throwing all that sugar cookie in the tank."

"What's wrong with that?"

Tony pulled into the street, turned the car around and headed downhill. "All that sugar? All that processed flour? You think that's good for them? I'm surprised you didn't toss in an ounce of scotch!"

"Hey, that's not a bad idea. They might've appreciated that even more."

"Oh, sure. Like Mrs. Clay is going to appreciate scooping dead seahorses out of her aquarium tomorrow morning."

"I didn't hear her complaining."

"I'm not sure she even noticed. But I'm pretty sure that fish don't eat sugar cookies."

"I don't see the big deal," complained Rock. "Besides, I'm not so sure that seahorses are even fish, are you?"

Kozol frowned. "No, but I sure know I wouldn't want to put a saddle on a seahorse or fry one." He twisted the wheel to avoid a cat. "Even if it had been plumped up on sugar cookie."

SIXTEEN

"WHAT ARE WE DOING back here?"

Tony shoved the car's nose up next to the rear wall of the Austinland Theater. A few empty cars and a couple of trucks were scattered about the back lot, but these were nothing to worry about. He turned off the headlamps. "Looking for an address on this Rick character. A phone number, anything."

Rock yawned and rubbed his jowls. "And you expect to find that here?" He looked at his watch. "Now?"

Tony gently closed his door. Not that it mattered since Rock gave his own door a gentle slam that sent the car rocking side to side. "Shhh."

"Sorry."

They approached the back door. There wasn't another sound.

Tony knocked. Hard enough to keep Rock off his back. Still, there was no response from within. He turned the dented knob. "It's locked."

Rock pushed Tony aside. "Watch out." He raised a boot.

Tony stopped him. "What are you going to do?"

"Kick it in," Rock replied matter-of-factly.

"In the first place, there could be an alarm and I don't feel like going downtown just now."

"We are downtown," quipped Rock.

"You know what I mean. In the second place, as I remember, this door opens out."

"Oh," said Rock, "yeah."

Tony scouted around the side of the building to the left. "You go the other way."

"What are we looking for?"

"A door, a window. There must be some other way in a big, old building like this."

There was. Tony spotted a smallish window on the wall around the corner. He called and Rock ran over. "There's our way inside."

"That window is fifteen feet off the ground."

"You can lift me on your shoulders."

"Yeah," Rock retorted, "but I can't help you fly. We'll still be shy a couple of feet or so."

Tony stepped back from the brick wall and looked upward. The window hung open several inches. But Rock was right. Even standing on the big guy's shoulders, he couldn't reach the sill. Then he snapped his fingers. "I've got an idea, Rock. Wait right here."

Tony jogged back to the car, started the engine and edged the rental up close along the wall below the open window. "Now," explained Tony, turning off the engine lest the car draw suspicion, and climbing out onto its hood, "all you've got to do is climb up here onto the car's roof. I'll climb up on your shoulders and I'm in."

Rock looked dubious.

"Come on," Kozol said, "it'll work."

"I don't know," Rock said tugging a silver earring. "What if the car can't hold us both?"

Tony thumped on the hood. "This baby's solid. Don't worry about it. What are you afraid of?"

Rock threw out his chest like a Neanderthal squaring off with a Homo Sapiens. "Nothing."

"Come on, then. Once I get inside, I'll go downstairs and let you in."

Rock put a knee up on the car. It tipped downward and Tony grabbed the windshield wipers to keep from sliding off.

"Easy," said Tony.

Rock clambered across the hood, slid up onto the roof and pressed his hands against the wall. Slowly he rose. The car bobbed and creaked. "I don't know about this," he said nervously.

"It'll be fine," promised Tony. "Bend down." He grabbed Rock's shoulders and inched up. "Okay, easy now."

Rock grunted and straightened his knees.

"Move forward a little," instructed Tony.

Rock leaned over. "Watch out!"

The roof of the car caved in by several inches and Kozol bounced off the wall. He held onto the bricks with his fingers while Rock struggled to maintain his balance. "Careful!" Tony cried.

"I'm trying," complained Rock. "I told you this was a bad idea."

Tony and Rock leaned against the building, atop the collapsing car, huffing.

After a moment, Rock said, "Can you reach it?"

"Yeah." Tony slowly pushed against the glass. The hinges were stiff but finally gave away. He lifted himself up and over the wooden sill. He fell into a low bookshelf below the window and it toppled to the ground, sending books, papers and bric-a-brac across the dark floor. Tony muttered an oath.

"What's wrong?"

Kozol stuck his head out the window and looked down. "Nothing. You move the car away from the building in case anybody comes by."

"What should I do with it?"

"Park it over there by those other cars." Tony tossed down the keys. "I'll meet you at the back door."

Kozol worked his way out of the shadowy office, down an unlit corridor, followed a stairs downward and came out near the dressing rooms. All along the way, he'd been expecting killer guard dogs with three inch fangs, armed guards with automatic rifles, infrared alarms or little old ladies in billowing blue robes carrying shotguns.

There had been none of the above.

The Austinland was quiet. Nice for a change, Tony thought, as he unlocked the back door and let Rock inside. There hadn't even been an alarm on the back door.

"So what are we looking for?" Rock asked. He followed Tony inside the deserted theater. "Kinda spooky. Especially when you think of Henderson's dead body lying around in here."

Their footsteps echoed up and down the black tiled hallways.

"Gee, thanks for that lovely picture," whispered Kozol. "We're looking for the business office. Personnel records. I think I know where to find it, too. The night Julian and I found Jack Henderson in the supply closet there had been a guy working nearby in one of the interior rooms. I think he said he was an accountant. Seems to me we'll find payroll and personnel records there."

"Makes sense."

Tony continued to lead the way. There was the storeroom where Jack Henderson had only recently been found. It felt like a hundred years ago. Then again, it seemed like if he opened the door right now, the body might just be lying there all over.

Tony didn't test his theory. Instead he tried the next door. It was locked. "This is it," he said, jiggling the handle. He cast the bass player a look. "What are you waiting for? Kick it in."

"What about alarms?"

"Get real, Rock. If there were no alarms on the perimeter, there sure won't be any here."

Rock grinned. "Wee-haa!" He leaned back and planted the bottom of his foot inches from the doorknob. The door splintered and Rock shoved. "Right this way, sir," he said, bending at the waist. "Your table is ready."

Tony fumbled around, found the light switch and soon the room was bathed in yellow fluorescence. "You look on that side," Kozol said, pointing to a row of painted yellow file cabinets, "and I'll try these behind the desk."

Rock started opening and closing file cabinets. Tony did the same. So much paper. Kozol barely knew where to start.

"I'm still not clear on what we're looking for," Rock complained as he slammed shut another valueless cabinet.

"I told you. Personnel records. A list of employees." Tony looked around the room.

"What's Rick's last name, anyway?"

"I don't know. Don't you?"

"No. I don't know anything. I'm following you, Kozol."

Tony sighed, hands on his hips.

"Here's one that says employee applications." Rock held up a telephone book thick manila folder. "You think we might find Rick's address in here?"

"I don't know," replied Tony, suddenly stiffening. "But it will have to do."

"Huh?"

"Look," whispered Kozol. A camera was flashing in the corner and a tiny red light was blinking furiously.

Rock cursed and dropped the folder. Papers flew across the tile.

"Pick them up, quick!" Tony dropped to the floor and helped Rock. "You hear something?"

"A siren?"

Tony and Rock grabbed the loose files and bolted up the way. "Come on, out the back way."

"What if the cops are waiting for us?" huffed Rock, holding up the rear.

"What choice do we have?" Tony leaned against the outside wall and slowly cracked open the door. The sound of the sirens was near deafening, echoing through the alley. "They must be out front." They had no choice now.

"Where's the car?" Tony asked. "I don't see it!" Panic raced up his toes and tickled his tongue.

"Over there," pointed Rock. Finger number two. Right hand. "Between the Chevy and the Dodge."

Tony and Rock bolted for the Honda and jumped in. Kozol's hand reached out to start the engine. The key wasn't in the ignition. Tony frantically searched his pockets. "Rock, I can't find the key!"

Rock dug into his front pant pocket. "Relax," he said, "you gave it to me."

"Relax? The cops are about to bust us for breaking and entering and you tell me—" Tony stopped suddenly. A tracing line of bright light shot up between the buildings. A flashlight. And whoever held it was coming around back now!

Tony jammed the key in the ignition. It was time to shut up and drive.

Kozol headed east, under the Interstate, twisted up and down sidestreets, past the historic French Legation compound, built for the French *charge d'affaires* to the Republic of Texas, and north again.

Tony parked amidst the hundred or more cars filling the Super 8 Motel parking lot on the east side of I-35. He looked over his shoulder.

"I don't know what you're so worried about, Tony." Rock

struggled to balance the stolen papers in his lap. "Nobody's following us."

"I hope not." He turned on the overhead interior light. The ceiling was as uneven as a Martian landscape but at least the light still worked. Who'd have thought the roof of a car couldn't stand up to a couple guys standing on it?

The rental company wasn't going to be happy. Neither was Johnnie. Tony hoped Beaton had loaded up on rental insurance.

"Give me some of those papers," said Tony. "Let's see what we've got."

They slowly shuffled through the disordered applications for employment. There had been two Ricks so far, but neither seemed to fit the bill. The first was too old and the second was a college graduate. That definitely let Rick out.

"Here's one," said Rock, handing Tony a penciled in form.

Atop the file was the name Rick Morgan, printed in big block letters. Tony glanced at the age. Twenty-four. High school graduate. Former bouncer. Last job was working the door at a local strip club out near the airport. Worked in a mall as a security guard before that. "This looks like our guy." Kozol read off the address. "You know where that is?"

"Not a clue."

"We need a map."

"Why don't we just go inside," said Rock, looking at the brightly lit motel lobby, "and ask them directions? Better still, let's do it tomorrow."

"Tomorrow?" Tony held Rick's application rolled up in his hand. "Tomorrow could be too late. Who knows where Julian and Claudia have gone or even Rick? We've got to track them down now."

"Why not call your friend, Izzie? He's a detective, after all."

Tony scowled. "And tell him what?"

Rock shrugged.

"That we broke into the Austinland Theater and swiped some records because Julian Santana drove off in a van with his sister and a guy that *might* have been Rick the security guard from the concert hall?" Kozol shook his head. "Oh, he'd love that, alright. He'd have no choice but to arrest me. *Us.*"

Rock threw open the passenger side door and jumped out.

"What are you doing? Where are you going?"

Rock snatched Rick Morgan's rolled up application from Kozol's hand. "I need this," the bassist said, waving Rick's employment form like a baton, "if I'm going to get directions, don't I?"

Rock returned some five minutes later. "Man at the desk says this address is out near Lake Travis or thereabouts."

Tony spread out a double-sided, four color map he'd found in the glovebox; the kind the car rental places dispense. "That means we go..." he paused. "West?"

"Yeah, the guy at the desk said the best way was to take the 35 to the 183, then catch the Loop 360 back down to—" Rock looked down at the notes he'd scratched on a hotel pad. "Looks like Bullock, er, Bullick Hollow Road and—"

"Whoa," said Tony. "Information overload already. First tell me how to get out of this friggin' parking lot and up the on-ramp of this perverse freeway system they've got here."

Rock looked forwards and back. "I dunno," he said. "We'll just have to go back the way we came and look for a sign."

Tony groaned and backed up.

He'd love to get a sign.

From Heaven.

Saying, "Yes this is it. You've finally found The Way."

A road marker, cookie crumbs... Anything?

SEVENTEEN

TONY SHUT OFF the engine and let the Honda roll to a stop by the side of the road. A driveway sloped upward about fifty yards to a long, low bungalow with a separate garage.

A car was parked near the front at an angle.

"That's Scott Day's Cadillac," whispered Tony.

"You sure? What's he doing out here?"

"And at this hour." Tony opened his door. "Come on."

"Where are we going?"

"You don't think I came all the way out here just to turn around again, do you? I want a closer look."

Sticking to the edge of the drive, Tony and Rock approached the house. Few lights were on.

Kozol crouched down and looked at the black Cadillac. "It's Scott's car, alright." The classy vehicle had a personalized KAUS plate on the front.

"So where's the van?"

Tony pointed at the dark garage and started over. On the far side, away from the house, they leaned against the garage and peered through a dusty window. "Wish we'd thought to bring a flashlight." Tony spit on his fingers and wiped the window.

"That's Rick's van. See the dent?" Rock said. "Just like Mrs. Clay described it."

"So Julian and his sister took off with Rick? What for? And that would mean that Rick and Claudia knew each other." Tony sighed. "This is getting way too complicated. Could it be Rick that Claudia went to see at the Austinland the night Julian says she disappeared and Henderson got killed?"

"We could knock and ask them."

"Yeah, and I could be the next Willie Nelson. All I need is a ponytail."

Rock crossed his arms. "So what did you have in mind, Willie?"

"Very funny. Let's check out the house. Quietly. Maybe we'll see something in one of the windows."

"Oh great. And maybe Rick will figure us for a couple of burglars and blow our heads off," Rock complained as he silently followed Kozol's lead.

A dog barked.

Rock stopped and cursed.

"Shhh. I'm pretty sure it came from the house."

"So? If that darn thing keeps barking somebody just might let it out."

"Don't tell me you're afraid of dogs?"

Rock huffed. "It's an allergic reaction."

"Right," whispered Tony. "Let's try that first window." Creeping low under the window, Kozol motioned for Rock to keep down while he tentatively raised his head. It was a large but spartan room, with a red leather sofa facing an unlit fireplace. White-shaded floor lamps stood like sentries on each side of the couch.

Most significantly, there were two people in wooden chairs with their backs to him. One was definitely Julian Santana. The other, with long dark hair could have been his sister. Their hands were tied behind their backs with clothesline.

Pacing back and forth, a look of worry and aggravation

branded into his face, was Clint Cash. His boots banged on the wooden floor like gunshots.

Tony pulled Rock up, gave him time to take in the scene and then pushed him down again. They hadn't been spotted. "What is going on in there?"

"I don't know. You think the girl is Julian's sister?" asked Rock.

"It must be. But what are they doing here? And what the devil is Clint doing holding them like that?"

"Maybe he caught them and is waiting for the police? Like you said, they could be drug dealers."

Tony sat on the grass. The dog barked again. And this time it was from the window. Glancing up, Kozol saw a big brown face with sharp teeth and drool pressed against the glass. Tony and Rock rolled away. Tony heard Clint yell at the dog to shut up.

Kozol and Rock hunched down at the side of the house. "Okay, let's think this through. Julian and Claudia come with Rick out to his house. For some reason, Clint shows up or follows them. He must have borrowed Scott's car, unless Scott is around here someplace, too." Tony looked side to side.

"So, where's Rick?"

"Who knows? Maybe he got away? You know, now that I think about it..." Tony paused. "When Julian and I found Henderson's body, Rick made a crack about finding him 'in the closet.' He was talking about Henderson being gay. I'm sure of it."

"So? It wasn't common knowledge but it was no state secret."

"Yeah, but don't you see, Rock? How did Rick know Henderson was gay? We'd only been in town a little while. As far as we know, Henderson and Rick didn't know one another. Or did they?"

"You think Rick killed Henderson?"

Kozol rubbed his temples with his fists. "I don't know."

A scream came from inside the house. It was a woman's voice.

Tony peeked around the corner. A low shrub provided camouflage. Moments later a young woman ran from the house and leapt from the porch. She was shouting in Spanish. And it was incomprehensible to Kozol.

Rick followed. "Hey come back here!" He started after the girl.

Tony couldn't make out her features in the darkness but she had long dark hair, the same length as the girl he'd seen tied to the chair beside Julian. But this girl's hair was fuller, wavier. So she was a new player. But who was she?

Rick caught the girl by the arm and pulled her back. She sobbed. "Quiet," Rick said harshly.

Tony jumped out from concealment before Rock could stop him. "Let her go, Rick."

The security guard dragged the girl along with him. She had a look of helpless terror in her dark, quivering eyes. She was small and vulnerable looking, dressed incongruously in a lacy red teddy with matching garters. Her feet were bare.

"What are you doing?" whispered Rock, still hiding behind the house.

"Quiet," whispered Tony through his teeth. "I'll try to get him to turn his back to you."

Rock nodded and clung to the wall, waiting to spring.

"You?" Rick said, coming closer. He gripped the young woman in front of him.

Tony could see a big, black bruise on her left thigh. "Let the girl go."

"Why should I? What business is she of yours? You sleep with her once and think you own her now or something?"

"What are you talking about?" Tony stepped away from the house and slowly turned. Rick followed him step for step. The guard held the girl pressed up against him. "I just don't think it's any way to treat a lady."

Rick laughed. "A lady, that's a good one! Look man," Rick suggested, "Kozol isn't it? Tony?"

Tony nodded briefly.

"If you're looking to get laid, come on in. I mean, Isabel here won't mind, will you, honey? Or maybe you'd like another girl?"

The young woman trembled, looking from man to man.

Tony reached for her. Rick swung out with a big right fist. Tony ducked and caught the blow on his shoulder. It hurt. But Rick had let go of the girl now. Tony pushed her back and leveled a left jab at Rick's chin. Something snapped.

Tony expected it was any number of his fingers. Rick laughed, rubbing his chin like he'd just been kissed by his high school sweetheart. In his case, probably a Jersey cow. No offense to the cow intended.

Tony swung again and Rick's feet flew out from under him. He hit the ground with a thud and an explosion of air leaving lungs much more quickly than the human body had been intended to allow. For just one proud second Kozol thought it had been his doing. But then he realized his punch had never connected. There stood Rock.

Rock had come up behind them and kicked the security guard off his legs. Rock planted a boot on Rick's chest and held a finger up to his lips.

Rick squirmed but kept his mouth shut.

The girl cowered in the bushes.

"What is going on in there, Rick?" Tony demanded.

Rick said nothing.

Tony nodded and Rock applied a little boot pressure.

"Look, you can threaten me all you want but I'm not talking. If you two are smart, you'll give me the girl and get the hell out of here. Forget you ever saw anything."

"Thanks for the warning," said Kozol. "But no thanks. I'd really like to know what's going on, Rick. I'm funny that way. So let's have it. Before I turn Rock here loose on you."

"Forget it," Rick said defiantly. "I'm just following orders."

"Whose?"

"Look, give it up, Kozol. You guys aren't going to hurt me. You're a couple of musicians for chrissakes, not hoods."

Tony leaned over the stretched out guard. He got mad when other people were right. Especially when they were people he didn't like. And in this particular case, despised.

Tony dug in his pocket, dreaming of pulling out a "rod" and forcing the jerk to speak at gunpoint. Instead he fished out his car keys and waved to the girl. "Take these," he said, dangling the keys to the rental.

She looked at him with incomprehension.

"Speak English?"

There was no response except for a dart of frightened eyes from side to side.

Tony took her hand and put the keys in her palm. "Car. Auto." He pointed down the hill. The girl's eyes followed his arm. That was something.

She nodded.

Tony grinned. "You understand?"

She nodded again.

"Good, good. *Bueno*. You go get police," he said. "Isidore Ibanez." There was that glazed look again. *"Policia?"* Tony tried. The girl's eyes showed some sign of life. *"Policia?"*

She shook her head.

"Good. *Bueno*. You go get policia. Car. Auto." He pointed. She squeezed his hand and took off down the hill. Red teddies, thought Tony, though not regulation jogging gear, should certainly be an available option.

"What are we going to do with him?" Rock said, giving Rick a nudge of boot.

Tony looked around. "Let's dump him in the garage."

They helped Rick to his feet and escorted him around the back of the house. A big veranda led to a pier. Two small motorboats were docked on one side, past a small boathouse along with a pair of Jet Skis.

"Lake Travis," Rock said.

Tony nodded. It was no time for sightseeing. He kept his eyes on the back of the house which showed little sign of life. One room toward the back seemed to have a light on, but the curtains were pulled tightly shut and it was hard to be sure.

Tony inched the garage door up just enough for the three of them to squeeze under. "Find something to tie him up with."

"Hey, you can't tie me up and leave me out here."

"Yeah, you're right," Tony said. "So, why don't you tell us who all is in the house besides Clint?"

Rick's eyebrows went up quickly.

"That's right, Rick," said Kozol. "We know he's in there. The question is why? Who else is inside and why are Julian Santana and his sister tied up?"

Rick wasn't talking.

"Fishing line," Rock said, holding out a spool. He flipped the roll to Kozol. "I'll hold his arms. You tie him up."

Tony wound about a hundred yards of fishing line around the security guard's thick wrists. "Sit."

Rick hesitated and Rock gave him a gentle assist to the ground.

Tony tied his feet together. He wasn't taking any chances with this one getting away. Rick complained the whole while.

"Will you please find something to shut this guy up?" he finally asked Rock.

Rock scoured the dimly lit garage and came up with a greasy rag. Bits of debris and spider web gave it that extra *je ne sais quoi*, as that goofy genie in that Bugs Bunny cartoon would say. Tony wondered why such childhood memories came to mind at times such as these. "Perfect," he said, stuffing the filthy thing into Rick's mouth.

Rock grinned. "I've never seen you look better, Rick."

Rick muttered something muffled and incomprehensible and twisted from side to side.

"What did he say?"

"No doubt something filthy. Good thing he's got that rag to clean it up with. Well, Rick," said Tony, "we'll leave you to ponder the error of your ways. Last chance."

Rick fought against his bonds and cast a defiant, if pointless, look at his captors.

Rock pulled the garage door down behind them. "Think that will hold him?"

"Long enough," Tony replied. "At least until the police get here."

"If they get here. Who knows what the girl is going to do. I mean, she doesn't even speak English."

"At least she can drive." Tony pointed. The Honda was gone.

Stepping out from the garage and keeping to the trees on the side of the drive, Tony surveyed the house. A woman stood on the porch, pulling on a cigarette. The light from inside highlighted her curves. And she had plenty of them. She wore a pair of cutoff black short-shorts which complemented legs that were about as curvy and long as the Colorado. A knotted white t-shirt kept her honest. If not decent. One thing for sure, thought Kozol, she wasn't packing any weapons.

The girl tossed the end of her cigarette off the porch and stepped back into the doorway. As if waiting for something. Or someone. Probably Rick to come back with that Mexican girl.

She leaned against the doorframe and drew another cigarette from the pack in her hand.

And then it hit him. Mrs. Emma Clay's words. *"She just stood over there next to that bookcase by the front door, looking like one of those flamencos in the zoo."*

"That's it," whispered Tony.

"What's it?"

"You remember what Julian's landlady said?"

Rock shrugged. "Lots of stuff."

"Yeah, but one thing in particular. She said that Julian's sister stood there waiting for him like a flamenco."

"You mean flamingo."

"Yes, I mean flamingo. She said flamenco but she meant flamingo—"

"Yeah, but you just said flamenco—"

"Yes," said Tony with growing irritation, "but that's only because I'm explaining what Mrs. Clay—" Tony stopped. "Never mind. That's not the point."

"So, what is?"

"The point," said Tony, doing a lousy job of hiding his frustration, "is that the girl isn't Julian's sister. Never was. Julian's sister is tied up next to him in that chair like we suspected."

Rock appeared to ponder this. "Could be."

"It must be. The other girl wasn't Julian's sister. Mrs. Clay got it wrong. She probably told Julian she knew where his sister was and so he came with her. And they've both got long brown hair and Hispanic features. I'll bet anything that's the girl that came by the Radisson claiming to be looking for me. Probably trying to get me to get Julian to back down."

"Yeah, I guess that makes sense. So maybe Julian and his sister aren't the bad guys after all..."

Tony bit his lip. "No."

"What are we going to do?"

Kozol considered their choices. And came up with only one good one. That made it easy. But following it up, that was another thing. "Rock," Tony said after a moment, "we have to get in the house."

"Shouldn't we wait until the police get here?"

Tony shook his head no and said in hushed tones, "No. You said it yourself. We can't be certain the police ever will get here. And Julian and his sister are tied up inside. Besides, my bet is that girl at the door is keeping a lookout for Rick. And if Rick doesn't come back with that girl soon they're going to get suspicious and who knows what they'll do."

"Yeah, you're right, Tony. Let's do it." Rock ground a fist into the palm of his opposite hand.

"Not like that," said Tony. "I'll walk up first and talk to the girl."

"Out in the open? Are you crazy?"

"Don't worry. I'll play dumb."

"That shouldn't—"

"No wisecracks," said Tony, cutting him off at the adverb. "You just wait for me to get close then come up on the side of the house. We can snatch the girl and toss her in the garage with Rick."

"Aw, he'll be so grateful for the company."

"Quiet. Here I go." Tony started walking slowly towards the house. The young lady apparently hadn't seen him yet. She blew out a small cloud of smoke and stared toward the top of the door sill.

Tony was only about fifteen yards away now. The woman turned towards him, sucked on her cigarette, then threw it into the bushes.

"Only you can prevent forest fires," Kozol wanted to say.

"Can I help you?" The young woman folded her arms across her peeking midriff. She was a looker. Even in the dark. Her breasts cast alluring hints from beneath the thin white t-shirt.

"I was looking—" Tony hesitated, unsure of what to say next.

She grinned. "For some fun?"

"Yeah."

"Sorry, we're closed."

"Oh." Tony wondered where he'd seen the girl before. Or maybe it was deja vu. Or his wetdreams. "I was hoping that maybe—" Kozol paused again. Rock waved from the opposite corner of the house.

The young lady stepped out on the porch and cast an eye over the lawn. Tony figured she was still looking for Rick. If she was, she was looking in the wrong direction though. Not that she'd find him anyway. Then she said, "Listen, maybe I can help you. Come on up."

Tony smiled. "Thanks."

She took his hand as he neared. "Where's your car, honey?"

"I—I parked it down on the main road."

"Okay. My name's Sherry. You?"

"T-Tony."

"Right, now tell me what I can do for you, big boy." She pressed against Tony and he nearly forgot what he was doing there. She had wrapped Kozol's arms around her willowy waist.

The abrasive sound of a loose floor board gave Rock away. The young woman turned her attention from nibbling Tony's neck to see what was happening. Rock came double time across the porch. She twisted free of Tony's embrace but he held her wrist with his left hand and wasn't about to let go.

"Help me here, Rock," Tony said as quietly as he could manage under the circumstances.

"I'm trying to," retorted Rock. "You're squirming too much."

The fiery young woman began to shout. Tony stuck his hand over her lips to shut her up. Sherry bit fiercely into the soft, fleshy side of Tony's hand and he screamed. "Hey!"

She broke loose and made for the door.

"Will you stop laughing and get her!" Tony shouted. "Come on!" He shook his hand. "I think I'm going to need a tetanus shot."

Shouting "Police! Police!" the young woman raced into the house and down the hall.

Confused—Tony wasn't sure if she was calling for the police or if she thought he and Rock were the police—he followed. At this point, it didn't much matter. Things were in motion. And he had no choice now but to follow them through.

The girl had turned to the left and disappeared.

"What's going on?" Tony heard Clint say.

"Two men," huffed the woman, running to the opposite side of the sofa and picking up the poker from the fireplace as Tony popped into the den and Rock tumbled into him.

Tired, frightened faces—Julian and the girl who had to be his sister—looked across the room in fear and amazement. Even in the chaos of the moment, Kozol saw the common ground in their eyes and foreheads. Gray duct tape covered their mouths.

"Tony! Rock! What are you two doing here?" demanded Clint.

"You know these guys?" shouted the girl, waving the poker with menace. She didn't look afraid to use it. "They aren't cops?"

Clint looked at the girl. "Of course not." He walked over and took the poker from her hands. "Give me that. And be quiet!"

A door slammed in the background.

Clint rushed toward Tony clutching the poker. A gun was tucked into his belt. "You guys have got to get out of here before—"

Rock reached out over Kozol's shoulder and clipped Clint in the chin. It was a good shot. Fingers one through five connected.

Clint himself connected with the floor. The poker went sliding uselessly against the wall. Clint groaned. The sharp tips of his boots pointed at the ceiling.

"What did you do that for?" Tony cried.

"I thought he was going to hit you," Rock replied, somewhat defensively. "You could say you're welcome."

"Clint wasn't going to hit me. I think he was trying to warn me." Tony looked at the wild girl who seemed frozen with indecision. "Quick," said Tony, he pointed to the girl, "go untie those two. Rock, you help her."

Rock and Sherry worked at the ropes.

The dog came almost unheard.

"Watch out, Tony!" Rock shouted.

Tony turned as the dog sprinted in through the door. "Whoa!" He jumped on the sofa, grabbed the nearest thing he could find, which was a nicely crocheted pillow saying what a "home, sweet home" it was and heaved it in the dog's snarling face. Not that the dog seemed to mind.

It turned into a game of tug of war. Man versus Beast. Tony had a feeling Man was going to lose. Probably sooner than later. "Hurry up and get them untied, would you!"

"Almost done," said Rock who attacked the ropes with renewed determination. Sherry seemed only to be going through the motions.

"You can stop now."

Tony took his eyes off the beast. Another beast filled the doorway. A beast with a shawl around her neck. "Tanya!"

She smiled. "Down, Demetrius!"

The dog yanked the pillow from Kozol's hands and retreated to his mistress's side. Smith & Wesson kept her company. She aimed Smith at Rock. "Forget it, Rock."

Rock stepped away from the chairs. Julian and Claudia's hands were free but their feet were still trussed and their mouths covered.

Sherry raced to Tanya's side. "They came out of nowhere. I tried to warn you."

Tanya nodded. "Don't worry, doll."

Tony said, "What is going on, Tanya?" He had a feeling it was about the hundredth time he'd asked that question of someone that night. Maybe this time he'd get some kind of answer.

Clint rolled on the floor, half-stunned.

Tanya laughed. "Sorry, Tone. What do you think? It's like the movies? I'm going to explain everything to you?"

Okay, he could forget about the answer part. Tony looked about the room. There had to be some way out of this. "Come on, Tanya, put down the gun."

"No can do, Tone. And I really am sorry. If Claudia hadn't run off and her brother hadn't started poking around..." She shook her head. "We could've avoided all this." She prodded Clint. "Get up, would you."

Clint struggled to his feet. "Tanya, this has got to stop. It's loco."

"Shut up and get the rifle out of Rick's room. Where is he anyway? That moron."

"I think he took off," Rock said.

"Yeah, maybe he went to get the police," Tony added.

"Sure." Tanya laughed. Apparently she was the only one with a sense of humor because nobody joined her. Still, she glanced out the open window and cursed.

Tony looked over his shoulder. Flashing lights were headed up the main road. The police!

Clint reached for the gun. A shot went out shattering the window over Tony's head. Tanya butted Clint with the weapon and screamed, "Kill, Demetrius, kill!"

The dog bared his fangs and lunged at Julian. Tanya ran in the opposite direction. In the struggle with Clint, she'd dropped the gun even as it fired. Clint scooped it closer with his boot, then picked it up but seemed unsure what to do with it once he'd gotten hold of it.

Kozol threw the floor lamp at the dog. "Sorry," he shouted as he lashed out at the dog. The dog yelped, stepped back and growled. "Get the dog, Clint!"

Clint aimed the gun but hesitated. "I can't shoot a dog."

"Don't worry, I've got him. Good doggie," said Rock, holding the dog at bay with one of the wooden chairs.

The big dog snarled.

"Oh, shut up, Demetrius," hissed Clint.

"I'm going after Tanya!" cried Tony. He pushed past Sherry and bolted down the hall.

"Wait for the police, Tony," Rock said.

"I can't! You wait for the police with the others," Tony yelled from the hallway. He tried to imagine where Tanya had gone. He heard a door slam at the back of the house and followed the sound.

"Be careful!" Rock shouted. "She may have got that other gun!"

Kozol didn't need a reminder. Cautiously, he opened the back door, expecting a volley of lead at any moment. Instead there was dead silence but for the occasional cricket and the lapping sound of water against the shoreline.

His eyes adjusted to the dark. A black, hulking shape was moving out near the lake. Tony jogged silently after it.

He reached the pier which stuck out into the water like a giant's wooden finger. Tony crept slowly. A crescent moon cast little light ahead. The boathouse was to his right. He tried the door. It wasn't locked.

Slowly, Tony pushed the door open. The boathouse was no bigger than six feet on a side. The stench of pent-up motor fuel filled the air and wormed its way up his nostrils. Tony's eyes took in the room. While cluttered, there was no place to hide. Certainly not someone as large as Tanya.

Kozol took a shallow breath and listened. She had to be out there somewhere. He stepped back out onto the pier.

Ching!

Something hard struck his shoulder then deflected off the aluminum siding of the boathouse wall. Tony shouted and fell back.

Kozol tumbled to the floor of the boathouse and winced as he felt his shoulder. It was warm and wet. He'd been stabbed!

Tanya rushed into the doorway, spear in hand. She lunged. Kozol rolled to the side and tossed a gas can in her face. "Are you crazy? You're going to kill me!"

She lashed out with the long pointed spear once again and Tony felt it brush through his hair. One more like that and he'd be mounted on a wall somewhere in some collector's den.

"That's the whole idea, Tone. If that bonehead, Rick, had toasted you proper, we wouldn't be having to do this the hard way now."

"Toasted?" Tony struggled to keep a tiny workbench between himself and Tanya. "You mean electrocuted? That was you?"

"Of course, it was. Rick was supposed to see you got fried like a chicken steak, instead you were only stunned." Tanya shook her head. "That's some brain that boy's got. Belongs on a meat counter." She jabbed and Tony sucked in his gut. "Want something done, do it yourself."

Tony edged his way towards the door and life.

"No you don't!" Tanya swung sideways, using the spear like a baseball bat and caught him in the ribs. Tony went down again.

"Come on, Tanya. Whatever is going on, give it up. It can't be that bad. Besides, why get rid of me?"

"Because you have a way of getting in the way." Tanya laughed and started for him.

Kozol kicked out and caught Tanya in the belly. His foot sank into soft flesh. She yelled like a mad banshee and started thrashing. The tip of the pole lodged in the wall and Tony grabbed the weapon from her before she could pull it free.

Tanya retreated.

Tony clutched his wounded arm and followed. The sound of a motor starting left no doubt where she'd gone. Tanya was astride a Jet Ski.

He raced to the edge of the pier. But he was too late. She was already out of arm's reach. "Tanya!"

He cursed.

There was no key in the other Jet Ski. He ran to the boathouse. The keys were hanging from hooks placed on a Peg-Board inside the door. Tony couldn't see a key for the other Jet Ski but there was a key labeled *motorboat*. He grabbed the key to the powerboat and cursed again. He abhorred boats.

Tony planted his feet on the pier. The whir of Tanya's Jet Ski was growing distant. He'd need something more powerful if he was going to catch her now that she had a head start. And the motor boat was his only hope.

Hating every moment, Tony hopped aboard, found the ignition and started the sleek little boat. Its engine growled. He thrust the throttle forward and the boat shot out. But the craft wasn't moving any further. He'd forgotten to untie the lines. He clambered back and detached the ropes that held him to the pier.

And regretted it.

The vessel kicked forward and Tony flew backwards. He grabbed the side of the boat, his head and shoulders dangling over the edge. The craft shot straight out into the lake, captainless. Unfortunately, Tanya was going along the shoreline.

The powerboat was bouncing madly. Cold water cut into his cheeks. Tony held on for dear life. With all his effort, he managed to hook a toe under one of the seats and push himself backwards. He fell to the deck on his knees. There'd be big, black bruises there tomorrow; Tony was sure of it.

Working his way to the pilot's seat. Kozol pulled himself up with the wheel and turned the powerboat around, following Tanya's dark shape as it grew ever larger. For someone who'd never operated a boat before, he prided himself now on how well he was handling himself and his vessel. Maybe he'd have to get a boat back in Florida. Keep it in one of those canals off the Intracoastal.

Yeah, right. When this was all over, Tony promised himself he'd never get near a boat again, not even a gravy boat.

He was gaining nicely. Then Tony noticed a strange sight. Tanya had turned about and was coming towards him. He slowed. Maybe she'd decided to give herself up. Not that Tony had any idea what all she was running from. He waved.

But Tanya wasn't slowing down.

Tony pulled the powerboat's throttle to neutral. She was going to ram him! Tony pushed the throttle into reverse. It was too slow and too late. "No, Tanya! No!" he shouted. Tony shut down the engine and braced himself.

Tanya had come along the opposite side and was headed straight for him. The Jet Ski hit the motorboat hard. Tony was flung into the lake. The water was bottomless and frigid. Tony came up from under, gasped and choked for breath. The powerboat rocked back and forth. "Tanya!"

Kozol thrashed about and, slipping and sliding, managed to climb up the back of the boat. He shut down the engine and leaned over the side. The Jet Ski lay floating on its right side in the water like an injured kingfisher. "Tanya?" He went to the other side of the boat. "Tanya?"

He jumped back into the icy water.

There was no sign of life. He barely had any himself. Tony caught a breath, dove again and came back empty. It was no use.

Tony crawled back into the powerboat. Water was leaking in from a hole somewhere but Kozol figured he could make it to shore, if he could keep the engine running. Looking ahead, Tony could see the flashing lights in the distance. It looked like a disco party at Rick's house.

He cranked up the engine and headed slowly back. He looked over his shoulder, expecting to hear Tanya calling his name or thrashing about. Had she managed to swim ashore?

But the only sounds were the motor, the boat skimming over the water, and the water seeping inside the hull and now up to his shoes.

EIGHTEEN

THE POWERBOAT THUMPED against the wooden dock and Kozol scrambled out and onto the pier. A pair of hands held the boat steady, then let it go, as Tony made it to his feet.

"So," said the ruddy faced man, with a GI build, and a bright yellow uniform, "where's the fire?"

"Fire?" asked Tony, somewhat dazed.

"Never mind." The man looked at the damaged boat. "What happened out there?"

"There was an accident. Someone's drowned."

"Yeah?" The Fire Rescue worker studied Kozol's shoulder. "First things first. You've been hurt. Let's get you inside and get that wound dressed."

Tony hobbled up to the house with his escort. A police officer, hand on holster approached them from the side of the house and crossed the porch to meet them. Somebody had tied Demetrius up to a post between the house and the garage. The big dog sauntered nervously back and forth.

"Anybody else out here?" asked the officer.

"He says there's another one in the water."

The officer looked at Tony.

"Tanya rammed the boat. I tried to stop her. Then she came at me. After—" He took a breath. "Afterwards, I couldn't find her."

"You'd better go on indoors," said the officer.

Inside the den, Rock was pacing. The Fire Rescue worker tore at Tony's shirt and called for his medikit.

"Mr. Tony!" shouted Julian. He ran to Tony and hugged him. He pointed. "This is my sister, Claudia!"

Claudia, quiet, dark faced and beautiful approached. "Thank you," she said with a thick Spanish accent. "My brother has told me how much you sacrificed to help him."

Tony shrugged. The kid was too generous with his descriptions.

"You okay, Tony?" Rock asked, looking at the fresh blood on Tony's clothes.

Clint sat in a corner answering questions. Izzie was asking them. "It's all her fault," he was shouting. "Tanya's crazy! She made me do it! I didn't want no part of it!"

Sherry stood looking like a sourpuss in one corner. Four other young women, all Mexican by the look of them, were squeezed together side by side on the leather sofa. One wore a nightgown, two wore robes and the other a pair of grey men's pajamas. The one in the middle was the girl Tony had sent for help.

"What did I miss? What's going on, anyway?" And who were these other women? And where had they come from? Even Rick was there, having traded his fishing line for a pair of handcuffs.

"Clint's spilling his guts," explained Rock. "I guess he figures he may as well, seeing as how he nearly had his own spilled for him."

"What's that supposed to mean?"

"I'd say it means our meal ticket has been pulled."

The Fire Rescue worker poured something on Tony's shoulder. Kozol had nearly forgotten he was there. The sudden sensation of burning liquid creeping into his skin reminded him. "Hey, watch it!"

"Sorry," said the man with an unmistakable grin.

Tony scowled. He'd find out what was going on from Izzie. "Hey, Izzie, what the heck is going on?"

Izzie stood and grabbed Tony by the elbow. "You okay?" Izzie was wearing gray slacks, sandals and his Clint Cash and the Cowhands tour jacket.

"Yeah, I'm fine. But what on earth is going on out here? And who are all these people?"

"Relax, Tony. In good time. I've got a job to do here and your boss is in a talking mood. I'll get to you in a little while. Relax. You look like hell. Get yourself some coffee."

Tony looked around the room. Sure, almost get killed, shot to death, speared to death, Jet Skied to death? Who wouldn't look like ripe manure?

Get some coffee, you'll feel better. The words echoed like billiard balls in Tony's dull, aching head.

"Are you okay, Mr. Tony?" Julian came up beside him.

"Yeah. Just dandy."

Julian, Rock, Tony and Claudia retreated to the kitchen. It looked out over the lake. It wasn't long before they were watching the first lines of the sun's long rays stretching out across the black water, turning it to blue.

Somewhere out there was a body. Tanya Tobler's body to be specific.

From the kitchen windows, Tony could see the police patrol boats just starting their search as the light caught hold and seemed to be sticking for the day. Kozol wondered what a body would look like after being in the water all night. No matter, it wouldn't be a pretty sight.

Izzie came in. He grabbed a mug from the tree on the counter and helped himself to some of Rick's coffee. "I wager you want to know what's going on."

Tony managed a smile. "I think I can guess. Part of it, anyway."

"So let's hear it, smart guy." Izzie set his cup on the windowsill.

Tony looked at Julian's sister. "I'm sorry," he said. "It was prostitution, wasn't it?"

Claudia dropped her eyes. Julian stared ahead. The girl nodded at the same time as Izzie.

Tony continued. "Clint and Tanya were running some kind of prostitution ring out here. Perfect spot. Isolated, yet close to town. And judging by those other girls out there, I'd say all the ladies," again he looked uncomfortably at Julian's sister, "came up from Mexico. Probably illegally."

Claudia interrupted. "Rick came to our town. He offered us to get into America. We had to pay. But once we were smuggled across the border the price went from five hundred dollars to five thousand dollars." Claudia sobbed. "It was all a trick. Then we had to work here. To pay off our debts, plus interest. We were prisoners. And no matter how much we worked, we were never done paying."

"And your boss, Clint, was in on it. In fact, it's been going on for several years." Izzie continued, "It'd be nice if this was the first and last time this sort of thing happened. But the truth is," he said between sips of coffee, "that we've busted operations like this before."

"So, I'll bet that's where Clint got the money to launch his career," Tony concluded.

"I expect so," Izzie replied.

"That louse," muttered Rock. "So who killed Jack Henderson? Clint?"

"No. That was Tanya," answered Claudia. "Margarita and I ran away and hitchhiked to town. We had been planning it for months. Ever since I'd heard that Clint Cash was coming to Austin. It was our chance for freedom. We knew Rick and the others would try to track us down and that we would not have much time."

"But when Margarita's body was found she was wearing your bracelet."

Claudia nodded solemnly. "I had given it to Margarita for luck." She twisted a silver ring on her finger. "And Margarita gave me her ring for the same. I suppose her ring has more magic than my bracelet..."

"I'm sorry," Tony said. "Was Margarita with you when you went to the Austinland? Julian never mentioned her."

Claudia shook her head. "No. When we got to town we decided to split up and meet again in three days at the capitol. I walked the streets during the day and slept in the parks at night, waiting to see Clint. I thought if we did that everything would be okay. He is a big star. He didn't need our money. He could let us free." Her chest heaved.

"Margarita never showed up." She stared across the lake. "I knew what must have happened. Margarita had been caught. But I never dreamed they would kill her."

Claudia's brother took her hand as she went on "That's when I ran into Julian on the street. I could not believe my eyes." She smiled wanly in her brother's direction and squeezed his hand. "I knew Rick was looking for me and I didn't want my little brother hurt. I didn't want him seen with me in case there was danger."

"I'm not so little. And I could have helped," replied Julian.

Claudia smiled bigger. "You did help, little brother. You helped rescue me."

Julian looked satisfied.

"Julian and I went to the Austinland. Rick was at the door so I had to wait. Then he left and another man took over and I approached."

Tony asked, "Jack?"

"Yes, Jack Henderson. Jack let me backstage and promised me he'd take me to see Clint. He seemed so kind."

She gazed across the lake. "But Tanya found him talking to me. She struck Jack with something and he fell. Then she and Rick stuck me in a trunk of some sort and put me in his van. They brought me back here and told me they would kill me, like they bragged they had killed Margarita, if I tried to escape again. They told me I'd be working in this house forever."

Claudia gripped her brother's hands. "That's why I disappeared. I'm sorry. I didn't want things to be like this, Julian. I am so ashamed."

Julian held her protectively.

Rock asked, "And who killed poor Hector? Clint?"

"No," said Tony. "Tanya is responsible for that murder, too."

"Very good," Izzie said. "What gave her away?"

Tony did the math. "It was that shawl." He thought back to the night of Hector's death. "When Grace and I left the Austinland, I made a comment about Tanya forgetting that black shawl she wears everywhere. Then later, when I was out shopping, I saw her dancing it up in some club up town. She had the shawl on then. That means she'd gone back to the Austinland in the meantime, though she'd denied it."

"That's right," Izzie added. "According to Clint, Tanya lured Hector to Clint's bus ostensibly to talk but actually to kill him. She was afraid he'd been asking too many questions. It seems he heard Tanya coming out of the storage room where Jack's body was found. She told him she had found the body and been too scared to do anything. Hector let it slide for a little while. She'd begged him not to tell anyone."

"But," Izzie shrugged and refilled his coffee, "I guess he was getting more suspicious. So Tanya decided he had to go."

"To protect her own hide and this nice little illegal prostitution business." Tony never ceased to be amazed at the lengths to which some people would go to keep what they had.

"I'd say so," replied Izzie.

Rock asked, "But why Clint's bus?"

"The way Clint tells it," explained Izzie, "Tanya was giving him a warning. Telling him to tow the line. Seems Clint was getting tired of running this house. Of course, he was finally hitting the big time. A place like this is small potatoes at that point."

"But not to Tanya," added Tony.

"So she was making him squirm to keep him in line?" Rock speculated.

"She was trying to seal the deal by getting Clint to get rid of Julian and his sister," added Izzie. "She wanted his hands to be as dirty as her own."

"So that's what we burst in on," Tony realized.

Izzie said, "Clint knew he had to do something. Tanya wanted Julian and Claudia Santana dead and expected Clint to do it to protect their mutual interests."

"But he couldn't do it." Rock snorted.

"Tanya might have killed him if he didn't," Tony added.

"I expect he knew that and he was trying to warn you two when you came stumbling into the middle of things." Izzie grinned. "Of course, he never got the chance."

"Of course," Tony said, giving Rock the one arch I-told-you-so eyebrow. "I still don't get why she tried to ram me like that." Kozol's eyes danced on distant waves.

"She was a desperate woman, Tony. Desperate people do desperate things." Izzie dropped his mug in the sink. "How about a little fishing in the morning?"

Lake Travis sparkled in the distance. Tony thought about the bloated corpse they'd be pulling up. Would they use a hook? A net? Was Tanya Tobler fishbait?

"It's not the same lake, for chrissakes," Izzie said, as if reading his friend's mind.

"All the same," concluded Tony, "I think I'll stay away from fish for awhile."

A parade of pink seahorses popped before his strained eyes, did the macarena, then popped away again. "Can we get out of here?" It wasn't that he was beat, which he was. It was because he didn't want to be around when Tanya came back. Like he knew she would.

"Sure," said Izzie.

"Just tell me one thing. What were the firetrucks doing here?"

"I can answer that," said Rock. He laughed. "That girl you sent for the police went to the fire department instead. They came screaming out like it was a two alarm fire. That's who Tanya saw coming up the road when she decided to take off."

"Then the fire department called the police. Standard procedure."

Tony shook his head. Everything was so normal, wasn't it?

NINETEEN

ROCK WAS WAITING for him in his hotel room. "Johnnie let me in." He was sitting on the edge of the nearest bed which bent like a tongue with a rock on the end of it.

"Where is he?"

"Out hustling up a gig, I expect."

"Yeah, it doesn't look like Clint's going to be keeping up his end of our bargain." In other words, he'd be holding onto the old Saab a while longer. "Especially since you punched his clock."

"Hey, I told you, I thought he was going to take a swing at you with that poker."

Tony waved Rock off. "It doesn't matter. I expect Clint will be doing time when this is all over."

"Yeah, give him something to write about."

"Sure and he can sing *Folsom City Blues* to the inmates in the prison rec room." Tony looked out the window. It was broad daylight. Congress Avenue was buzzing with commuter traffic. Kozol still couldn't figure out how a million bats slept through all that commotion. "So, what are you going to do, Rock?"

Rock beamed. "That's what I came to tell you. You remember Chico? My pal from the Chicotones?"

Tony rubbed his face. "Yeah, I remember. What about him?"

Rock rose. "He got us a job."

"Us? What are we going to do? Give mambo lessons after class at the local high school?"

"Very funny. Chico knows a guy who knows the fellow who runs things stateside for Luis Angel." He pronounced it An-hell.

"Who?"

"Luis Angel. Don't tell me you never heard of Luis Angel." Tony shook his head.

"He's only the hottest Latin crossover act going at the minute."

"Okay. So?"

"So Luis needs a new rhythm section." The big guy beamed. "That's us."

"You're kidding? Just like that?" Things were looking up.

"You got it." Rock snapped his fingers. "Chico's man talked to Luis's manager and we've got to hustle down there right away. Soon as we get our passports and visas in order, that is."

Tony stepped forward. "Whoa, cowboy. Get down where exactly?"

"South America." Rock scratched his head. He was desperately in need of a haircut. His hair was nearly three-quarters of an inch long, after all; the hippie. "Didn't I mention it?" Rock rubbed his hands together. "I can't wait, Tony. We'll be like Butch Cassidy and the Sundance Kid."

Tony made a face. "Butch Cassidy and the Sundance Kid?"

"Yeah, man!"

"Do you know what happened to Butch Cassidy and the Sundance Kid in South America?"

Rock appeared to give this some thought. He scratched his nose. "Not exactly. What?"

Tony turned up his lip. As he remembered it, Butch Cassidy and the Sundance Kid got shot to death in South America. Bodies riddled with bullets. And Rock looked so happy.

What the heck, thought Kozol, Life was all about attitude. So what could he say, except, "They had a blast."

Rock smiled. "Yeah, man."

A TORY TRAVERS/DAVID ALVAREZ MYSTERY

ROSEWOOD'S ASHES

by
AILEEN SCHUMACHER

New Mexico engineer Tory Travers is
summoned home to Gainesville, Florida,
where her estranged father lies in a coma
after a hit-and-run accident. While preparing
to face the demons of her past, Tory finds
herself unwittingly embroiled in a complex,
emotionally charged and deadly conspiracy
connected to a 1923 racial massacre—the
torching of a town called Rosewood.

*Available May 2002
at your favorite retail outlet.*

MYSTERY **W⊕RLDWIDE LIBRARY®**

WAS419